# Beasts

By

# Desiree Acuna

Urban Fantasy Romance

New Concepts                    Georgia

Be sure to check out our website for the very best in fiction at fantastic prices!

When you visit our webpage, you can:
* Read excerpts of currently available books
* View cover art of upcoming books and current releases
* Find out more about the talented artists who capture the magic of the writer's imagination on the covers
* Order books from our backlist
* Find out the latest NCP and author news--including any upcoming book signings by your favorite NCP author
* Read author bios and reviews of our books
* Get NCP submission guidelines
* And so much more!

Be sure to visit our webpage to find the best deals in e-books and paperbacks! To find out about our new releases as soon as they are available, please be sure to sign up for our newsletter (http://www.newconceptspublishing.com/newsletter.htm) or join our reader group (http://groups.yahoo.com/group/new_concepts_pub/join)!

The newsletter is available by double opt in only and our customer information is *never* shared!

Visit our webpage at:
www.newconceptspublishing.com

Beasts is an original publication of NCP. This work has never before appeared in book form. This work is a novel. Any similarity to actual persons or events is purely coincidental.

New Concepts Publishing, Inc.
5202 Humphreys Rd.
Lake Park, GA 31636


©Beast Master's Slave, Desiree Acuna, Nov 2009
Cover art (c) copyright Eliza Black, Nov 2009
© Summoning the Beast, Desiree Acuna, May 2010
Cover art (c) copyright Alex DeShanks, May 2010

All rights reserved, which includes the right to reproduce this book or portions thereof in any form whatsoever except as provided by the U.S. Copyright Law.

If you purchased this book without a cover you should be aware this book is stolen property.

NCP books are available at special quantity discounts for bulk purchases for sales promotions, premiums, fund raising, or educational use. For details, write, email, or phone New Concepts Publishing, Inc., 5202 Humphreys Rd., Lake Park, GA 31636; Ph. 229-257-0367, Fax 229-219-1097; orders@newconceptspublishing.com.

First NCP Trade Paperback Printing: June 2010

# Beast Master's Slave

By

Desiree Acuna

## Chapter One

Maura studied the mansion in the flickering light of the full moon, trying to dismiss the uneasiness creeping along her spine like invisible fingers. The place was clearly empty, she told herself for the dozenth time. She hadn't seen a sign of any movement of any sort beyond the shifting of the limbs of the mighty oaks that surrounded it and formed a natural tunnel along the long, winding drive that led from the gate through the park-like grounds that surrounded the place.

The drive disappeared behind the stone edifice on the southern side and ended in a carriage house cum garage in the back. She knew. She'd arrived before dark, parked her car in an unobtrusive tangle of honeysuckle vines, and walked the perimeter.

The high stone fence that surrounded the place was well maintained. She hadn't found a break or a single place where crumbling stone might offer an easy hand or toe hold.

The place reminded her of a mausoleum, she decided. That was what was creeping her out. The gothic style of the architecture looked like something straight out of Europe's distant past, not like anything that should be sitting next to a bayou in the U.S. of A.

And yet, it fit right in.

Did the owner fit in, as well, she wondered? Would she discover he was some modern day equivalent of Count Dracula?

It bothered her that she hadn't managed to get so much as a whiff of a description of the man of any kind—the beast master.

*There* was a weird moniker! Daegon, the beast master. That was all she had after weeks of digging. No last name, no history, no other aliases—Daegon, the beast master.

She hadn't even been able to discover why he was called that if, in fact, there was any reason behind it.

There usually was. She would've thought he'd be called the leather master, though, or maybe the pussy master considering the club he owned. Total freaks! Goths on steroids! She'd felt like she was dressing up for a Halloween costume contest when she'd donned the 'essentials' for getting past the barbarians at the gate, the behemoths that passed as bouncers.

She'd begun to entertain a lot of doubts about the case almost as soon as she began to delve into the dark world little Sheila had been a part of. As far as she could see, the woman had already had one foot in the grave the moment she embraced the lifestyle. She hadn't *seen* drugs, granted, but it seemed to go with the territory—the leather, bondage—and probably sadomasochistic—orgy-minded clientele of Noir.

If she'd been a betting woman, and she wasn't, *that* was the reason Sheila had decided to off herself—maybe not even intentionally. She certainly wouldn't be the first idiot that had accidentally hanged herself trying to get a sexual boost from autoerotic asphyxiation.

Her parents wouldn't hear of it, though. Sheila's parents. Her own parents, being best friends with them, were convinced there was something dark going on at Noir and dragged her into it or she wouldn't be sitting in the dark now, staring at the creepy mausoleum the owner of Noir called home.

Well, there *was* a lot of 'dark'.

What she didn't understand was that the place had never been raided—not once. She'd checked. She still wouldn't have allowed her parents to rope her into investigating except for one tiny little detail. Sheila was the third young woman to frequent the place who'd supposedly committed suicide in the five years since the place opened.

It wasn't much to go on even though her gut reaction was aroused suspicion. She'd studied the files backwards and forwards, talked to the coroner that had performed the autopsies and thoroughly pissed him off, and she'd had to conclude that it *was* suicide, or accident. There just wasn't anything to indicate anything else.

She wouldn't even have been able to put the three together if she hadn't noticed something nobody else seemed to have noticed—the mark. All three of them had it on the inside of their upper thigh. She didn't know what it was, but it damned sure wasn't a tattoo.

It *was* the only link between the three young women and

the club, though.

And it was probably nothing. She was going to get her ass booted off the force chasing ghosts!

Not tonight, though, she told herself. The owner wasn't home. She'd arrived well before dark. Even without any sign of movement either on the grounds or inside, if there'd been anybody home, a light would've come on long before the moon rose.

The longer she sat trying to think up excuses not to go in, though, the more chance there was that he would come home and catch her trespassing.

To go or not to go, she wondered, studying the house uneasily, feeling a warning prickling along her spine?

If she got caught, she was going to get her ass chewed out by the chief, at the very least. If she didn't at least find something to give her parents to give *their* friends she was going to have to endure accusing looks from her parents for months.

Shaking her head, she opened the car door and got out. After studying the narrow road leading back through the woods to the mansion for a few minutes, listening intently, and assuring herself there was no sound or sign of an approaching car, she moved briskly to the wrought iron gates of the drive and used the ornamental iron for the hand and footholds she needed to go over. She didn't like being so exposed, but she was pretty sure trying the stone wall would be an exercise in disappointment. The spikes at the top were a real bitch to get over without sticking herself, but she managed it, dropping to the ground on the other side.

She moved quickly then from the open drive to trees and shrubs that lined it. She was *positive* there was no one home, but she still didn't like the idea of boldly striding across such a wide expanse of lawn in plain sight. She hadn't gone far when she heard a low growl that didn't sound anything like any dog she'd ever heard. Unfortunately, even as she stiffened and glanced back toward the gate, she realized she was far enough from it that there was a good bit of doubt in her mind that she could reach it and climb fast enough to elude whatever it was that she discovered was staring at her from the brush no more than two yards from where she was.

\* \* \* \*

The hunger, never far, was already beginning to make itself known to him and yet Daegon resisted. Noir had seemed like the best solution to his needs when he'd started it, as perfect as anything could possibly be in such a world and considering his limitations. He could feed at will without arousing the sort of attention his overlord deplored—the sort that might inspire his overlord to summon him back to the underworld.

He hadn't been unleashed upon the mortal world to find satisfaction with his lot, after all, but rather as a sick punishment to begin with for displeasing the bastard. He wasn't *allowed* to feed as he pleased from them, to satisfy his cravings. Only to take what he needed to sustain him and to suffer the torments of the damned to be surrounded, always, by what he hungered for but could only sup from.

It almost seemed to him that it was worse when he'd nibbled at what he wanted to gobble, sucked the meager portion he was allowed. It seemed to make the hunger worse.

He should have known from the look of satisfaction in Trydan's eyes when he'd proposed the club as 'cover' that he was playing right into the bastard's hands, but he'd been too tormented with the pain to think clearly. He'd thought he could gather his slaves together and finally know true fulfillment, if only for a short space of time. He couldn't take all he needed from one of the puny mortals, but together they would make a fine meal.

Trydan hadn't been blinded by needs, though. He'd known immediately what Daegon had planned ... and it coincided nicely with his punishment. Daegon could draw his slaves into one place. It would attract far less attention, but he was still bound by the limitations set upon by the overlord. Only one every two to three days and only what they could give him without surrendering their souls.

He'd *still* thought it would be better, that he could hedge just a bit. They gathered for him. He didn't have to search, to wait for an opportune moment to feed discreetly. He could feed and the moment he was allowed to feed again, there would be one waiting.

It was almost worse, he discovered. No! It *was* worse! More torment to be surrounded by them constantly, to watch them feed upon each other and *know* that he wasn't allowed to touch!

He couldn't even bring himself to withdraw to a distance that made it more bearable at first. Night after night, he watched them, always hungry, always wanting, always waiting until he was allowed to nourish his needs.

He'd begun to fight it, however. It had almost been more agonizing at first, to know they were there and not go to watch at least, but he'd discovered when he persevered that he could tame the hunger with distance. Holed up in his mansion, so far from the smell and sight of them, he could bear the pain a little better. He still watched the clock, still waited impatiently, but the pain wasn't as searing. It was more bearable.

His thoughts gave him no peace. Dwelling on his circumstances only made it harder to control the hunger and he welcomed the distraction of his hawk with relief as it called to him and then lit on the balcony where he stood staring blindly at the lazy waters of the bayou that meandered along the rear of his domain.

The hawk tilted his head, fixing him with one beady eye. *Female.*

Daegon scowled at the hawk. "Why tell me?" he growled. "Go fuck her if you want to."

*Human.*

Daegon's anger vanished immediately. "A human female? *Here?*"

*Snooping. Go 'round wall.*

Disappointment flickered through him and his anger rose again. "That doesn't do me any bloody good! I can't entice her in! And I can't use a glamour on her if she's too far to reach!"

*No go. Look see.*

Daegon was tempted to ignore the hawk. In point of fact, it occurred to him to wonder if his overlord had sent the little bastard to torment him more, but the hawk had always been a loyal familiar.

On the other hand, there seemed little point in taking a look if she was beyond his reach. His retreat had become his prison. Trydan's stipulation for allowing him to create Noir was that *that* would be his hunting grounds forever more. He could feed on the mortals that came to him. He could no longer stalk prey beyond those walls, and his mansion was too remote even for the occasional prey to drop into his lap.

And he still couldn't resist. Nodding at the hawk, he cloaked himself and bounded over the railing. Landing in the yard two floors below, he glanced up at the hawk and then followed the bird as it led him around the mansion to the front.

Snooping, the hawk had said, he mused. A reporter? His mouth watered. Reporters—nosey fucking bastards, but pretty spineless for all that. Would her curiosity overcome her sense of self-preservation, he wondered? Lead her to him?

He could hope.

He discovered when he rounded the house that he hadn't needed the hawk to guide him. The cougar and the tiger were both perched in the trees near the gate to the driveway, staring at something beyond the walls with absolute focus. The cougar blinked as he approached them, sniffed the air, and went back to watching. *She's in the man box.*

Annoyance flickered through Daegon. He'd already caught her scent himself—and it was a delectable one. However, he curbed the urge to point out that, while his senses might not be quite as acute as the beasts that were his familiars, they were certainly far above mortal senses.

His familiars were useful to him. They guarded his back so that he had no need to guard himself. On occasion, they fetched for him and, even more rarely, they neatly disposed of troublesome mortals without him having to lay hands upon them himself and risk his overlord's wrath. They thrived as much upon his approval, though, as the care he gave them. They could feed themselves, if it came to that and often did. They were willing slaves, however, because they did thrive upon his approval and he made it a point never to chide them or punish them unless they actually stepped out of line.

Their conceit over their superior senses wasn't just cause for a reprimand only because he found their tendency to lump him with mortals annoying.

He spied her as soon as he reached the gate. She'd parked the car she drove, a light tan older model, in a thicket of vines that offered concealment.

His pulse leapt at that realization. She had a keen interest in him and she meant to do some serious snooping or she wouldn't have gone to those lengths.

Narrowing his eyes to pierce the cloaking shadows of dusk, he studied the woman, feeling his pulse leap a little higher when he saw that she was pleasing to his eyes. The scent alone had been enough to wet his appetite, but she was comely.

Not that it mattered. She was a mortal female. When all was said and done, there was very little difference in the sustenance he derived from them. In point of fact, he'd found the less attractive females were not only very eager to please, but extremely receptive. And the plump ones— well, they had more staying power and that was always a bonus.

This one looked to be a little on the thin side although, to his irritation he discovered he couldn't see her well enough to tell for certain. Disappointment still mingled with his excitement. She wouldn't make much of a meal. She'd be too weak to give him anything at all long before he was satisfied.

She would be a bonus, though, he thought, a tidy little snack his overlord would know nothing about, something to slake the pain.

If she nerved herself to come to him.

The temptation arose to open the gates for her, to try to lure her inside, but she was cautious even if she was curious. Opening the gates, he decided, might very well scare her off.

After studying her hungrily for some time, he finally decided to return to the mansion and wait. If she breached his walls, she was fair game.

\* \* \* \*

Running, Maura realized, was probably the worst thing she could do. The thought had no sooner settled in her mind, however, when the owner of the pair of eyes in the brush moved closer. She took a step back automatically, but froze mid-step on the second when the beast stepped forward again, rattling the brush that had concealed it, parting the leaves just enough that she realized the pattern of light and shadow *wasn't* light and shadow. It was the pattern of the beast's coat—a full grown tiger.

Her heart instantly began to surge against her chest wall in sheer terror. Her mind went utterly blank, struggling to discount the possibility that what her eyes beheld was actually real. The foot poised on one toe settled to complete the step she'd begun. Fighting the instinctive urge to whirl and flee, she commanded her other leg to take another step back. Even as she finally managed it, she heard another growl that froze her.

She stared hard at the tiger, trying to convince herself that it was he that had growled at her. The sound hadn't come from behind her, but the hair on the back of her neck said otherwise. It rose, prickling all the way up to the crown of her head.

Slowly, she inched her head around until she could check behind her.

A cougar was crouched between her and the gate.

The urge to scream for help or just scream clogged in her throat with the fear that it would be enough to make them charge her. She couldn't seem to command herself to move in any direction. She had a tiger in front of her and a cougar behind. She had far less chance of reaching the mansion than the gate, she realized, in any case, but it wouldn't help her to race for the gate with the cougar crouched there.

The tiger studied her for several moments and then began to move slowly to her side and then around her until he was between her and the nearest part of the wall. Without even realizing she'd done so, Maura discovered she'd rotated with the cat's movements until her back was to the house.

Cut off from the gate and the nearest segment of wall, she studied the two cats for several moments and nerved herself to flick a look around in search of another possible avenue of escape.

She discovered when she did that there were wolves—not dogs, *wolves*—ranged along the wall, guarding it as the cougar and tiger seemed to be, at least three that she could see.

They weren't going to let her out again, she thought. One step in any direction except backwards, she discovered, was enough to elicit another threatening growl. Trying to convince herself that they'd been trained to chase trespassers to their owner, she began to back slowly and carefully toward the mansion, hoping against hope that she could find a way inside if she did manage to reach it.

\* \* \* \*

*That's it,* Daegon thought, exhilarated, containing his impatience with an effort, enjoying the sense of anticipation. *Bring her to me.*

Discarding his cloaking, he abandoned his watch post when she was halfway across the lawn, strode briskly down the stairs to the entrance of the mansion and opened the door wide, watching as his minions stalked her slowly closer and closer.

The hunger added to his pleasure—now. He didn't have to fight it, didn't feel a need to ignore the gnawing at his vitals.

She was coming. He could feed. He could take as much as he wanted, he told himself as it dawned on him abruptly that she wouldn't have told anyone where she was going. No one would miss her and, even if they did, they wouldn't know where to look for her.

For a few moments he savored the thought while he watched her, but then his greed shifted focus. If he was a little more careful, he told himself, he might keep her a while.

Take all he wanted, now, knowing he could at least appease his hunger completely, for once? Or husband his new resource? Use her to supplement the meager feedings he was allowed at Noir?

He was torn. He would still be miserable, he reminded himself, but wasn't a little more better?

There was no ending the torment. Until Trydan decided he'd been punished enough, he had to suffer the fire eating at him, to remain imprisoned and surrounded by temptation he couldn't have.

She wasn't likely to last long regardless, his inner beast reminded him. Why drag it out when he might at least have one completely fulfilling night? Even if he took the chance, mastered his hunger enough to prevent himself from sucking her dry, his overlord might discover her and take her away from him.

He wrestled back and forth with his dilemma until she reached the stairs leading up to the stoop. Dismissing the internal battle, he strode swiftly through the door and wrapped her in an enchantment.

He'd feed a while, he decided, see if he could appease the pain and wait until she recovered enough that he could feed again.

## Chapter Two

Awareness came slowly and even as it began to blossom and expand, the sense that she was asleep, persisted, confusing Maura. There was an awareness of fear in the back of her mind, but she felt detached from it, as if it was nothing more than lingering echoes from a nightmare she could no longer remember. The urge to shake off the lingering dregs of sleep swept through her, but her mind and body refused to respond. She was still paralyzed in sleep, unable to expand her senses beyond her awakening mind.

She puzzled over it, wondering how she could feel awake and at the same time still frozen beyond the rim of true consciousness. Slowly, the thought began to form in her mind that she wasn't asleep at all. She couldn't move. She couldn't open her eyes, but when she realized she could command her vocal chords, she simply couldn't move her mouth, she became more certain she was awake and expanded her senses internally since she couldn't command them to offer anything else.

There was something over her head, she realized after a few moments, something tight enough she could feel the pressure of it, realized she couldn't see or speak because something outside of herself was preventing it.

Panic flickered through her until she realized she could breathe without difficulty—correction, much effort. Her nose wasn't blocked, but the moment she tried to expand her lungs to take in a really deep breath, she felt another restriction.

She was bound, she realized, struggling for several moments with the urge to give in to panic, fighting it to allow her mind to tell her just how much trouble she was in.

The moment she managed to focus, she realized she could feel something rope-like biting into her all over. That threw her for several moments. She could understand a binding on her wrists, even her ankles, but all over?

She hadn't been mistaken, though. When she focused,

she realized she was not only bound up completely, she'd been bound long enough that she could feel her blood pulsing all over, everywhere that her flesh poked through the binding. It brought to mind a fishnet, except she could feel knots at each intersection.

Her legs were bound tightly together all the way to her ankles, but she could wiggle her feet—a little, up and down, not in and out. Her legs were bound too tightly together to allow that.

Her arms had been bound to her sides and slightly behind her, even her hands, but she managed to wiggle her fingers enough test the rope and determine that it *was* rope.

There was something against her back. The realization disoriented her for several moments. If she was lying on her back, why did she feel as if her blood was pooling at the front of her body? That suggested she was lying face down.

Unable to unravel that strange circumstance, she dismissed it for the moment, her mind leapt to her fingers again and she brushed the tips back and forth against her buttocks.

She was naked!

That discovery threw her into disorder, not the least because she finally understood why her genitals and her buttocks were throbbing so painfully. The ropes binding her didn't just encase her. There were cords between her legs, as well, spreading her buttocks uncomfortably wide and pinching the fleshy outer lips of her sex tightly to her body so that her clitoris was fully exposed—worse than exposed—bound by the ropes on either side to make the blood pool in it until it felt swollen enough to burst.

She was still trying to assimilate that circumstance and grasp the design behind it when she felt something hot and wet close over one of her nipples. Any lingering doubts that she'd correctly assessed her condition instantly vanished. In took her several minutes, in point of fact to catch her breath.

She'd realized the binding had caused the blood to pool in every unrestricted area, but wasn't until something clamped tightly on one nipple that she realized her breasts were bound in such a way as to force the blood directly to the nipples. She almost blacked out with the first hard tug. Pleasure more closely akin to pain exploded through her, made her belly clench so hard it cramped.

She sucked in a sharp breath, felt the scream that rose to her lips trapped by whatever had been used to muzzle her and only managed a whimper. It wasn't merely a tug, however. Whatever it was, it continued to pull steadily sending one jolt after another through her so that darkness began to gather in her mind.

She tried instinctively to evade whatever it was after the first hard jolt and discovered she couldn't seem to move at all. The effort only sucked what little energy she seemed to have from her.

Gritting her teeth, she tried to endure since there didn't seem to be anything else she could do, but it was torture like nothing she'd ever experienced—pleasure so intense it was nearly unbearable.

It *was* unbearable! She struggled to drag enough air in her lungs to stave off unconsciousness. She'd just fought the darkness to bay when the suction on her left breast ceased.

She dragged in a shaky breath as she felt her nipple cool almost instantly. She hadn't managed to complete the act, however, when the mouth—it was a mouth, she realized—clamped onto her other nipple, sucking so vigorously that she fell into darkness—briefly. It was too brief to give her any respite. The sensation pierced her mind's determination to shut down.

She groaned, straining against the bindings mindlessly while the tugging continued, trying to close her mind to the sensation pouring through her like acid. The urge to weep assailed her. She fought it with the sudden realization that tears would clog her nose and make breathing completely impossible.

Her mind had begun to feel fevered by the time he released the nipple he'd been tormenting and she felt the soothing chill of the air. She struggled to orient herself, to force her lungs to cease the labored struggle and calm her pulse because each frantic pounding of her heart forced more blood into her nipples and her clit and created more pain.

She discovered why the protective outer lips of her sex had been peeled away to expose her clit. He latched on to it with the same enthusiasm that he had her nipples. The pleasure was a lot closer to pain that time, pitching her toward darkness for a split second before the next tug brought her back. She strained against her bindings again, tried to arch her hips to evade the torment and went limp when she discovered it was impossible. The tug became beguiling, in any case, within moments. Her body surged upward and exploded in a climax that threatened to rip her apart. For a few moments, she gloried in it and then, very quickly, even the climax became torture as he continued to pull at her clit, sending one shockwave after another through her—endlessly. She couldn't stop convulsing. It seemed to her that he pulled at her clit with more and more determination until the spasms began to weaken in spite of his efforts.

She was only dimly aware of the moment it finally stopped, too near unconsciousness to feel more than a flicker of relief before the darkness completely swallowed her.

Dread began to fill her mind even as she surfaced toward awareness. She wasn't certain why until she realized that her awareness instantly focused on the pulsing of blood in her nipples and her clit and the more aware she became, the more discomfort she felt until pain began to swallow her.

The mouth that clamped onto one nipple seemed hungrier than before, more demanding. The pain that surged through her was so blinding that it was several moments before she realized that pleasure lanced it like a knife. She hadn't even begun to acclimate herself to it as before, though, when he ceased to pull at that nipple and moved to the other. Even expecting it that time wasn't enough for her to brace herself.

She felt the edge of his teeth, banishing any doubts that it actually was a mouth tormenting her. She uttered a muffled scream against the thing covering her mouth, straining mindlessly to escape until he released it.

Her heart clenched. She knew what was coming next and she was still unprepared. Almost the moment he clamped down on her clit, she came. If that was his objective, though, to make her come, he wasn't any more easily satisfied than before. He pulled and sucked on her clit until she thought she would lose her mind, that her heart would stop. He refused to allow her to slip into unconsciousness even when her body began to shut down, sucking at her more determinedly, it seemed, dragging out her climax until she began to hope for death.

She whimpered when her mind dragged her toward awareness again and then cursed herself for alerting him. He didn't touch her until she was fully conscious, however, and she wondered dully if she *had* given herself away or if he could tell just by looking at her.

It didn't seem to matter. Even when she cautioned herself to be quiet, when she struggled to maintain the same breathing pattern, he seemed to know and he was waiting.

In time, in spite of her body's seeming willingness to respond, it grew sluggish. She'd come so many times she'd lost count. She'd climaxed so endlessly while he forced her body into spasms and then held her there until tears leaked from her eyes in spite of all she could do to contain the weakness.

He stopped. She could sense his frustration that he had to work harder to make her come.

She began to feel hopeful that the torture was over—at least for a while. The feel of a blunt object piercing her rectum didn't just send pain through her, it completely disoriented her. She'd been convinced she was lying on her back on something. She found she couldn't spare a lot of focus to figuring it out, however. The stinging pain eased after a few moments, but the sensation of being penetrated didn't. She felt whatever it was drive deeper and deeper until fear began to take hold of her. Relief flickered through her, briefly, when she felt it stop and begin to retreat. She'd barely felt the flicker of it, though, when she felt something clamp onto both nipples and her clit almost instantaneously and begin to gnaw her with a ravening hunger that blew her mind. It was several moments, in fact, before she realized that whatever had penetrated her rectum was being slammed in and out of her so hard that it was jarring her all over.

The realization had barely registered when she came. It seemed to inspire him—them—to great vigor. The rod driving into her began to work piston-like, feverishly driving faster and deeper. The mouths alternated between gnawing at her nipples and clit with the sharp bite of teeth and sucking harder. She couldn't assess what was happening. Her body was so racked with spasms, she couldn't think at all.

Blissful unconsciousness enveloped her after a few

minutes.

It didn't last long. Her body was still pinging all over from the aftermath of her last climax when she came around. It made it that much more tortuous when he—they—started again.

She struggled with that concept, trying to figure out why it had only seemed to be one before and now seemed like four, at least. She couldn't hear anything beyond the pounding of her own blood in her ears, though. She had no way to grasp who or how many surrounded her—or even if it was 'he'.

She knew it must be, but the how and why eluded her.

She discovered she was too tired to care. It took all she could do to endure and continue to breathe.

* * * *

Daegon was enjoying himself so much that it was a while before he realized that his slave was taking longer and longer to regain consciousness and it was growing harder and harder to make her come so that he could feed off of her. Reluctance to stop arose even when it dawned on him that he'd fed off of her until she was growing weak. He hadn't felt so gloriously fulfilled in longer than he could remember. Just a little more, he thought, and he would be completely satisfied—for once, for a little while.

He studied his slave hungrily at the thought, waiting for her to wake up. She'd been surprisingly responsive—surprisingly resilient.

The last time he'd fed so much on a mortal, the damned female had stopped breathing.

He frowned at the thought, feeling his anticipation wane a little, recalling he'd thought before that he should take care of his little pet so that he could feed on her again.

He'd have to let her go, though, and that thought instantly made him reluctant. He couldn't keep her locked away in his lair. Someone, eventually, might come to look for her and, if they did, his overlord would realize he had her.

He felt himself wavering between the urge to finish and take all he wanted and the reluctant sense of caution.

She was a prize. He didn't want to give her up.

If he sucked the life from her, though, he would still be giving her up. She would be useless to him.

He could have more if he let her go. Mayhap, she would even grow more accustomed over time and be able to give him a little more and a little more until he was completely satisfied?

If he was careful with her as he'd considered before.

It hadn't worked with the others he'd tried, he reminded himself, but then again they hadn't been able to give him nearly as much to start with. They hadn't had her passion.

It was worth a try, he decided with some lingering reluctance. She was his for the taking, after all. If he discovered she wasn't nearly as satisfying the next time he needed her, he could just take what she had and discard her.

Shrugging inwardly, he removed the binding spell and replaced it with the enchantment. Lifting her limp legs, he pushed them wide and lowered his mouth to skin above the thick vein that ran between her thighs and marked her as his own. He studied the mark for a long moment when he lifted his head and then his gaze flickered to her sex. It was still rosy with the blood that had pooled there for him and his throat went dry with the urge to drink a little more of her nectar before he sent her on her way.

Sighing, he dismissed it. No sense in being greedy. She was his now. She'd be back and, with any luck at all, he could feed longer on her.

Quality not quantity, he told himself! He could keep her in a state of climax longer than any mortal woman he'd ever had, feeding upon the energy her body released. She was too rare a find to be treated without consideration for the prize she was.

When he'd settled her in her car and carefully arranged her for comfort, he leaned close to her ear. "Come back to me tomorrow, slave," he whispered. "I want more of you."

\* \* \* \*

Maura awoke with the sense that she'd been beaten half to death—maybe more than half. For several moments, she struggled to retreat into unconsciousness again, but the light against her eyelids evoked a sense of 'wrongness' that she couldn't ignore. Shock went through her when she finally, reluctantly, opened her eyes and discovered she was lying in the front seat of her car. Feeling perfectly blank, she stared at the console for several moments, trying to figure out how she'd gotten in her car and why she was there. When her mind failed to produce an answer, she finally struggled to sit up and look around.

She felt more blank when she saw she was in the woods.

"What in the hell am I doing in the woods?" she muttered. The question triggered a flicker of memory, but it vanished too quickly to grasp it.

The only thing that was immediately clear was that she felt completely dehydrated and her bladder felt as if it was about to burst. She wasn't going to make it back to town, she realized irritably. Pulling on the door lever, she got out. She nearly passed out when she stood up and had to lean against the car for several moments until the darkness passed. She saw the mansion as soon as she opened her eyes again, however, and the instant she recognized it, memories began to flood her mind.

She'd fallen asleep on a stakeout? Good god! She hadn't done anything like that when she'd been a rooky!

Dismissing it for the moment, she found the privacy to relieve herself. The relief was almost orgasmic.

Oddly enough, that thought triggered another flicker of impossible to catch memory. Giving up on the elusive 'something' after a moment, she headed back to her car and got in, trying to shrug off the heaviness that clung to her. A brief search turned up a thermos with a little cold coffee at the bottom. She shuddered as she downed it, but it at least wet her mouth and throat, taking the edge off of her thirst.

She felt like hell! It was hard to blame it entirely on sleeping in the car, but she couldn't think of any other explanation. She honestly wasn't sure she was in any shape to drive herself back to her apartment, but she didn't think she would get to feeling any better if she stayed where she was. With that thought to spur her, she started her car and backed out of the brush in a tight turn. She glanced at the closed gates as she put the car into drive and spotted a sign she hadn't noticed the night before.

*Trespassers will be violated. Survivors may be eaten.*

She stared at it, feeling that strange flicker in the back of her mind again, like a memory trying to fight its way through her subconscious, but it remained maddeningly elusive.

"Very funny!" she said dryly, focusing on the road and heading back to town.

She made it to her apartment, but she was in doubt that she was going to actually make it inside for a while. She felt so drained when she got out of the car that it was all she could do to put one foot in front of the other and keep chugging. She headed straight to the kitchen once she was inside and drank water, juice, and the last of the tea she had in her fridge, until she thought she was going to throw up or explode.

Struggling with the queasy slosh of her stomach, she headed into her bedroom and sprawled across her bed without undressing. Despite the nausea, she was asleep within a few moments.

She didn't feel a hell of a lot better when she woke up. She debated briefly and finally yielded to the inevitable and called in sick. She'd barely hung up when her partner called back demanding to know what the hell was wrong with her. "I don't know, but I feel like I was rode hard and put up wet," she muttered in an attempt at humor.

"Well, if you don't think you can make it back tomorrow, try calling before your shift's over, how 'bout it?"

Maura frowned. "What time is it?"

"Oh, you are out of it! It's six o'clock."

"Morning or night?" Maura asked blankly.

"Shit! I was kidding. You *must* be sick as a dog. Evening, or afternoon. Why don't I just put you in for a couple of day's sick leave?"

Maura studied over the suggestion. Her gut reaction was to tell Bill hell no, but, considering the way she felt, she wasn't at all sure she was going to be in any shape to work the next day. On the other hand, two days out for sick was the limit unless she had a doctor's excuse. She compromised. "Day after tomorrow. I'm sure I'll be better."

She was tempted to climb back in bed and sleep more, but she decided she needed food before she collapsed from weakness. The bowl of soup and crackers were just what she needed to tuck her into her bed again. The second time she woke, she felt considerably better, however, thoroughly rested.

It sucked that it was nine o'clock at night! It was too late to go in to work, too late to try another stakeout, and too early to go to bed.

The chicken soup she'd had earlier seemed to have stoked the fires, though, and she headed into her kitchen to search for food. After considering and discarding half a dozen different options, she finally settled for a pan of scrambled eggs and sat down at her kitchen table to think while she ate.

It bothered her that she'd slept through her stakeout instead of executing the B&E she'd planned to see what she could discover about the owner of Noir. It worried her more that she'd spent most of the day in bed, asleep, and had felt like she was coming down with something horrible and now felt as fit as if she'd never been sick at all. What kind of ailment would have that kind of symptoms?

Her health was excellent. She rarely even caught cold. The only thing she'd ever experienced that even seemed to come close was when she'd been young and stupid and had gotten seriously stewed. Not only had she not been drinking, though, but there'd been one unmistakable side effect of getting drunk that she hadn't experienced with this—the dizziness that said she still had too much alcohol in her system. She'd felt lightheaded, but in the sense of weakness, not high.

It was baffling and more than a little disturbing that she couldn't account for it.

She pushed it to the back of her mind after a few minutes and tried to decide what she wanted to do when she'd finished eating. The moment she allowed her thoughts to travel that road, she began to feel antsy to do something. She'd wasted most of the day. She hadn't earned her keep or made any headway in the unofficial investigation she'd agreed to do for the friends of her parents.

Try the mansion again? As soon as the thought popped into her mind she felt both an odd sense of dread and anticipation. The urge to go was so strong, regardless of the strange sense of dread that she got up without finishing and headed in the bathroom to bathe.

She made a discovery once she'd undressed and climbed into the shower that was as baffling as the illness that had gripped her all day. Her nipples were so tender she could barely stand to touch them.

Premenstral tenderness? She wasn't convinced even before she bathed her genitals and discovered that her clit and her rectum were also extremely sensitive. Ruffies instantly leapt into her mind and sent her reeling with speculation.

## Chapter Three

Consternation washed over Maura along with cold dread. Foremost in her mind was the fact that she'd already washed off any evidence there might have been—unless there was evidence on her clothes?

Shutting the water off, Maura climbed from the shower, grabbed a towel and wrapped it around herself sarong-style, and moved jerkily to the clothing she'd discarded. No matter how she held her panties to the light, though, she couldn't detect any sign of semen, not on her panties or, in fact, on any of the clothing she'd been wearing.

Dropping the clothes in the hamper again, she headed into her bedroom, drying off as she went, and moved to stand in front of the larger mirror on her dresser. With the aid of a lamp, she found a tracery of strange, crisscrossing bruises in several places but they were barely visible and it was impossible to tell what had made them.

Frowning, she dug clothing from the dresser, moved to the bed, and then sat down without putting anything on. She couldn't think of anything to account for the bruises, but then again, they were faint enough she thought whatever had made them couldn't have caused her much pain. Pain was hard to forget. She couldn't even be certain they had anything to do with the unaccountable soreness.

In any case, she realized fairly quickly that it was unlikely that anyone could've spiked anything she'd drunk with the date rape drug. Sure, that would account for the fact that she didn't remember a hell of a lot about the night before but so would sleep, and she'd awakened in her car.

She hadn't had anything to drink, however, from the time she'd left her apartment to stakeout the 'Beast Master's' mansion but coffee from the thermos she'd made herself. The only time she'd left the car was when she'd walked the perimeter of the estate, looking for a way over the wall, and she didn't think she'd drank any of the coffee after she returned to the car, to say nothing of the fact that she'd locked the car when she left and it had been locked when she'd returned.

That didn't preclude the possibility that someone could've gotten into the car and spiked her thermos, but she still couldn't remember drinking from it until she'd woken that morning.

It was the case, she decided with a touch of disgust when she'd examined the 'facts'. It was just plain weird and she'd let her imagination run away with her, she decided. She didn't remember her breasts ever being quite as tender before a cycle, but that didn't mean they hadn't been. As for her nether regions—well, she'd had to relieve herself in the woods and that wasn't something she was used to doing. She might have gotten against something that irritated her. She could be chaffed for a number of reasons, including having spent so many hours bound up by her clothes in an awkward sleeping position.

Shaking the unnerving suspicions after a few moments, she put her bra and panties on then hesitated over the jeans and t-shirt she'd pulled out. The urge to head back out to the mansion hit her again, stronger than before. She didn't like the idea of trying to go in when she hadn't been watching the place long enough to be sure Daegon Buckmaster—the beast master—had left, but there would be some sign of his presence if he was there, she was sure.

She wrestled with the ... almost compulsion to go for a little while and finally decided she was just antsy from being so inactive for so long. She needed to do something and she wanted to do something that felt productive, not just veg out in front of the TV. Coming to a decision, she tossed her first selection of clothing aside and headed for her closet.

The leather outfit she'd bought to cruise Noir was so radical she cringed inwardly at the thought of anybody she knew spotting her in it, but she'd been assured she wouldn't get past the bouncers at the door without it. It was nearly midnight by the time she'd wrestled the tight leather shorts, corset, and thigh high boots on. Between the way she looked in the ultra short shorts, boots, and corset and the lateness of the hour, she was tempted to just drag them off again and stay put. If anything, though, the compulsion to do something was stronger than before and, after tossing a light coat over her getup, she headed out.

There was a line of freaks winding away from the door of the club when she arrived and parked. She studied them for a few moments, but it was actually a relief to see she wasn't going to stand out as a weirdo. Shrugging off the coat, she got out of her car and headed for the line, discovering once she reached it that she didn't fit in nearly as well as she'd hoped she would, despite the leather. There didn't seem to be anybody within view that wasn't tattooed over fifty percent of their body and studded with piercings.

The young woman directly in front of her glanced at her several times and finally spoke. "This your first time?"

Maura debated, but the woman had clearly deduced it was or she wouldn't have commented. "That obvious, huh?"

She grinned, giggling exuberantly. Either she was high as a kite or she was younger than she looked, Maura decided.

"You'll love it! It's like nothing else!"

"So I've heard," Maura said, hoping she would elaborate.

The woman glanced at the people in the line and moved a little closer to Maura. "Wait till you get a look at the beast master!" she said in a low voice throbbing with excitement.

Maura lifted her brows questioningly. "Good looking, huh? Who's the beast master?"

The woman looked shocked that she hadn't heard. "He owns the club. *God*, I hope he's here tonight!"

Disappointed when the woman didn't elaborate, Maura decided to give her a little push. "Why do they call him 'beast master'?"

The woman grinned secretively. "If he's here, you'll see."

Irritation flickered through Maura. "I won't if he isn't here," she pointed out.

"You wouldn't believe me if I told you. You'll have to see it for yourself," the woman murmured. She seemed to wrestle with herself for several moments. "Some people say he's an Incubus. I'm sort of leaning toward vampire myself."

Maura felt her pulse quicken, but she looked at the woman a little harder, wondering if she was just plain nuts rather than high. "He drinks blood?" she whispered back.

The woman giggled again. "Not blood, sexual energy."

Alrighty then! She was nuts! Maybe high, too, but

definitely nuts. "I'm not even going to ask how he manages that," she murmured dryly.

The woman looked vaguely offended, but she shrugged. "I would've thought you would've heard something about it or you wouldn't be here."

So maybe she wasn't quite as off her rocker as she'd thought? Maura shrugged easily. "I heard it was a BDSM club. Never tried it, but I'm curious."

"Ahh!" the woman said, nodding wisely. "I'm not sure this is the place for you if you haven't tried it. It's pretty hardcore." She thought it over. "Actually, it's seriously hardcore. I'd played around with BDSM a good bit before I came and I was still shocked."

Maura hesitated, but the woman seemed completely unsuspicious and she'd been a font of information already. "I hope to hell they don't get raided while I'm here."

"Oh! You don't have to worry about that! Cops can't get in the door. I told you the owner's an Incubus, or maybe a vampire."

"Meaning magical?" Maura asked skeptically. "He's got some kind of spell over the place?"

The woman shrugged again. "Supernatural. Something like that, I guess. I've heard they've never been raided."

Maura was more inclined to put it down to greased palms in the right quarters, but she kept that to herself. Unfortunately, the line had moved them to the door and she didn't get another chance to pump the woman for information. The bouncer looked her and the woman over and apparently decided they were together—a stroke of luck since the woman was clearly a regular!

She'd just breathed a sigh of relief when they stepped through the doors and she got the jolt of her life. There was a Bengal tiger sprawled between the door they'd entered and the door that led into the inner sanctum where all the noise was coming from. Despite the jolt it gave her, she was inclined, for a split second, to dismiss it as a very good reproduction—until it turned its head and looked directly at her.

Her heart leapt into her throat, but after staring at her hard for several moments, the tiger glanced at the woman taking money and blinked, slowly.

Maura followed the look and saw, to her surprise, that the

woman almost seemed to be taking her cues from the beast. She turned to Maura and held out her hand. Still unnerved, it took Maura a moment to figure out what the woman was waiting for.

"Twenty bucks."

Steep! Remembering she'd stuck her money in the top of her right boot along with her ID, Maura fished both out, peeled a twenty off and handed it to the woman. She barely glanced at the ID.

Trying not to feel insulted about it, Maura folded the ID in what was left of her cash and pushed it into the top of the boot again.

The woman she'd been chatting with had disappeared by the time she stepped through the inner door and halted to survey a scene that looked like something out of Sodom and Gomorrah. Maura was inclined to think that there wasn't much that could shock her after nearly ten years on the force, but she almost felt like she'd stepped on to the set of a porno. There was the usual nearly deafening music blaring from speakers around the place and in the center a large dance floor where men and women were gyrating wildly and rubbing all over each other, but that was where the similarity between Noir and any other club left off.

The place had the look almost of a coliseum—roman-style. It was tiered with what looked like stone benches that rose from the enormous dance floor at the bottom, which formed a pit, to about mid-way the height of the outer walls, which were four tiers higher than the entrance where she stood. Enormous columns studded the huge building and seemed to support the roof above. The ceiling was painted, but not just coated with paint. There was a mural painted on it where men, women, fanciful creatures from mythology and even animals cavorted in explicit sexual poses.

As Maura gaped up at the ceiling, trying to ignore the threesome engaged in sex not a yard from where she was standing, a hawk dove from the top of one of the columns with a high-pitched screech, swooped close enough to her that she could've identified what type of hawk he was even in the dimness if she'd known a damned thing about hawks, and then up again. Caught by the movement as much as her surprise at seeing it, Maura watched it glide above the uppermost tier and then alight on the back of a chair—throne—directly across from her.

The figure seated in the huge, stone throne was clearly a man, despite the fact that he had long blond hair that flowed loosely about his bare chest and shoulders and hung down almost to his waist. Even from where she stood, he looked massive—like a bodybuilder on steroids. He was sprawled negligently in the chair, his long, muscular legs clad in tight, black leather. He lifted his head and glanced at the hawk as it settled on the back of the throne with another high-pitched screech. Even as she watched, his entire demeanor changed from bored indifference to a tenseness that made her think for several moments that he would stand and stride down the stairs that led up from the dance floor to his throne. Instead, he merely turned from the hawk after a brief glance and looked directly at her.

Maura felt as if the breath had been punched from her lungs as she met his gaze across the wide expanse.

\* \* \* \*

Daegon was still in a towering rage when he arrived at Noir. He'd watched the road leading up to his lair for hours, most of the day, waiting in anticipation he could hardly contain for his slave to show herself. By the time dusk fell, doubts had begun to plague him that she would come at all. He dismissed it, pacing, waiting. He'd marked her. He'd planted his desires in her mind before he released her. She would come because she had to.

She didn't come.

When Daegon finally had to accept that she'd, somehow, eluded him, he unleashed the rage that had been building in him for hours. He might have completely destroyed his lair if it hadn't abruptly dawned on him that his overlord was bound to notice if he allowed himself to vent his frustration and fury as he wanted to. And, if he noticed, then he would begin to ask uncomfortable questions Daegon had no desire to answer. It took an effort to rein his temper in and contain it, but he managed.

The temper tantrum had still cost him. He'd expended far more energy than he could really afford. He had no choice but to seek the meager sustenance allowed him at Noir, although he was still so furious he knew he didn't dare seek even that until he'd gained a better control over himself.

He would be far too tempted, in his current state, to vent on whatever hapless mortal caught his eye and that would certainly draw unwanted attention from his overlord.

Above all, he had to keep his overlord from learning of his newest slave. He didn't know how she'd managed to thwart him, but she was his, and he would know how and why before he was done with her. Damn her! She was going to regret fighting him—deeply! She would regret displeasing him!

Mayhap the next time he wouldn't be as easy on her! Mayhap he'd just take all he wanted and throw the useless husk to his beasts when he was done with her!

He was still brooding over it, trying to decide which of the slaves that had dutifully presented themselves that he would feed on, when his hawk alerted him.

*Female here.*

*There are females everywhere!* Daegon retorted angrily.

*New slave!*

Stunned, Daegon turned and saw her standing directly across from him, poised like a startled deer. He narrowed his eyes, struggling with the surge of anticipation and rage that went through him. What the *fuck* was she doing here, he wondered furiously?

It hadn't been any part of his plan to feed on her *here*, where his overlord tallied every morsel he fed on!

Without even an acknowledgement that she knew he was her lord and master, she looked away after a brief moment and continued her descent to the dance floor. Baffled rage dogged her steps as Daegon wrestled with that stunning circumstance.

He was almost more inclined to think he'd somehow *forgotten* to mark her. That was incomprehensible, though, and beyond that he *knew* he'd marked her. He'd spent most of the day relishing that moment, congratulating himself on his restraint. As much as it had gone against his nature, he'd spared his little milk cow so that he could drink from her again and again. She was his secret weapon against his fucking overlord! She would end most of his torment, make his existence bearable.

He wrestled with himself as he watched her hungrily, trying to decide whether it would be safe to approach her or not, knowing if he did it was liable to draw his overlord's attention.

It wouldn't be safe, he finally decided. He was too hungry. He couldn't trust that he'd be able to refrain from feeding on her. Reluctantly, he dragged his gaze from her, noticing as he did so that he wasn't the only male in the room that was watching her hungrily.

It sent a fresh wave of rage through him. His cougar, he saw, was watching her, as well. He reached down to stroke his cougar's head. *Guard her for me.*

Obediently, the cougar rose and trotted down the stairs, pushing through the dancers and following her to the bar where she'd settled. Waiting until he saw the mortal males had gotten the not so subtle hint, he summoned his lead wolf. *Bring me the red head over there.*

The wolf stared at him. *One cougar watch?*

Daegon's lips tightened in annoyance. *Her hair's auburn, not red! And, as you pointed out, cougar's guarding her. The plump red head there.*

The wolf followed the direction of his gaze and stood up.

*And, after her, the dark one on the fourth tier there.*

\* \* \* \*

Maura was unsettled, to say the very least, when she'd gotten her mixed drink and turned to survey the club, or more specifically, the owner of the club, as casually as she could and discovered a cougar had sprawled on the stone floor not three feet from her. As if sensing her gaze, its head swiveled in her direction. It met her gaze for a long, long moment and then turned to study the other patrons of the club.

Without much surprise, Maura saw that everyone, regardless of how drunk, was giving the huge cat a wide berth. A tiger at the door, a cougar and a hawk inside, and none of the three leashed. She'd been certain the tiger must be, but the cougar sure as hell hadn't been there when she'd headed for the bar and she didn't see any sign of a collar let alone a leash.

She hadn't seen one on the tiger either, she realized abruptly. She'd just assumed ....

The stranger at the door had said she would see why the owner was called the beast master.

Trained pets? It still seemed inconceivable that the lunatic would allow wild animals to wander at will among his patrons, to say nothing of the patrons themselves! She could see, though, that while everyone seemed well aware of their presence and kept their distance, they didn't seem surprised or alarmed.

Maybe, given the fact that she'd seen no less than three couples fucking and two threesomes between the door and the bar, they were too drunk or too stoned to feel the alarm they should have?

She stared keenly at the people closest to her for some time, but she couldn't see anything that indicated they were either drunk or stoned beyond their wanton behavior and that didn't necessarily indicate drugs. Certainly not with people who clearly didn't have a lot of inhibitions to begin with.

When she glanced toward Daegon again, she discovered a large wolf had come to stand beside his throne where the cougar had been when she'd first noticed it. Daegon looked at it. The wolf met his gaze and then the wolf trotted down the stairs as if the two of them had actually exchanged words! Puzzled, she watched the wolf until he stopped behind a woman with long, unnaturally red hair and pushed his snout between the exposed cheeks of her ass.

Not surprisingly, it got the woman's attention instantly. Instead of turning and swatting at the wolf, though, she lifted her head, looked directly at Daegon and then an expression of eagerness lit her features and she made her way to the stairs, ascending them. Maura's belly tightened. She couldn't entirely decipher the emotion that rolled through her, but it wasn't uneasiness regarding the woman or her obvious intent.

The woman knelt in front of Daegon when she reached the top step, staring up at him worshipfully. Daegon's expression was harder to read as he surveyed the woman, but not only was his intention clear enough, Maura abruptly knew what the dark, churning was inside of her.

Jealousy.

She tried to dismiss it as ludicrous but it was hard to ignore when it only became more pronounced the longer she watched. Instead of rising and leaving, the woman turned and lay down on the step. Daegon rose from the throne without any appearance of the eagerness the woman had displayed and dropped to his knees between the woman's splayed thighs. Expecting any moment to see him unfasten his breeches and pull his cock from his pants, Maura watched in breathless anticipation despite the urge to look away. Instead, he merely leaned over the woman, bracing himself on his arms and staring down at her.

Almost immediately, the woman arched her head back, began to moan and gasp.

Not that Maura could actually hear her over the noise in the club, but her expression of ecstasy was eloquent. She writhed as if she was in the throes of sexual rapture. Her mouth dropped open.

Maura felt her own blood heat, felt it begin to pulse in her breasts and her sex. Confusion wafted through her, as well. She hadn't seen Daegon touch the woman at all. He hadn't kissed her. He remained braced on his arms and stiff above her. He wasn't even dry humping the woman!

She gave every appearance, regardless, of coming and it seemed to go on and on until Maura found herself squirming in her chair. Xcstasy, she wondered? It didn't make sense. He hadn't touched her. No matter how sensitive the drug might make her, she couldn't feel anything if he didn't *touch* her!

It was hard to argue with the fact that the woman came repeatedly while he hovered over her and could barely regain her feet when he finally sat back and motioned her dismissal with his head. She *crawled* weakly down two steps and lay down again as if she was too weak to move further. When she moved, another woman took her place.

As tempted as Maura was to move closer to see if she could see better from another vantage point, when a third woman assumed the position, she fought the urge to watch and turned around to face the bar.

She was aroused, she discovered, just from watching, so much that her hand shook when she tried to lift her drink to her lips. The burn of the alcohol didn't soothe her a hell of a lot either.

She didn't understand the arousal any more than she understood the sense of ... betrayal she felt, jealousy, resentment. None of it made any sense to her at all, but she decided she'd seen enough.

Emptying her glass, she set it down on the bar and turned

to leave. A jolt went through her when she discovered Daegon was standing directly behind her. She stared at him in stunned disbelief as he leaned toward her, bracing a palm on either side of her against the bar.

At such close range, she saw he had a hell of a lot more going for him than a physique sexy enough to make pretty much any woman that looked at him wet. He was so handsome it took her breath—literally. Without a word, he lifted his right hand from the bar, settled it on her bare thigh, and slid it upward until his thumb was resting on the pulse at the top of her thigh. Lightly, he brushed the pad of his thumb back and forth.

Maura's nipples tightened painfully. Her kegels began to spasm so wildly she thought for several moments she would come. Disappointment jolted through her almost painfully when he withdrew his hand and straightened.

Anger glittered in his strange golden eyes. "It's useless to try to resist," he murmured. "I always get what I want."

## Chapter Four

Maura was still thoroughly rattled when she got back to her apartment, her hands shaking so badly it was all she could do to ring the damned keyhole with her key. Relief flooded her when she'd gotten inside and locked the door behind her, but it was minor.

Her body felt as if it was on fire. It had since he'd touched her.

She was almost inclined to think she'd had some sort of bizarre hallucination. She didn't *know* him! Tonight was the first time she'd ever set eyes on him. She'd never so much as spoken to him! She found it hard to believe that he'd even spotted her in such a crowd. Why would he walk up to her as if he knew her? Touch her as if he had every right? As if she ... *belonged* to him?

And what had he said? *It's useless to try to resist. I always get what I want.*

Her response had been a gut reaction, not the product of thought, unfortunately.

*News flash, buddy! Nobody gets everything they want ... no matter how pretty they are!*

She squeezed her eyes closed, wondering if she'd actually said that or only thought it. She was pretty sure she'd said it. Rage had glittered in his eyes, but something else, as well. Curiosity, she thought, surprise, maybe.

And she didn't doubt he was! Not only did she think he was the most gorgeous man she'd ever lain eyes on, but it was clear all of the women who frequented the club looked upon him as if he was a ... movie star ... or a god!

She could hardly congratulate herself when the words had merely popped into her mind and fallen out her mouth! It hadn't been any part of her plan to insult or antagonize the guy! She hadn't really expected to get the chance to get close enough to him to pump him for answers, but she certainly hadn't had it in mind to totally blow the opportunity if it arose!

"Shit!" she spat in disgust, shoving away from the door

and heading to her bedroom.

She was seriously burning, she discovered in dismay when she'd peeled the leather off and flung it across the room. Was this what the drug X felt like, she wondered? And, if it was, how had she gotten it?

Her drink?

She'd watched the bartender mix it. She didn't believe he'd had an opportunity to slip anything in to it.

What about when Daegon had touched her, she wondered? She didn't think X could be absorbed through the skin, though. Of course, a lot of drugs could, but as far as she knew nobody simply rubbed it into their skin. They didn't want to take a chance that it might not work!

She didn't feel drugged, she decided—not that she messed with that shit! All of it was too damned dangerous, especially in her line of work. Anybody stupid enough to put themselves on the streets in less than tiptop condition was a fool that didn't last long.

Why, then, did she feel like her skin was too sensitive to touch?

Trying to shake the suspicion, she went to take a shower, hoping that that would ease her discomfort. She couldn't tell that it did. Worse, her mind kept replaying the images she'd seen in the club—mostly the image of Daegon and the women he'd .... She actually didn't know what he'd done beyond bringing them to climax.

She hadn't seen him actually touch them. Of course, she could've missed it. She'd been across the room and even though he'd been virtually on display, the room had been dim. He could've been rubbing himself on them, she told herself.

Except she hadn't seen him move.

Maybe the women had done all the rubbing?

She'd thought *they* must be on X from the way they were gyrating under him, moaning and shaking.

It wasn't helping her to allow herself to go over it in her mind.

Drying off, she discarded the idea of putting anything on and climbed into her bed naked. Almost as soon as she settled, the urge hit her to get up again, dress, and head out to the mansion.

It was almost as if she could *feel* him pulling her, *hear* him commanding her to go to him in her mind.

She struggled with it until it occurred to her that she'd left him at the club. She knew positively he wasn't at the mansion. Flinging the covers off, she got up, dressed, and headed out of her apartment.

If there was any sign that he'd returned when she got there, she promised herself, she'd just turn around and go back to her apartment.

The mansion, she saw when she pulled up and parked, looked every bit as creepy as it had the night before, just as dark, and just as deserted. She stared at it a long moment, wrestling with the urge to go in and finally got out of the car.

She was more than halfway across the lawn when she abruptly spied one of his wolves. She froze, staring at the animal for a long moment, and then slowly turned with the intention of racing back to the gate she'd climbed as fast as she could. When she turned, however, she saw the tiger and the cougar between her and the gate.

Swallowing convulsively, she slowly turned to study the house again.

Daegon was standing on the stoop, watching her. He lifted a hand in a summoning gesture.

Maura felt her belly tighten, but her feet began to move without her volition and she found herself staring up at him. An expression of satisfaction flickered over his handsome features. "I find your spirit ... intriguing, almost refreshing," he growled. "But I'm not particularly pleased with you at the moment. You'll have to be punished, of course. I never allow my slave's rebellion to go unpunished. And you are mine, aren't you, my precious?"

Maura's throat closed as if a hand had closed around it.

His expression tightened. "Say it."

Maura's mouth felt desert dry, but it flickered through her mind abruptly that acknowledging his demand was the last thing she should do. "No," she said in a hoarse whisper.

His gaze flickered over her. "And yet you're here. I see I'll have to convince you," he murmured lifting one hand and making a brushing gesture in front of her face.

\* \* \* \*

Dread flickered through Maura before awareness was much more than a faint budding. A strange sense of déjà vu followed as her awareness expanded and she became aware that she couldn't open her eyes because there was a tight band around her head. She couldn't move because she was bound with something net-like from her shoulders to her ankles.

Warm air brushed her neck, making a shiver skate down her along with the realization that she was completely naked. Her nipples throbbed painfully from the blood pooled at the tips and her sex countered that refrain.

"I see no reason to deprive myself merely because you deserve to be punished for your rebelliousness so we'll play this little game until I tire of it. You aren't allowed to come until I give you permission."

She recognized the voice immediately and instinctively strained against her bonds.

"You should conserve your energy. You'll need it."

Fear made her heart pound. "I'm a cop. You'll never get away with this."

He chuckled. "Ah! That explains it."

She discarded the question that immediately rose to her mind as to what he was referring to. "I'm Detective Maura Downy. If you don't believe me, search my clothes for my badge."

"Maura," he murmured, almost as if he was tasting the name. "It doesn't matter to me what you were ... only what you are."

Maura swallowed convulsively. "What do you mean?"

"Mine."

Before she could demand to know what the hell he meant by that, she felt his mouth clamp down over one nipple. It sent such a hard shaft of pleasure and pain through her that she nearly blacked out. It fried her brain and made her belly clench so hard it cramped. She struggled to muffle the whimper clawing its way up her throat and was only partially successful as he sucked and pulled at her nipple as if he meant to gnaw it off. She couldn't speak. She couldn't think. She was barely conscious when he finally ceased, but before she could even drag in a breath of relief, he caught her other nipple in his mouth. She came as close to passing out as she'd ever come in her life without actually achieving that avenue of escape.

There *was* no escape. Strain though she did, she couldn't

pull away from him, couldn't move at all. She couldn't do anything but endure the tortuous pull of his mouth and try to catch her breath. He would suck and gnaw at one with the edge of his teeth while the pressure built in the other and then, when the blood had begun to pound painfully, abruptly seize it and torture it as he had the other, back and forth, on and on until she began to pray that she'd pass out.

When he finally stopped long enough she managed to drag in a breath, she searched her mind frantically for something to say to make him stop. "I'm sorry!" she gasped.

"Not yet, but you will be," he responded.

She nearly lost her mind when he caught her clit as he had her nipples, stripped it with the edge of his teeth, and then sucked it into his mouth. The muscles along her sex seized. Her heart hammered with incipient climax, and then ... nothing. Disappointment didn't begin to describe how she felt. Mindless was closer. She felt her body straining toward release and yet it continued to elude her until she was fighting tears.

She ceased trying to grasp her release when she couldn't stand it anymore and began trying to divert her mind from what he was doing, but she discovered it was useless. He seemed to know her body better than she did. He pulled until the sharp sensations gentled and then he moved to one of her nipples, which had had just enough time to reach the point where the pressure of the blood made it sheer torture for him to touch her, let alone to pull at her flesh so vigorously. It took every ounce of determination she could muster to keep from crying out each time, and it didn't get any better.

Hours, or so it seemed, passed. She didn't know. It seemed to her after a very few minutes that she'd been tortured forever, and yet as fevered as her skin was, despite the painful quakes that traveled through her, she couldn't achieve release.

She felt like crying when he finally stopped and allowed her to catch her breath, allowed her heart to stop its frantic pounding, but even she wasn't certain if it was from relief or disappointment. Her body throbbed all over. Her breasts and her sex throbbed far worse, however.

She'd begun to entertain some hope that he'd finished

with her, despite the fact that he hadn't made any attempt to loosen her bindings, when he began again. She was barely conscious when he stopped the second time, but, again, the hope rose that he was done tormenting her and, again, he dashed it.

She didn't make the mistake of thinking he was done the third time. She knew he wasn't. She tried to brace herself for the next assault and she still wasn't prepared. A mouth clamped down on both breasts and her clit at the same time. She should have exploded in climax. Instead, it seemed to be her mind that exploded. She couldn't catch her breath for several moments. She certainly couldn't grasp what was happening, although her mind scrambled in an effort to try.

She'd thought she was alone with him. How?

It flickered through her mind that she couldn't possibly be alone with him, but she was in too much pleasurable agony to think past that. The pulling stopped as abruptly as it had begun and it finally dawned on her that he wasn't stopping to rest or even to give her the false notion that he was done with her. He was waiting for the bindings to force the blood to pool again to achieve maximum sensation.

Her determination to endure in silence didn't last past the second three way assault. Nor did it occur to her to beg him to stop or release her. She began to beg him to let her come.

He didn't respond—not verbally. Instead, he continued the three-way assault until she thought she'd completely lose her mind and had begun weeping and begging and shaking all over.

She didn't feel movement, but she wasn't certain if it was because her senses had all been fried and gone haywire or if he didn't actually change her position. She didn't actually feel the bindings loosen, and yet she felt the pull of his hands on her legs, spreading them wide where before they'd been clamped tightly together. She whimpered when she felt his fingers stroke her cleft and then felt the pull of fingers on either side, spreading her cleft. Something enormous probed the mouth of her sex and a second probed her rectum at the same time, speared into her with little warning. Hands clasped her hips, driving her down onto the twin shafts, stretching her flesh until she whimpered again with a mixture of fear and anticipation, pain and pleasure, driving so deep she began to fear she'd be mortally impaled.

"You belong to the beast master," he murmured in a husky voice near her ear.

The words wafted over her, through her, made her shiver. She searched her beleaguered mind, trying to decide if there was a demand in the statement.

"You're still not certain?" he purred.

"Yes!" she gasped. "Please!"

He seemed to consider it for so long that she began to be more afraid he'd stop what he'd offered—what she thought he'd offered.

She thought he'd decided to punish her more when she felt his mouth clamp on her nipples and then her clit. Her mind went wild with the attempt to figure out how he could do that when she'd thought she was impaled on his cock, but then she had two huge rods in her and he certainly couldn't have two.

She ceased trying to understand or figure it out when she felt herself lifted and slammed down again, driving the rods deeply into her. The muscles along her sex quaked painfully, but again release was denied. The shafts began to move faster and faster, driving almost painfully deep each time, pistoning in and out of her until she couldn't catch her breath. And all the while she felt the unrelenting tug on her nipples and her clit.

She couldn't stand it! She was going to die, she thought weakly.

"Say it!" he growled.

She couldn't think. "I'm yours," she gasped.

"You're my slave, Maura."

"I'm your slave," she groaned.

"And you'll come to me each night."

"I'll come."

The thrusting increased. The tug on her nipples and her clit began to feel more like pain than a mixture of pleasure and pain. "Come for me, Maura."

The convulsion that hit her dragged a choked cry from her. She jerked as the spasms tore at her, flinging her toward unconsciousness and then snatching her back over and over until she was screaming hoarsely.

A profound relief swept over her just before she passed out.

She came to with a groan of despair, knowing it wasn't over, praying it was.

It wasn't and the climaxes began to be as much torture as withholding release from her had been. She came over and over, on and on, until she was hoarse and finally sank into an oblivion so deep her last thought was that she wouldn't ever wake up again.

\* \* \* \*

It was the sunlight beating against her closed eyes that finally roused Maura enough to open them. She stared blankly at the console of her car, struggling with a strange sense of déjà vu. Groaning, she pushed herself upright and looked around.

Her car was parked in the brush outside the walls of the mansion as it had been the last time she'd awakened in her car.

Frowning, Maura struggled to shake memories loose, but the only thing she could remember with any clarity was the decision to head out to Daegon's mansion to see if she could snoop while he was gone. She couldn't even remember parking the car when she'd arrived.

"What the hell?"

Her throat felt as if it had been scoured with sandpaper. Her mouth and throat were beyond dry, painfully parched. A brief search of the car revealed that she hadn't even brought coffee with her.

Shaking the sluggishness with an effort, she started the car, turned it around and headed into town. She felt worse, if possible, after spending her second night in the car.

Too weary to try to make any sense of what had happened, she drank until she'd managed to banish the 'dried husk' feel and collapsed in her bed. She was so sore she could hardly move when she woke up. Groaning, too needy for food to ignore it in favor of pampering her sore muscles, she went to the kitchen and wolfed down a sandwich.

She discovered when she got back to her bedroom that it was nine o'clock. A glance out the window was all it took to assure her that she'd slept all day.

Something wasn't adding up, but she was damned if she

could figure it out. It was bad enough that she kept falling asleep in her car, but to turn around and sleep all day?

The thirst and hunger, she supposed, was understandable. She couldn't recall that she'd had anything to eat or drink after the scrambled eggs she'd had before she'd gone to the club Noir. She didn't understand the weariness when she'd slept so long. She certainly didn't understand the soreness.

She supposed sleeping in her car wasn't the most comfortable place and, maybe, that accounted for some of it. But every muscle ached as if she'd had a thorough workout and she certainly hadn't.

It bothered her even more that she remembered so little about what had happened and what she'd done. The visit to Club Noir seemed pretty clear in her mind—almost too clear. She also remembered she'd felt like she was on X when she got home, so wound up her bedpost looked good to her.

She'd still felt that way when she'd headed out to Daegon's mansion, and yet she didn't now.

Actually, almost as soon as she began to think about it, she began to feel warm and as soon as she began to feel warm, she began to feel the urge to head out to his mansion again.

She shook her head at herself. Two nights she couldn't account for and she was thinking about going back?

She'd lost her marbles!

Trying to shake it, she dressed and headed to the kitchen for a snack and a tall glass of water when she saw she'd drank everything else in the house. Turning the TV on, she flopped on her couch and tried to focus on the screen. It didn't help. The longer she sat staring blankly at the tube, the stronger the urge became. Feeling a mixture of dread and determination, she got up after a little while, turned the TV off and headed out of her apartment.

She was almost relieved when she pulled in to what was rapidly becoming 'her' parking space and saw that the gates to the mansion were open and there was a light on in one of the rooms on the second floor.

Daegon was home. She certainly couldn't go in.

She turned off the car anyway and sat staring at the house. The sense began to settle in her that he was waiting for her, that he knew she'd come.

She had no idea where the notion had come from, but she couldn't shake it. The certainty became more pronounced and, from it, sprouted the compulsion to get out of her car and see if she was right.

Maybe she would just walk boldly up to the front door and ring the bell, she thought? She wasn't getting anywhere. Beyond that brief encounter at Noir that she'd found so disconcerting, she hadn't even managed to get near the guy. She wasn't going to learn anything sleeping in her car outside his gate.

Coming to a decision abruptly, she got out of the car and started toward the gate, more than half expecting it to close before she reached it since it had always been closed before. It didn't. The hair on the back of her neck prickled as she passed through. She glanced around the darkened grounds a little uneasily, but she didn't see any sign of the 'beast masters' pets roaming the yard.

The front door opened as she reached the steps to the stoop and Maura felt a jolt go through her as she looked up and met Daegon's gaze.

"Good girl," he murmured. "You're late, but you're learning."

Dread settled in Maura's belly. "Late?" she echoed shakily.

"Mmm." His eyes gleamed. "I begin to think you enjoy being punished for your rebelliousness. Do you, my pet?"

Maura's throat went dry as a collage of fragmented memories collided in her mind. She glanced back toward the gates uneasily. "I don't think so."

"No?"

She looked at him again. "No," she said more firmly.

He made a tsking noise, but his voice was a low growl when he spoke again. "You should try to be on time tomorrow, then. If you aren't ... well, I may have to get more inventive. If you'd learned your lesson last night, you would've known better than to keep me waiting. I don't have a lot of patience when I'm hungry."

## Chapter Five

Maura realized as soon as she surfaced that something was different. She'd experienced 'the waking' before. It wasn't like waking from sleep. It was more like reviving from a faint, and yet even as dread and anticipation mingled inside of her, she realized it wasn't the same before she even tried to open her eyes and discovered she could.

The room was shadowy, but there was enough light to see it looked like some sort of medieval torture chamber—not a cheesy mockup but real. It sent her mind into chaos. It wasn't until she tried to move and discovered she couldn't that she looked down at herself.

She was naked except for the intricately tied, knotted rope that bound her, forming diamond-like patterns across her bare flesh, but even that was different. Her legs had been bound together before. Now her knees were drawn up, doubled up and slightly to either side of her hips, spread far enough she began to feel the discomfort even before she looked down at herself. Her arms were behind her back as before, but tighter, drawn upward so that her back was arched, her chest thrust forward.

Her breasts had been bound tightly into pointy cones and her nipples were already tightly distended with the blood pounding in the tips. She couldn't see her genitals, but she could feel that the ropes running between her legs pulled the flesh to either side, leaving her cleft fully bared and worse, tightly bound enough the blood was pulsing there, as well.

A jolt went through her when she looked up and discovered Daegon was standing in front of her, watching her, his eyes narrowed. He lifted a hand, skating it lightly along her inner thigh until he reached the juncture of thigh and hip. He skimmed the pad of his thumb lightly back and forth along the artery and Maura felt heat rise inside of her, felt her kegels spasm.

She licked her dried lips. "You don't have to do this."

Amusement gleamed in his golden eyes when he met her

gaze. "I know I don't. This little mark makes you mine and I can do whatever I like ... and I enjoy it ever so much more this way."

The mention of the mark, to say nothing of the brushing motion of his thumb that was driving her crazy, abruptly made a memory surface. "They were yours, too," she said abruptly.

Something flickered in his eyes, but it wasn't wariness. His amusement deepened. "It that what brought you to me, my precious? The others?"

"Their deaths."

Surprise flickered in his eyes, but it was gone so quickly she might almost have imagined it. He shrugged. "Mortals. Unfortunately, as sweet as the meat is, it's tender."

"And you're not?"

He lifted a brow questioningly and finally lifted his hand, to her temporary relief. It was short lived. He 'tested' her nipples, watching her face as he pinched them. Maura swallowed with an effort. "Not mortal?" she said shakily.

He smiled. It sent a shiver along her spine. "You haven't guessed yet?" He studied her thoughtfully. "You aren't easily frightened. Would you like to see?"

Maura wasn't certain she did. He didn't wait for an answer. He waved a hand in front of his face and carried it downward. Her gaze automatically followed the movement.

One moment, he was fully clothed, the next instant naked—and not merely naked. Maura found herself staring at genitals like she'd never seen before. Two thick, long, obscenely huge cocks stood out from his lower belly. His flesh was an angry red, darker than her own blood-flushed sex and it went beyond his genitals. She followed the trail of knotted muscles up his belly to his face and sucked in a sharp breath.

Something flickered in his eyes. "You prefer the glamour?"

Maura swallowed with an effort, blinked, and when her eyes focused again, she saw Daegon as she'd come to know him. He leaned close, nuzzling her cheek and then licking a trail from her jaw to her ear. "I am the demon, Daegon, an Incubus to be precise."

The statement pitched Maura into complete turmoil. Her

body responded to his touch by catching fire, and yet fear and disbelief, dread and reluctance chased one another around and around in her head. "An Incubus? You killed them?"

He lifted his head. "I released them. They bored me. As tempting as they were, they failed to appease me. You won't, will you, my precious?"

She didn't know, but she was afraid it wasn't possible, not if he was, in truth, an Incubus. She was still trying to decide if there was any hope of escape when he caught her hips and impaled her on the double shaft protruding spear-like from his lower belly. Despite the heat he'd already aroused in her, despite the moisture coating her sex, his enormous cocks stretched her as he pushed her inexorably down over them until she felt the burn of being stretched beyond her limits. She gasped, tensed and then struggled to relax when she realized she couldn't evade him and she was only causing herself more pain in trying. She was panting for breath and so dizzy when he finally stopped that darkness invaded her sight when she opened her eyes.

"It hurts?"

She didn't know what answer he wanted, but she felt as if she'd been impaled on two posts. Almost the moment he spoke, however, the pain began to recede and pleasure began to take its place. His eyes were gleaming knowingly when she met his gaze. "That's part of the punishment," he murmured. "You haven't forgotten you displeased me?"

She realized abruptly what was coming and a mixture of dread and excitement began to pound through her. "You didn't say what time I was supposed to come."

"Didn't I?"

She blinked at him, but she didn't remember him telling her to come to him at all. In fact, until she'd woken bound, she hadn't remembered any of this.

But he was a demon. As hard as that was to grasp, she either had to accept what she'd seen with her own eyes or assume she'd lost her mind. And demons deceived, didn't they?

"You know what comes next, my sweet little mortal?"

Maura swallowed, tried to shake her head and finally answered when she realized she couldn't. "No."

He smiled. It was almost a sweet smile, but the demon gleamed in his golden eyes. "You're not allowed to come until I allow it."

"Oh god!"

He chuckled. "There is no god here—only you and me."

She tried to brace herself when he lowered his head to her breast, but she might've saved herself the effort. Acid boiled through her when he raked his teeth along the tender captive and lava flowed behind it when he closed his lips around it and sucked. She closed her eyes, trying to shut out the sensations pouring through her but realized almost immediately that it was a mistake. Closing her eyes only focused her entire being on the tortuous tugging of his mouth. She opened her eyes again, staring down at him and felt him bite her other nipple.

Confusion tore through her with the pain and pleasure. He hadn't touched her there. She could see he wasn't even touching her with his hand.

And then she felt a tug on her clit that nearly made her black out. Unfortunately, it didn't. She bit her lip until she tasted blood, fighting the urge to scream. Nothing she could ever have imagined could have felt so exquisitely wonderful and torturous at the same time. Her kegels clenched madly around the cock he'd driven deeply inside of her. Her sphincter tightened spastically around the cock in her rectum. Her body gathered itself to find release and hovered there, endlessly.

He fed on her flesh until she felt as if she was being eaten alive, pulling so hungrily at her that a constant war raged between pleasure and pain. She almost felt like weeping when he finally stopped, partly with relief, and partly because he hadn't assuaged the need pounding through her for release.

He waited until her body had begun to calm itself and started over. She'd given up trying to hold her cries inside by the time he stopped again.

"You won't disappoint me again?"

Maura couldn't even grasp the question for several moments. When he started again, though, it jogged her mind. "I won't! I swear I won't!"

Either she was too slow to answer or he hadn't intended to stop regardless of how she answered. He continued as if he hadn't heard her. The cocks began to move, as well, knocking the breath from her as they were withdrawn and slammed deeply again, faster and deeper until he was ramming into her steadily and she felt like she would go up in flames.

"Do you adore me, my slave?" he murmured when he finally released her breast.

"Yes!" she gasped immediately and discovered as soon as she said it that she *felt* it, adoration, need.

"Come for me, baby."

She screamed when her climax tore through her and kept screaming until he finally allowed her to stop coming.

She'd barely managed to catch her breath when he began again. She groaned, feeling the familiar mixture of dread and anticipation, wondering if she would survive.

She was nearly comatose when he finally decided he was satisfied.

\* \* \* \*

Daegon didn't particularly want to stop, but he felt the encroachment of dawn and knew he had to send her home. A strange sort of uneasiness flickered through him when he studied her limp form. He frowned, trying to determine the source of it and finally realized it was her near lifelessness that had caused it. He'd gotten carried away, he realized with annoyance, wondering uneasily if he'd broken his favorite toy. It didn't make him feel any better when he discovered how weak her pulse was.

It did occur to him rather forcefully, though, the moment he realized how wonderfully satisfied he felt, that he'd been incautious. He'd gotten too wrapped up in his pretty little slave. He hadn't even gone to Noir the night before as he should have.

His overlord was going to grow suspicious and put her beyond his reach if he wasn't careful.

He studied her face thoughtfully, reluctantly, and finally decided it would be better all the way around if he steered clear of her for a few days. She would have time to recover, he was sure, and he could manage on the meager feedings allowed him at Noir.

He would have to, he told himself, else he ran the risk of losing her entirely and as reluctant as he was to give her up for a day or two, giving her up altogether didn't bear thinking on.

Two days, he wondered? Three? More?

He couldn't stand more, he decided. He was reluctant to give her up for three, but he didn't want to risk discovery and Trydan would certainly become suspicious if he seemed too satisfied.

"Three days, Maura," he murmured in her ear when he had settled her in her car. "Three days, no more. Come to me. I will be hungry then. I can't contain the hunger longer or guarantee that I could stop if you disappoint me again.

\* \* \* \*

"You look like death warmed over, Downy," Thompson growled.

Maura struggled and finally managed to shoot him a bird. "Bite me."

"Looks like something already did. Why didn't you just call in sick again?"

"Because I didn't feel like dragging my ass out of bed to see a doctor. I figured if I had to get up anyway, I might as well get paid."

"You get sick pay," Thompson said pointedly.

"Whatever. I was planning on adding my sick days to my vacation time."

"Well, maybe you ought to consider taking a vacation. I'm serious. You look like hell."

"Thanks."

"You're welcome. Why don't I head back to the station, you grab the paperwork, and I'll take you home?"

"I need my car," Maura said pointedly.

Thompson looked her over doubtfully. "I'll get a patrolman to drop it off."

"Fine!" Maura said, too sick to care. She was glad her partner had been so insistent by the time she got home again. She'd filled out the papers on the trip and handed them to Thompson as she got out.

"I'll give you a call tomorrow and see how you're doing."

Maura turned to look at her partner in surprise. "I look that bad, huh?"

He shrugged. "Take it easy. The city won't fall apart without you—it's pretty quiet anyway."

It was. That was the only reason she'd allowed her parents to badger her in to investigating Cheryl Malone's suicide on the side.

*Not* that she was in any shape at the moment even to consider it!

She was asleep almost before she hit the mattress. She

didn't feel a whole lot better when she woke up, but thirst and hunger drove her from the bed. Discovering she had next to nothing in the apartment, she jogged her mind, trying to remember the last time she'd shopped for groceries. Giving up after a few minutes, she settled for a can of soup and as much water as she could hold and went back to bed. It was morning when she woke the next time and she almost felt normal.

Well, until she got up. Dizziness assailed her the minute she stood up and she thought for several moments that she was going to faint. Thankfully, it passed after a moment and she headed into her bathroom to attend her needs and bathe.

There was barely enough coffee in the jar for a weak half cup. When she'd downed it, she felt like she might be able to make it to the grocer, however. Her car was parked at the curb when she went out. She studied it for a moment. Ordinarily, she would've walked, but she discovered she didn't feel like it. Besides, she was out of everything. Walking with one or two bags was one thing. Trying to carry three or four didn't appeal to her at all.

The shopping itself was an exercise in endurance. By the time she had the buggy half full, she was ready to collapse. Gritting her teeth, she finished up as quickly as she could and headed home again.

There was a wolf crouched by the shrub near her steps when she got out. It sent a jolt through her. After staring at it for several moments, trying to convince herself it was just a big dog, Maura finally turned away and reached back inside the car for her bags. When she straightened again, the wolf had disappeared.

Frowning, she glanced up and down the street, but there was no sign of it. Wondering if she should add hallucinations to her repertoire of symptoms, she dragged herself upstairs to her apartment, dropped the groceries on the table and headed into her room for a nap.

Her cold stuff was room temperature when she woke, but the nap had refreshed her considerably. Settling at the table in the kitchen, she searched the bags until she found the ready to eat items she'd bought and munched chips and swigged juice from the bottle until she felt like getting up. Promising herself a real meal next time, she stowed the groceries and headed into her living room to flake out on the couch.

It dawned on her as she lay the couch staring out the window instead of watching what was on the TV that she'd seen that wolf before—the one she'd thought was a hallucination. She'd seen him at Noir the night she went.

She'd seen him before that at Daegon's mansion—or since.

Closing her eyes, she struggled to summon the memory and finally produced it.

The wolf was one of the animals that had herded her to Daegon's door.

The beast master.

The incubus.

She swallowed convulsively several times, but once the memories began to filter into her mind, they quickly became an avalanche. She rubbed her eyes, clamping her hands around her head as if that would stop the flow of images. It didn't, but she discovered that fog seemed to enshroud them, making them fuzzy and indistinct around the edges—almost like remnants of a dream.

Was she remembering some bizarre dream, or dreams?

What would make her dream that she'd been bound and fucked half to death by a demon?

Discovering she had a blinding headache in a matter of moments, she got up to search for a painkiller. After popping a couple of ibuprofen and chasing the pills with juice, she returned to the living room and turned off the TV.

It was hard to accept what she thought she could remember as reality, far easier, she discovered, to think it was dreams.

It almost made sense that way. She'd been struggling to find out what she could about Cheryl Malone, turned up nothing, and her dreams had attempted to fill in the blanks.

Except she could remember things she rarely remembered from dreams. She could remember being bound so tightly she couldn't move a muscle. She remembered feeling pleasure and pain so keenly her body responded to the memory, remembered feeling it in a tortuous mixture that made her feel like she was dying.

A super wet dream slash nightmare?

There was no denying there was a dream-like quality to the memories, but wouldn't that explain, at least in part, why she felt so drained when she woke up? Not just tired, but as if she'd had the life nearly sucked out of her.

It would if Daegon was a demon, an Incubus.

Frowning, she got and grabbed her lap top. When she'd connected, she did a search for information about the Incubus. She supposed it shouldn't have come as a surprise, much less a shock, to discover they fed on sexual pleasure. He'd told her he was hungry, she remembered abruptly, that he wasn't patient when he was hungry.

He'd also told her that he hadn't had anything to do with the death of those women. He'd discarded them when he was done with them.

Her belly tightened and a wave of nausea rolled through her.

She shied away from the reasons behind it, trying to focus and remember what else he'd said. She discovered she couldn't actually remember a hell of a lot. She could remember his voice. A shiver skated through her even at the memory.

Unfortunately, she couldn't convince herself that it was a shiver of fear or revulsion. It was hard to deny the way her kegels clapped at the memory.

What the hell had he done to her? Besides screwing her brains out until she nearly expired?

He'd touched her between her legs. He'd told her that was his mark and she belonged to him.

And maybe that explained the wolf at her door?

That time the shiver was definitely from nerves. She didn't have to look at the mark. She knew it was the same, strange mark she'd found on the women who'd committed suicide, but she undressed and examined it anyway. It didn't make her feel any better when she'd confirmed it. It was the same strange symbol, darker than she remembered, almost blood red, but definitely in the same place and definitely the same mark.

What the hell had she gotten herself in to?

How was she supposed to get rid of a demon, assuming she wasn't crazy as a loon?

Wait until he got tired of her, her mind told her.

The sick feeling that washed through her that time was harder to ignore. She struggled with it for a moment and finally met it head on.

She wasn't afraid that he wouldn't let her go, she realized.

She was afraid that he would discard her ... just like he had the others.

"Jesus!" she muttered, curling into a ball and holding her head in her hands. Maybe she *did* need her head examined?

She shook that thought. As long as she was still sane enough to question her sanity, she was sane. She'd heard that somewhere and it gave her some comfort.

Beyond that, and as unbelievable as it seemed to her when she'd always had her feet planted firmly in reality and never believed hocus-pocus, she had *seen* him transform himself into demon form. She didn't remember anything very clearly but the two cocks, but she sure as hell remembered them! She remembered what they felt like when he worked them inside of her, when he'd been thrusting into her frenziedly.

A shudder rippled through her—of remembered delight. She'd enjoyed it. As much as she hated to admit it even to herself, she'd enjoyed it even when she thought he was going to rip her in two. She'd enjoyed the pain, not for itself, but for the possession and with the absolute certainty that he would give her pleasure that matched or surpassed it.

He'd teased her about wanting to be punished. She hadn't even realized at the time that that was what he was doing— not threatening her, *promising* he'd give her what she wanted.

She wasn't crazy. She was a sick puppy! How could she have endured it let alone enjoyed it?

But she had. She knew she had, even when she'd always thought the BDSM crowd was off their rockers, had sneered at the idea of wanting to be treated that way!

He'd done something to her, she decided, knowing even as the thought came to her that she was grasping at straws because she didn't want to know that side of herself existed.

And when all was said and done did it really matter how it had come about? She couldn't deny she enjoyed it any more than she could refuse him.

He owned her. She was the beast master's slave until he decided to set her free.

## Chapter Six

Maura was torn the moment she remembered that Daegon had commanded her to present herself to him in three days—instantly torn. The first impulse that hit her was dismay that she had to wait three days. Hard on the heels of that, so close behind that she barely had time even to acknowledge the longing she'd begun to nurture, alarm went through her for the same reason. Three days wasn't much time to think of a solution to her problem, especially when she'd slept through the first!

She was reasonably satisfied that she'd solved the mystery that had thrown her in his path to begin with. No one was going to like it, but she felt that it was the truth.

Cheryl Malone, and the others, had simply become dependent upon Daegon in a very big way when he'd taken them as his slaves and when he'd discarded them they'd caved in. In some ways, it didn't make any more sense than any other suicide which, unfortunately, didn't preclude the possibility in and of itself, especially since the investigators and the coroner were satisfied in their findings. They hadn't been able to cope and that had seemed like a solution to them.

There were plenty of people, men and women, who sought suicide as a solution to various problems they couldn't deal with and dependency on a person who'd dumped them was one of those, maybe one of the biggest causes.

Although she was beginning to understand far better than she likely would have if she hadn't been caught in the same net, she certainly couldn't tell her parents, or Cheryl's, why it made sense to her. Daegon wasn't just any man—or even a man at all. Cheryl might have become just as attached if he had been, but Maura doubted it.

In any case, that particular part didn't matter. The bottom line was that Daegon had no reason to lie about it that she could see. He was a demon. He wasn't worried in the least that she was a detective when he'd taken her because he had no reason to worry about their laws.

That train of thought finally led her to something that had been nagging at her.

If Daegon wasn't constrained by human laws, was he constrained in some way by his own? She thought he must be. From what she'd read—and granted it was debatable just how much of it was reliable—as an Incubus it was in his nature to feed until he was satisfied and that usually resulted in death for the mortal unfortunate enough to catch his interest.

She couldn't be certain, of course, but she was fairly sure that *something* had stopped him from doing that with the women who'd ended up committing suicide. Something had prevented him from doing it to her. Considering how dehydrated she'd been after these sessions, she was pretty sure the coroner would have detected signs that Daegon had at least contributed to their deaths if he had.

Whatever had constrained him, it certainly wasn't love or any kind of affection as mortals thought of it. As unhappy as it made her to consider it, she realized she actually fell in the category of food, not companion or lover.

Of course she did love her favorite donuts, but not in the same way she held people in affection. Daegon wasn't human and couldn't have human emotions so his motives would be different than human motivations—at least to an extent.

Noir must be his primary feeding grounds, she realized abruptly. Maybe he was only allowed to feed there? Well, she supposed he must be allowed to take 'food' home since she knew that was where she'd been, but if she accepted that he was a demon, then she also had to accept that he wasn't even restrained by the *physical* laws of her world, let alone the manmade laws.

It seemed like a sound deduction. As far as she knew he was never seen outside of those two places so it seemed reasonable to assume he wasn't allowed to hunt outside those areas. Otherwise, surely he would've? It must chaff him not to be able to hunt at will, to be prevented from roaming as he pleased, possibly even restrained from feeding as he pleased.

So another demon, stronger than him, or at least more powerful in some way, was holding the reigns?

If she was right, did that mean that she could escape him simply by avoiding those two places?

*That* was why he had the beasts, she realized abruptly! That must be it! *He* couldn't breach the boundaries and he sent them when he couldn't!

Did she dare test the theory, though?

Did she want to?

By the end of her second day, she realized she had a serious problem. She'd begun to feel like an addict that needed a fix.

On the level of reason, she didn't want to go back. She wanted to test the chain and see if she could break it and have her life back the way it was. She should've felt that even more strongly on an emotional level. She *should* hate him. He hadn't used drugs to take her will to resist or refuse, but he'd used magic and that was pretty much the same thing in the end.

She couldn't get around the fact that she didn't feel violated, however. It should have been her first reaction as soon as she'd finally remembered, but it hadn't been. She would've liked to put it down to shock, but she wasn't much for self-deception. On some levels she *was* angry. He'd shown her a side of herself she hadn't known existed and hadn't *wanted* to know was there.

But she didn't feel violated.

She toyed with the idea that, maybe, he'd used some kind of magic to make her feel like she liked it and wanted it when she really didn't, but she had to discard it. No amount of soul searching unearthed anything but her unhappiness at discovering she enjoyed being dominated and used almost beyond what she could bear physically or emotionally.

He was an evil bastard, she was sure. He was a demon after all, but she didn't loathe him.

Truth be told, she discovered she actually pitied him in a way. He couldn't help what he was. However he'd come into being, he'd come as an Incubus and he was as bound by that as any mortal was bound to being human. He was a sentient being, which meant he could make choices, good or bad, but to eat or not to eat wasn't actually a choice. What one fed on, might be. Whether one was a glutton or conservative might be, depending on one's nature, of course—that was hard to fight, too.

The one thing that really stood out in her mind, though, was his hunger—and hunger translated to suffering.

Maybe she was crazy to think like that, but once that understanding settled in her, she began to see him in an entirely different light. She began to think that, just possibly, he was being punished for something.

And maybe he deserved it. Maybe she would never know why and maybe if she did know she would agree that he deserved to suffer.

All she did know was that she didn't hate him for being what he was and that she couldn't help but view him as a lover even knowing he viewed her as food.

And that brought her to the physical level—a growing addiction that was something she should be worried about. By rights, she should be sexually satisfied enough to last her a life time. She might not clearly remember all of it, but she remembered enough that she knew she'd climaxed more in the time she'd been with him than her entire life previously. Beyond that, they hadn't been 'simple' releases. He didn't just know how to prevent her from coming until he was ready. He knew how to hold her at her peak and keep her convulsing with waves of pleasure until she thought she would die.

Playing with Daegon the Incubus was as bad or worse than playing with fire. It wasn't safe to indulge her sexual fantasies with him even though, physically, she'd already developed a strong craving to do so. *Particularly* because she had.

Strong enough that as soon as she'd recovered she'd begun to feel the pull to go back for more.

She might not have any choice in the matter. She might have to wait until he got tired of her and discarded her as he had the women before her, but her rational mind was warning her that she had to try. There was a real danger for her even if he was prevented from feeding on her until he sucked her dry.

Her understanding of and empathy for him was part of the problem. She would've been better off if she'd been able to simply view him as a beast. There wouldn't have been a danger then that she might become emotionally entangled as well as physically dependent. *That* was dangerous enough in and of itself.

She was pretty sure he'd already ruined her for mortal men, though. The best—mortal—dom in the world wasn't going to be able to do for her what Daegon could as easily as breathing.

She could live with it, she told herself firmly. It wasn't as if she hadn't already had disappointments in her life. As bad as her dependency was already, though, she would be worlds better off to cut the cord herself, as quickly as possible. She'd learned what she'd set out to discover. She needed to put the incident behind her as quickly as possible.

She went to bed the second night with that firmly implanted in her mind and woke up the following morning feeling energized. She wouldn't go back. She would ignore the pull. No doubt, like any addiction, it would be hard at first, but she was confident she could do it.

Too antsy to stay cooped up, Maura decided to take care of errands she'd been neglecting. Her first stop was her parents' house. She explained to them that, as far as she'd been able to determine, Cheryl Malone had gotten deeply into the BDSM crowd and had become involved with a man. When he'd broken it off, she had become so depressed, she'd killed herself.

They weren't satisfied. She wasn't surprised. Nobody wanted a simple answer when they weren't willing to accept the truth to begin with and she imagined Cheryl's parents would be even less willing to accept. She refused to give them the name of the man Cheryl had been involved with, though. It would lead them straight to Daegon and that might well end in tragedy for Cheryl's parents. They were just going to have to accept that their daughter had become dependent to an unhealthy degree and couldn't handle the rejection.

She was almost sorry she'd made that her first stop, but it had always been her habit to take care of the most unpleasant tasks first. Putting them off didn't make them go away. It only allowed one to become increasingly reluctant to take care of it at all.

Her other errands weren't particularly 'uplifting' if it came to that. She dropped her car off to be serviced and walked to the cleaners to drop off clothes and then returned to pace until the car was ready. The service set her back enough to depress her and then there were the bills.

Discovering when her head began to pound that she'd missed lunch, she decided to treat herself before she headed home again—nothing like spending *more* money to perk one up after paying bills!

It *did* lift her spirits, however, until she caught a glimpse of the wolf. Her heart instantly went into overdrive. As before, he vanished the moment she was distracted and took her eyes off of him, but it didn't matter. She'd seen him. It didn't even do any good to try to convince herself it was pure imagination. *Thinking* she'd spotted him was enough to focus her mind in a direction she'd been working hard to prevent.

And it couldn't have come at a worse time! It was late in the afternoon by then. She'd finished her errands and had nothing to do but return to her apartment and think and pace.

Naturally enough, as soon as she began to dwell on it, she began to feel the pull. It made it worse that she abruptly remembered Daegon's warning—'Don't test me. I'll be hungry and I don't have much patience when I'm hungry'.

"Shit!" Maura ground out angrily, feeling her belly knot with a mixture of dread and, loathe though she was to admit it, excitement.

In all her plan making, she'd carefully avoided considering that her determination to break the hold he had on her might incite Daegon's wrath. She thought that was because she'd convinced herself that, as long as she avoided him, he couldn't get to her.

It resurrected another memory, though, reminded her that Daegon had speculated that she enjoyed the 'punishment'. She might. She didn't think she'd deliberately provoked him before, though. The spell, or whatever, that he put over her to control her had also seemed to have the effect of locking the memories in her subconscious.

Maybe subconsciously, she wanted to provoke him so that he would punish her?

She hated to think so, but she couldn't discount it. Was that what she was feeling now, though?

Or was she using it as an excuse to convince herself to go to him because she wanted to anyway? I *have* to go, otherwise it could be worse?

Maybe, but she also wanted control of her life back. She also thought he was very bad for her and she was concerned that she would only become more deeply dependent on him if she continued to put herself in harm's way.

If he truly was suffering as she thought, she empathized, but it wasn't her job to make it better. He'd managed just fine before she came along. He would manage if she left.

Of course, that might lead him to snatch another 'slave' and then another woman might lose her life, but she couldn't do anything about that. Daegon hadn't done anything 'illegal' beyond forcibly seducing her, and *she* sure as hell wasn't pressing charges! As far as she knew or had been able to discover, Cheryl and the others had presented themselves for use, just like all the other women she'd met at Noir.

If the stranger she'd spoken to was any indication, and she thought she probably was, every woman that entered Noir *hoped t*o catch his eye and become his love slave. And they didn't seem to be laboring under any deception. The woman had told her right off that everyone thought he was either an Incubus or a vampire.

None of that helped her at the moment. She either had to present herself as ordered or risk the consequences if he did manage to get to her. Which, she wondered, was more risky to her? Going and hoping he'd get tired and let her go before she was really ruined? Or taking the chance that she was right and he couldn't do anything as long as she stayed clear of his domain?

And did she actually have a choice?

She'd seen the wolf twice. She had a feeling that he'd deliberately shown himself so that she would know she was being watched by Daegon's minions, or familiars, or whatever they were called. They'd herded her to him before, though, because she'd placed herself in a position where they could. She didn't think they had magic of their own, which meant all that they could do was scare her—or possibly eat her.

She paced her apartment for hours, wrestling with her thoughts and the need that blossomed and steadily grew stronger until she couldn't ignore it anymore. When she reached that point, however, she discovered to her horror that it was nearly ten o'clock at night. She'd missed her call. She'd missed her chance to present herself as ordered, at dusk, and Daegon was probably already pissed off.

That unnerved her enough that she had to fight the urge to dash off to his mansion immediately, but when she managed to calm herself a little, she realized that it might be a good thing. The die had been cast. All she had to do was stick it out, refuse to go, and, hopefully, eventually, she would cease to feel the pull. Hopefully, he would turn to someone else and she could have her life back.

It was the shakiest resolution she'd ever made. Nothing she tried served to cool her blood or shake the growing anxiety about angering Daegon. It wasn't much of a relief that he didn't appear in her apartment and vent his rage on her. She could *imagine* it reaching the boiling point and spilling over. She was just glad her imagination failed her when she tried to envision the extent of Daegon's wrath. She was sure it must be terrible.

\* \* \* \*

It had been far harder to wait the three days he had convinced himself he needed to than Daegon had thought it would be and that unnerved him. He did his best not to think about that aspect of his situation, but it was hard to ignore the uneasiness that twisted his belly when he considered what he might feel like if he didn't have Maura to look forward to.

It almost seemed to him that it was *more* tortuous knowing he had her waiting at the end of his self-imposed fast than it had been when there had been nothing to look forward to.

Not that that mattered, he assured himself. He *did* have Maura and she appeased him as no other mortal he'd found before. He'd been as close to complete satisfaction as he'd ever come before in his entire existence when he'd, very reluctantly, sent her on her way to 'plump up' for him.

He was so complacent, in point of fact, that it was nearly his undoing. He had realized it was necessary to give Maura time to recover. She was mortal, after all, and there was a limit to the energy she could expend and still recover. If he was careful with her, she could be almost an endless source to him to stave off the endless gnawing within him.

It was hard to be practical about it, but he'd accepted that it was his best option.

Unfortunately, he'd not only been thoroughly sated when he'd finally let her go to rest for him, he'd been looking forward to her return and that had been enough to tamp his appetite sufficiently that it had caught his overlord's attention. He'd recovered his mistake. He thought he had, by feeding wildly enough the second night that his overlord had banished him to the mansion, but he couldn't shake the fear that he'd aroused his overlord's suspicions and not completely appeased them.

He would have to be more careful, he cautioned himself.

That worked right up until dusk settled on the third day and Maura didn't come. Struggling with his anger, disappointment, and the gnawing hunger, he'd questioned his beasts. He'd set them the task of guarding her and protecting her if necessary from would be poachers and the like. She was mortal after all. They were so fragile there was never any telling what might snatch their souls from their bodies and leave them useless.

That reassured him, briefly. She was fine. She seemed strong and healthy, fully recovered. She'd been up and about, running around the city performing 'man tasks'.

That had reminded Daegon that mortals had regular tasks they had to perform to provide for themselves and he'd begun to think that, maybe, her work was interfering with his needs. Not that that was an excuse! She was his. She didn't have to do those things. If she had needs, he could take care of them. All she had to do was tell him.

She hadn't, though. He'd been too busy feeding on her to consider any of that and he hadn't spared the time to question her.

He should do that, he told himself. Not that he meant to excuse her on those grounds, but it wouldn't inconvenience him again if he took care of it.

After questioning his beasts carefully, though, he discovered that wolf had overheard the man in the 'man box' mention 'vacation' and Maura seemed to be completely free to come and go as she pleased.

He knew that word. It meant they weren't required to work for a time. It was rather along the lines of what he'd done—given her free time to recover.

It thoroughly pissed him off the minute he realized she didn't even have the excuse of being tied up with mortal concerns.

She'd defied him! Again!

His rage boiled over. He expended it on his 'prison'. The beasts, wisely, made themselves scarce. By the time he'd demolished everything he could—which included everything inside the mansion, everything except the mansion itself—there was nothing but rubble around him and he'd weakened himself to an alarming degree. That only made his hunger worse and brought his anger to a boil again.

"She will regret it!" he stormed. "She will suffer as I have before I am done with her—*more* than I've suffered, damn her! She has no inkling of the lengths that I can make her suffer and *still* prevent her from slipping away from me in death!"

The echo of his own voice through the cavernous mansion unnerved him, brought him crashing back to reality with a vengeance. He froze, more than half expecting his overlord to appear, triumphant that he'd given himself away.

Relaxing fractionally when he didn't, he glared at the shambles he'd created for a while and finally decided that it might be best to put it back together. Chances were, his overlord would only view it as a tantrum he'd thrown because he'd been barred from Noir and gloat over it, but he didn't want to take the risk, not when Trydan had already become suspicious. He could only hide just so much from the bastard!

Maura would come back—eventually. He was confident she would. She was amazingly strong willed for a mortal, but she couldn't fight him forever. He'd marked her. She could resist—she had—but the pull would only become stronger the longer she fought it.

He was going to *enjoy* teaching her a lesson she would never forget! She was going to be *begging* him to give her release before he did! And maybe he'd leave her clinging to a thread of her soul and maybe he wouldn't!

## Chapter Seven

Maura wasn't sure whether it was fear of Daegon that kept her tossing and turning most of the night or if it was the growing need, but by mid-afternoon the following day she no longer had doubts. She needed him and not even the fear of what he would do to punish her for trying to elude him was enough to prevent her from getting in her car and driving out to the mansion.

She was so anxious, in fact, that she left well before dusk only to discover that she was barred from entering. She felt perfectly blank when she discovered that not only were the gates not standing open for her, but she couldn't scale the gate.

A different sort of fear gripped her then. What if he'd gotten so furious he'd discarded her?

She couldn't believe he had and she couldn't convince herself he hadn't. Giving up finally, she tried to sit patiently in the car and wait for dusk. When she found she couldn't, she got out again and paced.

To her vast relief, as dusk fell, the gates opened. With relief, anxiety, and need churning in her until she felt sick with it, she braced herself and went in. Daegon met her on the stoop and one look at his face was enough to assure her that he was more than a little pissed off. There wasn't a trace of gentleness or amusement in his expression. He was seething, so furious he didn't even speak.

Her knees turned to water. If she could've mastered any coordination, she thought she would've tried to run regardless of his beasts, despite the very real possibility of angering him more.

He narrowed his eyes at her. "Don't even consider it, woman!" he growled.

It was almost as if the words unfroze her. Maura managed to whirl away from him, but she hadn't taken two steps when the darkness engulfed her.

\* \* \* \*

Maura wasn't certain if it was the discomfort of rough fingers pulling at the tender flesh of her cleft and genitals that roused her toward awareness or if he'd lifted the veil to be certain she was aware, but it didn't take her mind long to grasp what was happening, regardless. He pried his flesh into hers with a ruthless determination that she knew was intentionally hurtful. It was her instinct to deprive him of pleasure in knowing that made her try to contain the sounds of her distress, but she discovered fairly quickly that she didn't actually have an option. Her entire head, with the exception of her nose, was encased in something as it had been the first time.

"I made these especially for you," he muttered in a purring growl near her ear, "a perfect fit for your body to be certain I caused no harm."

Disbelief instantly flickered through her mind. It hurt. If he was trying to say he was tender, he was way off the mark and she wasn't buying it. Relief filled her, though, when he finally achieved full penetration and stopped. The instant he did, the burning pain began to ease and her body warmed with gratitude at the cessation of pain.

"I could have made them thicker, longer—big enough to cause real pain, injured you—killed you outright or allowed you a slow death. The energy is the same to me, whether its pain or pleasure for you."

He *did* think he was reminding her that he had been careful with her, she realized, outraged!

"Your life means nothing to me, mortal! *Nothing!* You infest this world like annoying insects. There are millions more just like you! I *chose* to give you pleasure, more than any mortal will ever give you, and you repaid my kindness with betrayal, rebellion ... torment."

Anger had swept through her at the beginning of his speech. The last word gave her pause, however. *She* had tormented herself by refusing to answer his call. It had been a hellish two days—more actually, because as soon as she'd recovered the heat had begun to eat at her and it had grown worse by leaps and bounds the longer she refused to acknowledge her 'addiction'.

Had it been as bad for him? Worse?

It was hard to grasp that it might have been even though she'd acknowledged that he was a creature that drew his sustenance from the energy mortal bodies expended in the throes of passion, that it was as necessary to him as water and food were to her. She might accuse him of being a self-centered bastard, but she certainly hadn't given any thought to his suffering when she'd been fighting returning to him. She knew she hadn't and, worse for her, *he* knew she hadn't.

It flickered through her mind that that was the root of his anger. Maybe he was trying to convince himself as much as her that she was insignificant to him in any way, but she'd already deduced that she *was* at least in the sense that she was his primary source for his needs.

He didn't allow her to dwell on it long. Once he began the assault to her senses, her thoughts refused to make connections in her mind, scattered and rolled in drunken circles like beads tossed carelessly on the floor. It was almost more than she could endure, the exquisite torture of unrelieved pleasure, endless. The brief moments of respite weren't for her benefit, she knew, but to allow her to cool enough so that he could start again with optimum effect. It seemed to go on for hours and hours, but she had no concept of time encased as she was in the hood of darkness.

The time came, regardless, when she began to anticipate release. Before, when he'd punished her, he'd given until she thought she couldn't stand it anymore, withholding release until she thought she would lose her mind. In time, though, he'd given her release, allowed her climax. That had been as much torture in its own way because he hadn't simply allowed it. He'd made her convulse with pleasure until she'd thought she would die from that.

She dreaded it in a sense, but she began to look forward to it with desperation.

He didn't give it to her. Instead, after arousing her over and over until she couldn't keep tears of weakness and frustration from seeping from her eyes and rolling down her cheeks, he simply stopped and left her.

She was in too much agony at first to realize she was no longer bound—not as she had been, at any rate. She'd been curled into a fetal position for some time before it dawned on her that she'd been allowed the instinctive urge to curl into herself.

She was still naked, still blinded by whatever covered her eyes, but the heat radiating off of her skin began to cool by degrees until she was shivering. Discovering she could move her arms, her hands moved to the thing covering her eyes of their own accord. If it was a blindfold, however, she couldn't find a knot or pull it off. Giving up after a while, she lay panting, trying to regain her strength and then explored the surface where she lay. She thought it was a bed. The tightness around her throat was a collar studded with wicked points that pricked her fingers. A heavy chain led from it across the bed.

She was so thirsty she felt like her tongue was swollen. It was the demands of her body that finally led to the notion that he'd allowed her the freedom to take care of them and that thought drove her to explore further. The heavy chain struck stone as she wiggled to the edge of the mattress, the sound startlingly loud. She froze for several moments and then pushed her legs over the side and pushed herself into a sitting position, waving her arms in front of her blindly.

Nothing met her fingers. Dizziness and an acute sense of disorientation swept through her when she struggled to stand on her feet. The muscles in her legs quivered, threatened to give out, but once she'd stood for a few moments, the feeling passed. Moving slowly, sliding her feet alone the cold stone floor, she explored the limits of the chain and found a narrow door. The certainty leapt into her mind that it was a bathroom for her needs and she felt her way inside and discovered she'd guessed right.

She relieved herself and then scooped water from the lavatory and drank it until her tongue and throat didn't feel as swollen with thirst, bitterly grateful that he'd at least uncovered her mouth. Using the chain to guide her, she found her way back to the bed and discovered the other end embedded in the wall. A few tugs were enough to convince her she couldn't pull free. When she dropped the chain in defeat, it clanged dully against wood before it hit the floor. An exploration with her hands produced the information that it was a table, or maybe a low chest beside the bed. She found a plate of food and a mug.

Her belly tightened. He had no intention of releasing her—certainly not any time soon if he'd provided for her needs, she realized. It was small comfort that he clearly didn't intend for her to starve or die of thirst.

She wasn't hungry. She was too thirsty to feel any hunger, but it certainly wasn't in her best interests to allow herself to grow any weaker. She ate what she could of the bread and cheese and drank the juice in the mug, wishing it was something alcoholic instead so that she could drink herself into a stupor.

Truthfully, she was as near a stupor, she supposed, as she needed to be—except her flesh still felt as if ants were crawling over her, stinging her. She lay down again after a few minutes, searched the surface until she found a thin sheet to cover herself with and curled into a tight ball. Torn between the coolness of the room and the heat still radiating from her body, she lay still, trying to control the shivers, trying to empty her mind.

It wasn't as difficult to empty her mind as it should have been. She couldn't seem to manage much besides disjointed thoughts. Dread permeated her, though, the certainty that she'd so enraged Daegon that he might well have decided to torment her until she died or went completely insane.

She thought she'd slept for a time. The sluggishness of being awakened before she'd completely rested gripped her when she aroused to awareness again and found herself bound for his torment. She groaned aloud when she felt his thick flesh invading her. The sound startled her, but it also made her aware that, this time, he wanted to *hear* her—maybe wanted to wring pleas from her.

She didn't know and she couldn't gather her wits enough to figure it out. Determination settled in her to deny him the satisfaction, however. That sustained her for hours, or what seemed like hours, but she reached a point where she ceased to care whether her complete surrender brought him satisfaction or not.

When that settled inside her, it took hold of her mind that that was what he was waiting for, surrender, complete and utter defeat and she stopped fighting it. She was defeated. All she wanted was surcease and he could give it to her.

She began to plead with him then to bring her to climax and give her release. Her pleas fell on deaf ears, however. She begged until she finally realized that no amount of pleading was going to do any good. He wasn't tired of tormenting her. He hadn't appeased his anger, and he wasn't going to give her what she desperately wanted until he'd reached that point.

She ceased begging, but resentment took its place and then anger—weak, but sustaining. She began cursing him then, called him every foul name that came to mind.

"Give it to me!" she screamed at him. "You low down

son-of-a-bitch! I hate you! Hate you! Hate you! Hate you!"

He stopped so abruptly when she screamed at him that surprise and fear jolted through her.

"Do you think I *care* if you hate me, mortal?" he growled after a long pause. "The only thing that matters to me is your passion and, either way, love or hate, I have that!"

He was lying. She knew it instantly. Why would he roar at her as if she'd stabbed him if it didn't matter?

A jolt went through her when she felt his mouth settle over hers. He didn't have to force her lips apart. They went slack with stunned surprise. She was completely unprepared for the invasion of his tongue, the conquest. His essence flowed into her like a potent drug, sending her reeling. Even as he swept her meager defenses aside, she felt the pull of his mouth on her breasts and her clit as before and he began to drive his cocks into her almost frenziedly. Her climax hit her like an atom bomb, shattering her, splitting her atoms. She flew apart with the searing heat, jerking in nearly unbearable spasms on and on until she lost herself to the darkness.

She was shivering when she came to and she was alone. Too thoroughly confused to assimilate where she was or how she'd gotten there, she lay perfectly still for a while, staring blankly at the ornate armoire across from the bed where she lay. As memories trickled into her mind, she roused enough to search for the collar and chain and found they were gone.

Pushing herself up with an effort, she shoved her hair from her face and looked around the shadowy room. Moonlight, she saw, was spilling through a huge window big enough to be a door, limning much of the room in its gentle light, enough that she could see the room where she lay looked like something from an old world palace.

Her heart jerked painfully in her chest when Daegon stepped from the shadows and not merely because she hadn't realized he was there. He'd dropped his glamour. It was the beast that approached the bed.

"Why?" he demanded, baffled fury eloquent in the single word.

Maura blinked at him, searching her mind for the answer to the question. Try though she might, though, she couldn't figure out what he was asking. He launched himself at her, pinning her beneath his weight. "Explain to me, woman!"

Maura swallowed with an effort, but he'd caught her completely off-guard and she couldn't seem to command her thought processes. "I don't understand."

He growled in frustration. "I have wrung pleasure from your body as no mortal ever has, damn you! I gave you more than I have ever given any mortal! The others adored me, begged for more, wept when I withheld it. Why do you hate me when I have adored you as no other?"

Doubt flickered through her, but Maura felt her heart squeeze with compassion—and something else she didn't even want to consider. "I didn't seek this," she said angrily. "I didn't want it! I don't want to be enslaved by you and I certainly don't want to be enslaved by my desires. You showed me a part of myself that I hate! You *made* me a monster!"

Something flickered in his eyes. "I made you for me!" he growled. "No pale, weak mortal can ever please you like I do!"

Maura felt her throat close. It was all too true and it made her angrier to acknowledge it. He kissed her before she could respond, fiercely, as if to drive home the fact that it no longer mattered whether he donned a glamour to seduce her or not.

And it didn't. His taste and scent were as powerful a narcotic as before, drawing heat from her.

"Touching!"

Daegon broke the kiss at the intrusion, his head jerking upward as if he'd been scalded. Before Maura could even search out the source of the beastly voice, Daegon was lifted and hurled across the room as if an invisible hand had slapped him. She sat up with a jolt of horror.

The demon standing beside the bed was horrible to behold, sent such a wave of stark terror through Maura that her mind seemed to shut down. Uttering a roar, Daegon flew back across the room, slammed into the other demon and drove him into the wall, crumbling plaster and furniture.

Maura screamed, leapt from the bed and scurried to the far side of the room without any awareness of moving.

"I ... release ... you!" Daegon roared without even turning his head in her direction, every muscle on his body straining as he struggled to keep the other demon pinned against the wall. "Leave!"

Maura gaped at the two demons, unable to assimilate that Daegon meant the words for her.

"Get out, Maura! Go!"

Feeling almost like a puppet, as if something was controlling her from outside her body, Maura jerked upright, glanced wildly around for an exit, and raced to the door. It flew open before she reached it. She raced through the opening as it began to slam closed again. The edge of the door struck her, nearly sending her sprawling. Instead, she stumbled into the wall on the other side.

Righting herself, she glanced around with no notion of where to run. The cougar bounded into view, butted her with his head to get her moving and then chased her down the hall, down the stairs and across the foyer to the front door. She grabbed the handle, wrestling with it, nearly pulling her shoulders from the socket in her effort to pull it open. Abruptly it gave inward. She stumbled back, managed to catch herself and charged outside.

Daegon's beasts, she finally realized, weren't chasing her. They were fleeing the battle inside the mansion just as she was. Beyond the cougar nipping at her heels to make her run faster, none of them seemed interested in her. The gate at the drive banged open just before she reached it. In the dim recesses of her mind, she realized the demons were battling for possession of the barriers between her and safety and also that safety lay beyond the estate.

It spurred her to more speed. She managed to squeeze through before the gates banged shut again, but she kept running until she reached her car, wrenched the door open, and dove inside. The cougar tried to get in with her. She hit him on the snout with her fist. He reared back with a feline yelp, lost his balance, and rolled on the ground. She slammed the door shut before he could regain his footing and locked it for good measure.

She heard the great cat bound onto the roof of the car as she grabbed the key and turned it, but she was still running on automatic. Her instinct for self-preservation had her firmly in its grip and thought wasn't part of the process, merely action, reaction, and habit. When she jerked the car into reverse and twisted around to see what was behind her, she saw the ass end of Daegon's beasts—both cats and two or three wolves—as they disappeared into the woods.

It was a good thing for her that heading to the 'stable' was an automatic response. She hadn't recovered her wits when she parked in her usual spot and leapt out. It was probably fortunate. She didn't realize until she'd raced into her apartment and slammed and locked the door that she didn't have a stitch of clothes on.

She looked down at herself blankly when that dawned on her. Shivering uncontrollably, she headed into her bedroom, climbed into the middle of her bed, and pulled her covers around her. For a while, all she could do was stare blankly into space, shivering until her teeth rattled in her head, listening for any sound that might be a threat.

Slowly, the shock began to ease its hold on her. Every creak and groan of the building sent an electric jolt of fear through her, though, and it wasn't until the first fingers of dawn began to lighten the sky that weariness finally overcame all other considerations and she passed out.

She awoke with the sort of jolt a nightmare produced, her heart hammering uncomfortably in her chest. Her familiar surroundings produced a sense of safeness that began to calm her almost immediately, however.

Relaxing fractionally, she searched her mind for the nightmare that had awakened her. There was little comfort when she found what she was seeking, though, and realized it wasn't a nightmare at all that had awakened her.

Shuddering when her mind produced an image of the demon that had attacked Daegon, Maura tried to banish the image. Her confusion demanded answers, however, and her mind began working at an understanding that she wasn't sure she wanted.

It occurred to her after a while that she'd suspected Daegon was controlled by something, some force that made him as much of a prisoner as he had made her. The demon had found him out, she realized. He'd given himself away, maybe, or the demon had simply stumbled upon his secret—her.

She didn't know which, but the certainty settled in her that that was what she'd witnessed—maybe Daegon's battle for his life.

Her belly clenched at the thought. In spite of all she could do to ignore it, the fear began to grow in her that Daegon might well have lost that battle. She tried to convince herself that she was glad if that was the case, but it was useless. Even the certainty that he'd weakened himself just to punish her for defying him didn't give her any satisfaction. It filled her with remorse—and guilt.

She'd punished *him* first by refusing to acknowledge her need for him.

It wasn't logical, at all, for her to feel that she'd hurt him, that *she* had tormented him until he'd grown incautious and the other demon had discovered what he was up to.

It began to play back through her mind, though, the hours he'd spent 'punishing' her, his anger when she'd told him she hated him, his baffled anger when he'd demanded to know why.

He was a beast, she realized. He truly didn't understand and his confusion wasn't only because he was a demon and couldn't grasp human emotions. Every female he'd dealt with was 'in' to BDSM. They *wanted* him to treat them that way, relished it, adored him for mastering their bodies and their minds.

At least three that she knew of had been so despondent when he'd discarded them that they'd killed themselves.

As twisted as it seemed to her, she began to think that, in his mind, he truly had worshipped her.

It made her feel much, much worse. It made her feel as if *she* was in the wrong, that she'd been so stupid as to play with a dangerous animal and then stabbed it when it behaved according to its nature.

Driven from her bed by her needs after a while, she showered and dressed and searched for food. She couldn't manage much of an appetite for all that. It kept running through her mind that she'd been the instrument of Daegon's destruction.

Not that he'd seemed weak to her mind, but how weak had he been compared to his 'normal' self when he'd expended hours tormenting her instead of feeding? Weaker than the other demon, she was sure.

It dawned on her after a while that he'd been holding the demon off to allow her to flee. The entire battle, she realized abruptly, had been to save her from the other demon's wrath!

## Chapter Eight

Despite the guilt and anxiety for Daegon that rattled around in her mind, relief was uppermost when Maura finally realized that a full day had passed and not only had neither Daegon or the other demon come after her, but she didn't feel the heat that she'd come to dread. As soon as that occurred to her, though, confusion followed.

Daegon had marked her as his slave. She'd tried to fight it and failed. Why didn't she feel that nearly painful pull to go to him?

After a brief search for a hand mirror, she stripped and examined the mark Daegon had left on her thigh. A jolt went through her when she saw that it was different, paler, almost invisible—like the marks she'd found on the dead women.

He'd released her. Her heart seemed to stutter at that realization. She waited in vain for a feeling of freedom, release, gladness. Instead, she flung the mirror across the room where it shattered against the wall, threw herself onto her bed, and wept like she'd never cried before.

"I'm so happy!" she wailed. "So relieved! I'm free!"

She wasn't! She'd never been so miserable in her life!

He'd let her go to save her from the other demon. She knew it.

Maybe it was in the hope that she would come back to him, though?

That thought dried her tears. He was a demon, she told herself, deceptive, manipulative. He was playing with her mind!

He no longer had control of her, though. He'd removed the mark, knowing that the mark was all that had brought her to him before and then only reluctantly.

For two days, she struggled to pick up her life, to convince herself that she was fiercely glad if Daegon *had* been destroyed. On the third day, she acknowledged that it wasn't working.

She just wanted to know, she told herself as she drove out

to Daegon's mansion and parked near dusk. After staring at the mansion for a while, she got out and approached the gate. There was no sign of his beasts within the grounds, but then she'd never seen them before until she climbed over the gate.

It didn't stand open in welcome, but then it hadn't before.

She encountered a wall at the top. Disbelieving at first, she felt the invisible barrier with her hand and discovered it seemed to go on forever, as far as she could reach. Disconcerted, she climbed down, planted her hands on her hips and studied the gate. Maybe it was just the gate?

It took her nearly an hour to find and move a limb that she could climb. She discovered when she'd wedged it against the wall and scaled it, though, that the same invisible wall barred her from the premises. Anger and disappointment began to nag at her. Instead of stalking back to her car and leaving, though, she pulled the car closer to the stone wall in another spot, climbed on the hood, and tried again. She couldn't even get up on the top of the wall to walk along it and search for an opening. It was as if a glass bowl had been turned down over the entire estate.

Thwarted, angry and disappointed if the truth were told, she finally gave up and headed back into town.

She'd been discarded—just like the others.

He was done with her. The gates to 'heaven' were closed and the key had been taken from her.

Maura was still pissed off when she got back to her apartment. She paced for a while, resisting the urge to dash off to club Noir, but she finally decided she needed to vent.

How dare the bastard just toss her away!

She was horny, god damn it and it was all his damned fault!

More than half expecting to discover she'd been barred from the club as well, Maura felt a vast sense of relief when she discovered that wasn't the case. It didn't tamp her resentment, however. That boiled over into real anger when she got inside and discovered that Daegon was sprawled in his throne, none the worse for his battle that she could see.

She'd spent *days* worrying about the son-of-a-bitch, crying her eyes out thinking he'd been destroyed and it was her fault!

Ignoring the people around her, she descended the steps, stalked across the dance floor and began to climb the stairs determinedly. She managed to get all the way to the top before she encountered the 'wall'. She met Daegon's angry gaze. For several moments, she was so angry herself she was blinded by it. As his gaze moved over her hungrily, however, it pierced her self-absorption and by the time he met her gaze again, she realized Daegon wasn't the source of the wall. It was clear as a bell that he would've grabbed her right then and thrown her to the floor if he could've reached her.

Misery flickered in his eyes and disappeared so quickly she knew she would've missed it if she hadn't been staring straight at him.

"I freed you," he growled.

Maura swallowed with an effort. "I know."

His face twisted. "Go!" he snarled. "I cannot bear the sight of you."

It hurt, stabbed her to the core, and yet she didn't see loathing in his eyes. She saw hunger. She saw suffering and pain.

She stared at him for a long moment. "I didn't mean it—what I said to you."

Something flickered in his eyes and then he looked away. "It doesn't matter to me one way or the other, mortal."

She studied his handsome face—his façade. "It does," she whispered.

He flicked a quick look at her. "It doesn't!" he roared. "Go!"

Maura didn't bother to look around. His vehemence was enough to convince her he was being watched. There was almost a thread of panic in his voice that she took as a warning. Nodding stiffly, she turned on her heel and stalked out the way she'd come.

She was shaking all over long before she reached her car. She almost felt too weak to unlock the door and get in.

\* \* \* \*

"I understand that you're as close to an authority on demonology as there is around here," Maura said to the elderly man hunched over the book on his desk.

He lifted his head after studiously ignoring her approach and stared at her speculatively through his thick glasses.

He looked completely ordinary, she saw with a touch of surprise—nondescript even.

"You are Dr. Claus, correct?"

His gaze flickered over her. "I am. And you are?"

"Detective Maura Downy."

The speculative look intensified. "This is a police matter?"

Maura debated. "No. Personal."

He gestured toward the chair on the other side of the desk. Maura was too tense to feel like sitting down, but she did anyway.

"What would you like to know?"

"How to free a demon from another demon."

The wave of shock that rolled over the man seemed almost physical. He rocked back in his seat. "I beg your pardon?"

Maura didn't especially feel like beating around the bush. She'd wrestled with this for days and finally concluded that, however insane it was, she wasn't going to be able to simply forget Daegon and go on with her life. It had taken nearly another week to track down Dr. Claus. Desperate didn't begin to describe the way she'd begun to feel. "Theoretically, suppose a demon, an Incubus, was ... being controlled by another. How would one go about ... destroying the demon and setting him free?"

He grasped that and she felt her face heat slightly at the speculation in his eyes. "You don't. There is no such spell." He shook his head. "I'm not even going to ask why you might want to do something like that, but humans—mortals—are far better off leaving the demon world to deal with its own issues. If this theoretical situation existed, it would mean that the Incubus is constrained by his master, or overlord, and that demon is more powerful than you can imagine. An Incubus has unimaginable powers in their own right. Any demon powerful enough to control one ...."

Maura felt almost sick with disappointment. "You're saying it couldn't be done?"

He shrugged. "If the Incubus isn't strong enough to free himself—no. A mortal couldn't, not with the most powerful spell. I'd have to think the Incubus must be weakened, to speak plainly, before he could even be controlled by another—overlord or not. You do know *how* an Incubus derives his power, I assume?"

Maura felt a flash of heat that wasn't just from discomfort. "I understand that part. What you're suggesting, then, is that he would have to ... uh ... feed to gain the strength?"

The man blushed faintly. "Yes."

"What if the other demon, this overlord, was preventing him from feeding as he needed to?"

"Then he could retain control."

Maura frowned, feeling defeat settle over her. "There isn't a ... back door? There isn't a spell of some kind that could ... allow a mortal to slip past, feed the Incubus to give him strength?"

The man looked startled, but he settled to pondering it and Maura waited hopefully. "I don't honestly know the answer to that. I suppose a summoning might work," he said doubtfully.

"A summoning?"

"A dangerous undertaking," the man said warningly. "Worshippers throughout the ages have tried it. It works—after a fashion."

"Meaning?"

"They aren't easy to control," he said dryly. "That's the objective of the summoning, to pull a demon from the underworld and harness his powers. It generally ends badly for the human even if they succeed—*especially* if they succeed. They're tricksters. The spell does bring them forth if done properly and it does exert a hold on them, but they aren't pleased at being enslaved by mortals ... and their wrath is ... terrible when they break free."

"You mean if?" Maura asked uneasily.

"I mean when."

Maura considered that for several moments, but she couldn't *un*convince herself. She'd grown more and more certain that, regardless of how it had begun, despite the fact that Daegon was a demon, he *felt* something for her. If he was angry that she'd summoned him, she reasoned, she could just let him go back. She had to know, though. Not knowing, feeling as if he wanted and needed her, was driving her nuts, especially when she felt like it was her fault he was suffering.

Particularly when she'd had to face the fact that she cared that he was. "Where would I find the spell to summon?" she asked firmly.

The man blinked at her. "Have you heard anything I've said?"

"I heard it. There's a risk, but it's my risk."

"We aren't talking theory."

It wasn't a question and she didn't bother to answer it. "Can you tell me? Or do I need to keep looking?" she asked tightly.

He looked angry. "I'm almost tempted to tell you to keep looking!" he said angrily. "But I can see you're determined and it would be worse if you stumbled upon some dabbler in the black arts and tried one of their sloppy spells!"

She waited impatiently.

He shook his head at her. "You can't summon one particular demon! You do realize that? You can only open the gateway. Without his name, any demon could come through that happened to be snagged by the spell."

"I know his name."

"You think you do!" he snapped. "They won't give a mortal their name! It gives the mortal power over them, and they never do that."

Doubt flickered through her, but she dismissed it. "I suppose I'll need a spell to send one back, too, then."

He spent an hour trying to convince her that she didn't want to do what she'd already made up her mind she was going to do and finally gave up. Opening up his laptop, he printed out the two spells—one to summon, one to banish and carefully explained the procedure.

It sounded like a lot of ritualistic mumbo jumbo to her, but she listened carefully and repeated it back to him. When he seemed at least satisfied that she knew how to repeat the ritual he'd explained, he gave her the copies of the spell and told her to destroy them when she was finished playing with fire—if she was still able to.

Folding the papers, she left him to search for the things she needed to perform the ritual—or rituals. Fortunately, he'd given her directions to a shop that catered to followers of the black arts where she found everything she needed.

She was shaking with a mixture of sheer terror and hopefulness when she got back to her apartment. Doubts began to surface as soon as she began to set up. Over and over in her mind, she heard Dr. Claus' warning that she needed the demon's name to summon him, reminding her that they were deceivers, they never gave a mortal their true name.

Did she really want to take a chance that she might summon some other demon?

If his name wasn't Daegon, what was it?

She settled crossed legged in the center of the pentagram she'd drawn on her floor when she'd finished setting up, staring at nothing in particular, wrestling with fear and hopefulness.

It was insane to feel anything but disgust, fear, revulsion! Daegon had never done anything to deserve the feelings she had for him! He'd tortured her with pleasure, withholding release until he'd broken her, she told herself. He'd bent her mind!

She managed to cling to those thoughts briefly, and then an image of him as she'd last seen him formed in her mind. Maybe he didn't feel as a mortal would. Maybe he couldn't, but she mattered to him—enough that he'd sent her away to protect her. She knew she wasn't wrong about that.

Dragging in a deep breath, she let it out slowly, focusing, and finally opened her eyes to stare at the spells she'd laid on the floor.

Daegon. It wasn't his name. It was the name he used at Noir. Even if he'd trusted her enough to give her his true name, he certainly wouldn't have allowed everyone that came to the club to know.

Noir. Black. Dark. She considered that for several moments.

Daegon---Day gone.

Abruptly, she knew what his name was, with a certainty that gave her the confidence to begin the ritual. Contrary to what she'd more than half believed, she felt the power of the spell immediately, and it grew the longer she chanted the words. She *felt* the gateway open.

Doubt shook her. Was the spell the same if they were already on the Earthly plain?

Had she guessed the name wrong?

She moved the summoning spell aside to reveal the

banishing spell and continued the chant. "Nite!" she said when she knew the gates had opened wide. "Come to me! I command you!"

The crackle of flames and the smell of sulfur sent a shudder through her.

"Who summons ...!"

Maura's eyes flew open at the roar of their own accord. Her heart nearly beat its way out of her chest before recognition struck her. Daegon was staring at her in blank disbelief. He blinked even as she met his gaze, his face contorting in a ferocious scowl as he looked around.

A shiver clawed its way up her spine when he slid a speculative gaze at her. "You summoned me," he growled. "What do you want, mortal?"

A little damned appreciation, Maura thought angrily.

He was a beast, she reminded herself. It wasn't even logical to expect him to behave like a mortal would. It relieved her, though, when she saw his gaze flicker over her hungrily. She unfolded her legs and planted her feet on the floor, making no attempt to block his view of her sex. She'd 'dressed' herself in her own concept of bondage—a black leather camisole that bracketed her breasts, leaving them bare, and ended mid-hip, and nothing else.

Her throat closed at the look in his eyes. "I want you to feed upon me, Incubus, until I tell you to stop. Punish me until I beg for release and then give me release."

She heard him swallow. He looked doubtful, suspicious, but he dropped to his knees, his expression slack with hunger. "Feed?"

"Yes."

He moved toward her almost as if he was fighting the urge, jerkily. Her eyes rolled back in her head when he covered the tip of one breast with his mouth and began to suckle her ravenously. She had the sense that he expected her to shove him away at any moment and he was desperate to feed as much as he could before she did.

She settled back, enjoying the torture as he moved from one breast to the other and down to her clit. "Tongue fuck me," she demanded abruptly. "But don't let me come."

His head jerked upward at the demand. He stared at her a moment and dropped lower. It was sheer delightful torture to feel his tongue trusting inside of her. "The clit, too," she gasped. "And my nipples."

She thought she was going to die. It took everything she could do to hold still for him, to fight off the urge to demand release, but she fought it for all she was worth as long as she could bear it.

"Make me come!" she gasped when she couldn't stand it anymore.

He surged over her as if he'd only been waiting for the command, spearing his double cock into her almost violently and driving deeply. He'd barely sunk to the root when he began to pump into her feverishly. She climaxed. He held her there, convulsing in rapture until she was gasping for breath and then allowed her to relax for a moment and brought her to her peak again and then again.

She had to keep reminding herself it wasn't only her needs that she'd meant to appease. She'd summoned him to give him what he needed. She fought the urge to command him to stop until she realized she'd reached a dangerous level of weakness. It took an effort to find the strength to tell him to stop, to banish him until she summoned him again.

She felt his heated gaze on her for a long moment and then his weight vanished and she fell into a deep, dark pit. She had no idea how long she lay comatose on the floor, but it was long enough she felt pain when she finally surfaced toward awareness and the numbness of poor circulation. It took all she could do to get up. Bathing was out of the question and, in any case, she didn't particularly want to wash his scent from her. She relieved herself, drank as much juice as she could to chase the dehydration and collapsed on her bed.

She was still so weak when she woke again that it unnerved her. Selflessness was one thing! Allowing him to feed until he'd nearly sucked the life out of her was just plain stupid!

Nearly two days passed before she even began to feel close to normal, but she decided she'd recovered long enough. He couldn't go long without suffering and it hadn't been any part of her plan to punish him.

He looked more sullen than angry when she summoned him, but eagerness glittered in his eyes for all that. She patted the mattress beside her. "Come. Lay with me a moment, Nite."

He scowled at her, but he climbed onto the bed, staring hungrily at her.

"You know how much you can take without harming me?" she asked tentatively.

Surprise flickered in his eyes when he jerked his head up to stare at her. "I know," he said a little hoarsely.

"Then I give you leave to take what you want as long as you stop before you become a danger to my life."

Confusion flickered in his eyes. "Is that a command?" he growled.

"It is. Feed. You must stop before you harm me. And then you must go until I summon you again."

She wasn't at all sure he'd grasped the command or had any inkling how much was too much. He ravaged her until she lost consciousness.

It took her the better part of three days to recover enough to summon him again. He was definitely sulky when he appeared. "I displeased you, mistress?" he demanded angrily.

Maura sighed testily. "You took too much!" she said testily. "I'm mortal!"

He studied her thoughtfully. She had no idea what was going through his mind, but once she gave him permission to feed on her she didn't have room or enough mind to spare for figuring it out.

## Chapter Nine

Daegon startled Maura when he settled beside her on the bed and sought her lips. Except for that last time in his mansion when she'd been his slave, he'd never shown any inclination toward having interest in anything but pure, raw, animal sex. His mouth was ravening, demanding, and yet it gave her the sense that he was making love to her—whether he intended it that way or not.

"I can give you my essence," he murmured raggedly when he broke the kiss. "Only a little, my precious, and it will give you more strength for me."

"Your essence?" Maura gasped dizzily, confused.

"Demon seed."

Maura's heart lurched in her chest. "Your baby?" she gasped.

Daegon jerked away from her as if she'd punched him. His eyes narrowed with suspicion. "Why would you want my spawn, mortal?" he growled.

Maura stared up at him blankly. "Because I love you, you idiot!" she snapped angrily.

It sent a shockwave through him. She felt it, but aside from momentarily leaving him slack faced with stunned surprise, the statement clearly did nothing to assuage his suspicions. If anything, they grew more pronounced. Anger glittered in his eyes. "I am not such a fool as to believe that, mortal!" he snarled.

The depths of Maura's disappointment only added fuel to her own anger. "I didn't ask, damn it! You offered!"

"Not my spawn," he growled. "My seed."

"Shove it up your ass!" she snarled back at him. "You can keep your damned precious seed! Just take what you need and go the fuck away!"

He took her at her word. Despite the roughness of his caresses, it was a while before Maura began to get an inkling that she was in trouble. Even then, she dismissed it. It was always as much torture as pleasure when he fed on her, draining her until she thought she barely had the strength to breathe. As she began to sink toward oblivion, though, it crossed her mind that he'd taken far more than she could afford to give.

"Command me to stop, Maura!" Daegon growled as if the words were forced from him.

The urgency in his voice roused her slightly, but it confused her. Hadn't she told him that he was to stop before he took too much?

He gripped her arms painfully and shook her. "You will die!"

She didn't care, she realized abruptly. She was beyond caring. "Better," she whispered, realizing that she didn't want to live like she had been. She'd never wanted to enslave him, but that was what she'd done. "I release you."

"No! Command me to give you my essence, damn you! Don't send me away!"

She discovered he was coiled tightly around her as if he thought he'd be sucked away if he didn't hold on to her.

"Please, baby! Please!"

It sounded more like a demand than supplication and she still couldn't resist the urge to comfort him. "Give ...."

He uttered a choked sound and she felt heat fill her belly. Her body tingled all over. For a handful of moments, pleasure filled her and then she drifted away.

The ringing of her phone penetrated Maura's consciousness but by the time she'd roused enough to figure out what the hell the noise was, it had stopped. Exhaustion dragged at her. She was tempted to roll over and go back to sleep, but something nagged at her mind and made her struggle out of the bed instead.

The phone rang again as she left the bathroom. "Jesus fucking Christ, Downy! What the hell is up with you?"

Maura glanced at the clock in dismay. "Shit!"

"Shit is right! You're going to get fired if you keep this shit up!"

"I'll be ready in fifteen minutes. Can you pick me up?"

"I'm at the curb," her partner growled.

"I'll be down in fifteen, then."

It was hellish getting through the work day and it had nothing to do with the case load. She chugged juice a while and coffee a while to try to pump some life into herself. She was more relieved than she could ever recall when her partner dropped her off after shift.

The relief lasted right until she went to her apartment and found Daegon. She halted on the threshold, staring at him blankly. Finally, remembering she was still standing in the doorway, she stepped inside and closed the door behind her. "Did I ... summon you?" she asked a little weakly, knowing she hadn't.

His eyes narrowed but he didn't make any effort to hide the satisfaction that flickered across his features. "You released me."

"Oh ... uh oh."

He cocked his head, studying her almost thoughtfully for several moments and then, in the blink of an eye, he was no longer standing at her window but directly in front of her. "Who was that mortal?" he growled.

Maura blinked at him. "My partner. We work together," she stammered.

"Not anymore," he said, tossing the veil over her so that she slid into darkness with the words still echoing in her mind.

She woke to find herself in the room where Daegon had battled his overlord. Daegon was lying on his side on the bed beside her, studying her. She stared at him for a long moment and then scanned the room. There was no sign that there'd ever been a battle in the room and confusion settled in her.

"This is the room," Daegon answered the question in her eyes.

Maura frowned. "Your overlord?"

His grin was feral. "I don't have one. I crushed the bastard."

Maura felt a wave of weakness. "So you're ... uh ... free?"

His gaze flickered over her. It was warm in a way that wasn't entirely desire and it made her heart flutter uncomfortably. "Yes."

"So ... we're even?"

His eyes shuttered. "Was that your objective? To repay what you thought was kindness? I'm a demon. I don't 'do' kind."

Maura swallowed with an effort. "I know what you are. I did it because I love you."

He frowned. She had the sense that she'd thrown him. "You're mine," he growled.

"Because I want to be," she countered.

"You enslaved me—*me*! Daegon!" he growled angrily.

"To free you from your overlord. It was the only way I knew to do it and I didn't know that it would work."

"Why?" he demanded, clearly baffled.

"Because I love you and I couldn't bear to think of you suffering."

"You did it because you wanted me to fuck you! Because no one else can do the things to you that I do!"

Maura couldn't help but smile. "True. I guess you want to punish me for summoning you?"

He surged toward her, pushing her to her back and manacling her wrists to the bed on either side of her head. "There is nothing to stop me from sucking you dry, woman!"

A flicker of fear went through her, but she'd known the risk she was taking. She was gambling that a beast that had no concept of human emotions would feel something. "No. Nothing."

She thought for a while that she'd lost the bet. Even as she felt herself sinking, slipping away, however, he drove deeply inside of her and stilled. Uttering a choked, pained sound, he spilled his seed into her, gave her his essence. Warmth and reviving strength flowed into her.

He was watching her when she woke. She had the feeling that he'd been watching her for a while, waiting for her to wake up. It almost surprised her to discover that she felt like she'd woken from a restful sleep.

"Why would you be willing to bear my spawn?" he asked curiously.

She was a little startled that he'd brought it up when it seemed to have made him so furious before. "Because I love you."

He frowned. "Why?"

It was her turn to feel confusion. "I don't honestly know."

His look was knowing. "It's because I give you pleasure."

She reached up and touched his face. "That's part of it," she agreed.

He caught her hand. For a moment, she thought he would thrust it away. Instead, he stared at it a long moment and lifted it to his mouth, nibbling at her palm. Emboldened by the caress, she wiggled closer and tilted her head up to nibble kisses along his throat. He went perfectly still. He searched her gaze when she lifted her head. "You like this glamour."

It was a statement, not a question. She thought it was also a test. "I know what you look like. I know this is just a human-like façade you wear."

He banished it and she found herself staring at the beast he truly was. Holding his gaze, she lowered her lips to his and kissed him lightly. Uttering a growl, he rolled with her and tortured her for the better part of an hour before he finally gave her release. To her surprise, he rolled away when she'd spent herself.

When she'd caught her breath, she rolled over and began to caress his chest, first with her hands and then her mouth. He stiffened at her first touch, lay tensely while she explored him, but he neither objected nor encouraged her. She paused when she reached his genitals, wondering if she was giving him any pleasure at all, wondering if she should do what she was thinking about doing.

Shrugging inwardly, she captured one thick member and covered it with her mouth, stroking the other with her hand. It gave her pleasure, his taste and the feel of him in her mouth. She had no idea whether it pleased him or annoyed him.

He burrowed his fingers in her hair after a few moments, stilling her movements briefly and then applying enough pressure to let her know he wanted more. Feeling more confident, she complied eagerly, stroking him and sucking at his flesh more hungrily as she felt her excitement rise. She hesitated when she felt his cock jerk and then pulled at him with more determination until he groaned and his seed spilled into her mouth.

It was like nothing she'd ever tasted. Surprise flickered through her. Swallowing, she sucked harder and finally desisted with a touch of disappointment when she couldn't draw more from him.

There was a mixture of amusement and satisfaction in his eyes when she righted herself and met his gaze. "Why did you do that?"

The question burst her bubble. "It didn't ... give you any pleasure?" she asked doubtfully.

He captured her head between his hands and dragged her closer, kissing her with a hunger that set her blood to pounding in her veins. "Everything about you gives me pleasure," he murmured when he broke the kiss. "Even giving you my essence."

She studied his face curiously. "It makes me stronger," she tentatively.

"It will make you into a demon."

Surprise flickered through her and a mixture of reluctance and doubt. "Will it?"

He tilted his head, studying her. "Part demon ... I don't want to change you."

"If you think it will, then don't."

He nibbled on her throat. "I must before I give you my spawn else you'll never survive its birth."

Maura's heart tripped over itself. "You'd ... be willing to do that?"

"There's very little I wouldn't be willing to give you, my precious," he murmured lazily. "I will give you a houseful of the infernal things if you want."

Maura couldn't help but chuckle. "That's a terrible thing to say about your children!"

He grunted. "Wait till you see the first before you judge," he muttered wryly.

The End

# Summoning the Beast
by
Desiree Acuna

## Chapter One

On some levels, Cara was aware that what she was about to do wasn't rational. She'd established a fairly lucrative business around such ancient, pagan beliefs, but she wasn't a believer. She had her feet firmly planted in reality and knew such things didn't exist.

Thankfully!

Desperation and grief, although she knew she was suffering from both and that they'd warped her sense of reality, weren't adequate excuses for her behavior when she knew with some part of her mind that it was a waste of time.

It was the almost infinitesimal possibility that there might be something to it, though, that drove her—and grief and desperation.

She couldn't face losing her mother. She'd tried to prepare herself when they'd run out of options, but she simply couldn't.

All she could think as she moved around her living room, preparing for the ritual, was that it couldn't hurt. It might be useless, but she'd exhausted every other possibility— every sane, rational possibility. They'd thrown everything known to modern medicine at her mother's cancer and hadn't succeeded in anything but putting off what seemed to be the inevitable, torturing her mother in the process when she was already suffering.

Pushing those thoughts from her mind, she focused on studying her preparations, trying to think if she'd left anything out. There was no telling what might be important, she thought.

Not that it was likely anything would happen regardless.

She shook that thought off.

Deciding she'd prepared everything for the ritual as nearly as she knew to the way it was supposed to be, she left the living room and went to prepare herself—the offering. When she'd soaked for a little while in the hot water where the herbs had been steeping, she got out, patted herself dry and donned the ritual robe.

Returning to the living room, she lit the ceremonial candles and settled cross-legged within the pentagram with the book containing the summoning spell. Dismissing her qualms, she began to chant the ancient words of magic that would open the doorway to the netherworld. She repeated the chant over and over, demanding, cajoling—until her throat felt dry and raw, and her back and butt ached from sitting so long. She chanted until the candles melted down and began to gutter—and nothing happened. Nothing at all.

The urge to cry assailed her when she finally gave up and fell silent. She swallowed against the tightness in her throat, ignoring the urge as she focused on what she'd done, going over it again in her mind. She'd done everything right, she finally decided—everything except performing the ritual on the night of a full moon.

Why would that have anything to do with it, she wondered angrily? But she realized that it might actually be the most important part of all. She'd thought that when she'd hatched the crazy notion of summoning a demon to heal her mother. She'd dismissed it because she'd been afraid it would be too late to help her mother if she waited until the next full moon. She might not live that long!

"Open damn it!" she screamed abruptly, flinging the book away from her. Not surprisingly, nothing happened except that she turned over a candle and broke the magic circle she'd drawn around herself.

Surging to her feet angrily, she leaned down to blow the rest of the candles out and stalked back to her bedroom, flung herself down on her bed and wept as she hadn't in weeks. She'd tried hard to hold her emotions in check. She hadn't wanted to upset her mother when she was so sick, but her mother wasn't there to be disturbed by her wails of anger and grief.

Soon, her mother wouldn't be there for her at all anymore.

She wept about that, expelling the grief she'd been holding back and her frustration that she'd resorted to such a crazy thing and it had still been for nothing! She fell asleep railing against the unfairness of life. Her mother was all she had! What was she going to do when she was alone? Who would be her ally against the rest of the world?

Exhaustion from her emotional outburst carried her from consciousness to the dream world without any awareness of the transition. One moment she was struggling to cope with a situation that seemed beyond her and the next she found herself in her living room once more, lighting the ceremonial candles and carefully drawing out a pentagram and then marking a circle around it with the magic powders she'd obtained.

An odd sense of déjà vu swept through her. Hadn't she done this already?

She frowned, studying the preparations she'd made, checking everything carefully. When she started into her room to undress, to bathe in the ritual bath, and don the ceremonial robe, though, she discovered she was already wearing it.

Confusion flickered through her briefly, but she dismissed it. She'd just been too focused on preparations to remember she'd prepared herself first.

Settling in the center of the protective circle, she opened the book of spells and began to chant the summoning spell. The words seemed to flow from her as if she'd memorized them. That seemed odd, too, but she dismissed it, concentrating. When she'd reached the end of the spell, she began again. On the third repetition, she noticed that her skin had begun to prickle, almost as if with a static charge.

Uneasiness slithered through her. Sternly, she reminded herself that she was doing this for her mother and continued the summoning chant. The prickling intensified. The flames in the candles surrounding her elongated, began to dance—not as if the air currents were controlling them, but something else.

She fell silent when she'd finished the third repetition of the chant, waiting, unnerved by the strange currents she could feel crackling in the air. Abruptly, the flames of the candles seemed to combine, to form a fireball. Her heart leapt into her throat, but before she could react to the certainty that she'd just set her living room on fire, a shadowy figure emerged from the center of the flame. For a handful of moments, it looked like nothing more than a shadow and then it became solid.

Cara stared at the being that stood before her, absolutely frozen with sheer terror. His flesh was as red as fresh blood. A pair of great black wings sprouted from his back and curled around him, keeping his face in deep shadow.

"Why did you summon me?" he demanded in a deep, resonating growl of a voice.

Cara swallowed convulsively several times, trying to find her voice. "To make a bargain with you," she managed finally.

He seemed to consider that curiously for several moments. Abruptly, he folded his wings and crouched down so that his face was level with hers. A jolt of surprise went through her. Despite the fact that he was like nothing she'd ever seen, his face wasn't a horror mask as she'd expected—far from it. It was startlingly handsome.

"What sort of bargain, mortal?"

It took an effort to gather her wits. "My mother's dying."

"Mortals die—that's why they're called mortals," he said dryly.

The awe vanished and along with it her fear. "I can't bear to lose her! Heal her for me. I know you can do it. I'll do whatever you want, if you'll just make her well again."

He tilted his head, studying her. "This is why you summoned me?"

"Yes," Cara croaked.

"And to seal the bargain you wish to make with me, you offer whatever I should ask for?"

Cara blinked at him. "Whatever I can do. Whatever I can give you."

He frowned. "You aren't asking for anything else? Riches? Fame? Power?"

Cara felt her pulse leap at the suggestions. Wealth, fame, power—who wouldn't want such things? In the scheme of things, though, what use were they without health? In any case, she knew what she was asking for was not only the greatest prize she could've requested, but she wasn't willing to risk asking too much, more than he was willing to give. "None of those things would give me comfort without my mother and I know demons are inclined to use trickery. I just want my mother healed. Take the cancer away and make her better. It's all I ask."

"And you're willing to pay whatever I ask?"

Cara swallowed. "If I can."

He sent her a sardonic look. "You."

Cara blinked at him. She'd known there was a strong possibility that that was what he would ask and she'd thought it was worth it. She still did, but if she gave him what he was asking, she still wouldn't have her mother.

Her mother would have her health, though.

"You mean my soul?"

He lifted his brows. "Aye ... and the vessel that contains it."

She frowned. "I still wouldn't have my mother."

"She would be well."

It was selfish to think, she knew, but she realized she didn't want her mother to leave her alone ... and yet she was contemplating leaving her mother alone.

"Could I ... delay payment?"

He tilted his head, eyeing her sardonically. "You want me to give you what you're asking now and to pay at some distant date?"

Cara sucked in a calming breath. "It isn't as if it would be any great hardship for you!" she said tightly. "You're immortal! My entire lifetime would be barely a blink for you!"

"Ah ... but that's the point, little mortal. You will fade in time. Why would I have any interest in a faded blossom when I might have a fresh one?"

She frowned. "Well, I suppose that depends on what you have in mind for the vessel! I thought demons only wanted to collect souls for their master to torment!"

He laughed. It sent shivers through her. "Which only goes to show that you've no understanding of what you're dealing with."

"I guess I don't."

"If I told you that I am an incubus would you have a better understanding?"

A jolt went through her. She swallowed convulsively several times. "You're an incubus?"

He grinned. "I didn't say that. I merely asked if you knew what one was."

"A male demon that has sexual intercourse with mortal women while they sleep."

His eyes gleamed, turning from black to flame. "You

have some inkling then."

Cara considered it, feeling oddly relieved and unnerved at the same time. How bad could it be, though, to have sex with a demon? And wasn't that better than giving up her life or her soul? "What you're saying is that I would be accepting that you would come to me in to my dreams and have sex with me as your part of the bargain?"

"I would feed on your desires and your pleasure."

A shiver skated through her but this time it wasn't entirely due to fear. "You wouldn't require me to give up my life and my soul? I could still see my mother? Be with her?"

He hesitated briefly. "I would not require that ... only your willingness to allow me to feed."

Cara dragged in a shuddering breath. "Then I agree. Heal my mother. Make her well again and in return I'm willing to allow you to ... uh ... feed."

He straightened abruptly. "Then I'll consider the bargain you wish to strike. I warn you, though, if I do decide to favor you I will not tolerate treachery. Once I have given, I will take what I'm due and if you attempt to bind me once more, you will regret it."

* * * *

Cara woke with a jolt as if she'd fallen and landed hard. Still groggy, she searched her mind for the nightmare that had pitched her toward consciousness but, as it happened so often, the moment her mind became alert the images that had frightened her disappeared and she was left with nothing but a sense that she'd dreamed something frightening.

Struggling to throw off the jitteriness the nightmare had left her with, she rolled over and opened her eyes. Daylight spilled into the room. Climbing from her bed with an effort, she staggered into her bathroom to perform her morning ritual and then headed into her kitchen in search of something to rid herself of the lingering sluggishness.

Settling at her kitchen table with a steaming cup of coffee, she found herself trying to recapture the elusive dream that had awakened her. Indistinct images flickered through her mind, but they flitted just out of reach. Dismissing it finally, she fixed herself a second cup of coffee and wandered into her living room to boot her computer.

A different anxiety churned in her stomach as she studied

the orders she'd gotten since the day before. The sales were actually pretty good. She'd sold a dozen pieces of jewelry and several charms.

Unfortunately, although those sales would've been a cause for celebration before and would've been sufficient to carry her for a week, at least, they fell woefully short when compared to the mounting medical bills for her mother's care. She'd begun to feel as if she was drowning in debt, something she'd tried hard to hide from her mother.

It made it worse that her mother was so apologetic about it and continued to argue about every new treatment they'd tried. What good was money, though, if it couldn't buy the most important thing in life? Life!

It was hard to convince her mother that she didn't count the cost, though, when she was worried sick.

Checking the time, she got up to begin working on filling the orders. The remains from the ritual she'd performed the night before caught her attention as she did and she stopped, staring at the candles for a long moment as something tickled at the back of her mind. Unable to grasp it, she dismissed both the sense that there was something she needed to remember and the mess she'd left in her crazy attempt to summon 'other worldly' help and headed into her workshop.

## Chapter Two

Discomfort brought Cara drifting toward awareness, and yet the drugging mists of half sleep seemed determined to cling to her mind, leaving her with the sense that she was dreaming. Trying to identify the cause of her discomfort and even the location, she struggled to direct her mind, to sift through the sensations.

She was lying face down ... she thought. Even that confused her, because although she felt pressure against the front of her body rather than the back, she couldn't feel any pressure against her face or anything to indicate her head was turned to one side. She did feel a strange sort of pressure against her forehead, almost like a band. She couldn't seem to open her eyes. She tried for a few moments and gave up, searching with her other senses once more. It was uncomfortable but not the source of her discomfort.

Her arms were out to her sides, seemed to be parallel to her body. She tried lifting them, failed, and then tried moving them up and down and discovered she couldn't seem to move them in any direction. More confused than alarmed, she abandoned that puzzle since it didn't actually seem to be the source of her discomfort either and focused on her breasts.

There was every reason to feel discomfort there, except it wasn't like it should have been. They weren't crushed flat by her weight. Instead, it almost seemed as if they protruded from something, like a sleeve—or a manacle because it was tight, she realized, around the base of her breasts—all the way around. The tips of her breasts didn't seem to be restrained at all, but either her position or the tight bands around the top that felt as if they'd forced her rounded breasts into a more tubular shape seemed to have forced the blood to pool at the ends of her breasts. They were throbbing like an aching tooth.

The pulsing throb held her attention for a few moments and then her mind wandered again in search of the other area of discomfort. Her clit was throbbing, too, she realized, and seemingly for the same reason. The outer lips of her sex had been peeled back, not merely exposing the far more tender inner flesh to currents of air, but restricting blood flow and making it pool in that sensitive area so that it rivaled the uncomfortable pounding in her nipples.

Having identified the source of her discomfort, her mind seemed to focus on them and it seemed the more pointed her focus became the more intensely they pounded until discomfort began to give way to pain and she began trying to free herself from the restraints causing it—uselessly—because as soon as she did, she realized it was as if she was glued to the hard surface that supported her. She couldn't so much as shift a hair in any direction.

She was so focused on that disturbing circumstance, she didn't realize that her legs were being slowly drawn upward by pressure beneath her knees until she began to feel the strain in her tendons. She realized fairly quickly that she wasn't in control, though. They were pulled upward until her thighs were parallel to her body as her arms were. The pressure had curled her hips upward and tautened the pull against her nether lips until it almost felt as if the inner area of her cleft was bulging, until she could feel that the mouth of her sex was stretched open.

Alarm struggled to penetrate the strange fog gripping her mind as something pressed against the mouth of her sex. It was hard and thick enough it spread the mouth wider and wider as it was pushed deeper inside her until she began to feel uncomfortably stretched and then painfully stretched. She began to pant, her entire focus on the burning resistance of the mouth of her sex and then the muscles along her channel as her flesh yielded with great reluctance to the enormous thing being driven with slow deliberation inside of her until it was pressing against her womb.

The pressure eased, but she felt little relief. The fog had begun to churn as thoughts flitted through her mind, but she couldn't identify what had been pushed inside of her. It felt too big to be a cock, too hard and unyielding and yet beyond stretching her until she thought her flesh would tear, it had seemed as smooth and cylindrical as a cock. The tip first inserted had seemed rounded like the head of a cock, hadn't seemed as big as the shaft.

So abruptly that it sent a wave of shock through her, creating further chaos in her mind, something hot closed over both of her breasts at once. She realized she hadn't merely imagined that the blood was pooling in the tips. It had been. They'd swollen and, in doing so, become so intensely sensitive that she nearly blacked out as the heat engulfed her. It was only as the darkness parted a little that she realized that it was mouths clamped over the ends of her breasts, sucking and pulling at them with such vigor that she wove in and out of the darkness. Pain and pleasure so intense it bordered pain poured through her body like fire, closing her throat and squeezing her lungs until she couldn't manage more than choked gurgles of sound while her mind screamed at the torment to her nerves.

Even as her system began to acclimate to the horrendous sensations, another mouth clamped over her clit with the same ferocious greed, sending her spiraling toward oblivion once more. It eluded her. She skated the edge, hoped for it, and yet she couldn't reach it because of the intensity of the sensations pouring into her. The muscles along her channel fluttered abruptly in reaction, clamping around the shaft so tightly her belly cramped.

The shaft began to move then, withdrawing and then slamming back into her jarringly. She began to come with the third jarring thrust, the convulsions wracking her until she thought they would shake her apart and still the cock pounded into her and the mouths fed greedily until she reached maximum overload and blacked out.

When she surfaced again toward awareness, every pulse point on her body seemed to be sizzling and throbbing. Slowly, her breath returned to normal and her fevered flesh began to cool. It still throbbed. She could still feel the bindings that made the blood pool until the flesh was so swollen it ached, but it settled to mild discomfort again—briefly.

Without warning, a mouth settled on her clit with a fierce hunger than pitched her toward the abyss. Before she'd even managed to catch a decent breath of air, the twin tormentors of her breasts returned, throwing her into a mindless, drunken fever. The muscles along her channel fluttered madly. As if summoned, she felt the pressure of the cock, felt insistent penetration despite the resistance of her body to its girth—she knew it was a cock, so thick it was sweet agony to feel it ram into her.

She sucked in a sharp breath as she was impaled fully on

the enormous shaft. Even as she did so, she felt the pressure against her forehead increase, tilting her head back. A thick cock was forced between her jaws. Her senses rioted. The sensations were too intense, too much for her mind to handle at once. She sucked on the cock in her mouth mindlessly as she was penetrated from both ends at once, almost in sync. The tug at her breasts and clit became so savage pain and pleasure collided, sent her body barreling toward a climax that was so explosive that it flung her from consciousness.

She was jolted awake by burning cold against her clit. She gasped, squirmed to evade it, but it coasted around and around her clit until it was numb. Dread clawed its way up her throat, but despite the fact that she'd guessed what was coming next, the ice on her breasts knocked the breath from her again. She didn't manage to regain it until her breasts grew as numb as her clit. She was shivering all over by then, her jaw cramping from the effort to keep her teeth from chattering.

The ice disappeared. Slowly, the numbness dissipated. The bindings drew the blood to pool once more until she scaled the rungs from discomfort to aching sensitivity. She whimpered when she realized she'd reached the peak in sensitivity again, struggling to brace herself. It was an exercise in futility. She was as sensitive when the twin mouths latched onto her breasts once more as she had been the first time and as it had then, it nearly pitched her into darkness. The disembodied mouths seemed more feverish than before, though. This time instead of merely sucking and tugging out them, she felt sharp teeth digging into her. It didn't prepare her for a similar assault on her clit and yet, despite the searing pain, she felt her kegels convulse, threatening a hard climax.

Before it could gain ground and become a full-fledged climax, she felt fingers prying at her buttocks and then pressure against her rectum. Sucking in a sharp breath, she struggled to relax the muscles and it still burned like fire as he drove deeply inside of her. The burning eased as he withdrew and thrust again. She'd almost managed to regain some semblance of sanity when she felt pressure against the mouth of her sex. It threw her into a total state of chaos all over again as he drove the thick member to the hilt inside of her. As he withdrew, the cock in her ass drove deeply. The counter thrusts pistoning inside of her one behind the other catapulted her into a climax within moments, holding her at the apex until a dark cloud enveloped her. She never actually touched down. Her body convulsed, rested briefly, and spasmed again. The third time she hit orgasm, she passed out.

She roused fully enough when she came around again to begin to feel dread fill her, to feel it seep into every pore. Just as she'd fully tensed with it, they began the torment all over again, pulling frantically at her clit and then her breasts. A cock was forced between her jaws and moments later, the thick shaft was forced into her channel again. They began to pump in sync as before, driving her toward another climax. Before she could achieve it, a third cock was rammed into her ass. Already mindless with a mixture of pleasure and pain, the pounding cadence of the triple penetration sent her over the edge, sending one hard shockwave after another through her until she passed out.

There were two things Cara noticed almost immediately when she surfed toward awareness again. She could move when she hadn't been able to during the hours she'd been bound and fucked within an inch of her life and she ached as if she'd been beaten half to death—seemingly everything on her body. She thought her arms ached from nothing more than straining to move when she couldn't. Her neck and legs were sore from the awkward position she'd been bound in, her stomach from climaxing over and over. Her jaws, her ass, and her pussy ached from being thoroughly reamed out, though, and beyond that her skin was still so sensitive the slightest movement sent jarring sensation along every nerve ending.

There was no possibility of convincing herself it had been a dream or a nightmare. Nothing purely of the mind could've made her so miserable.

Dread filled her, but when she'd searched her surroundings with her senses, she couldn't detect anything indicating she wasn't alone. Nerving herself, she opened her eyes. The room she was in was dim, but not pitch black as the room before had been—as she believed it was. She was no longer certain whether she hadn't been able to open her eyes or if it simply hadn't made any different when she did.

She could see that she was alone, though, and a modicum

of relief flickered through her. Lifting her head, she scanned the room. A jolt went through her. She was in her own room, her bedroom! The discovery made her feel perfectly blank. Questions crowded into her mind to fill that void within seconds, but she couldn't shake any answers loose.

Had she been in her own bedroom the entire time?

If she had, there was something seriously wrong with her mind!

Shaking that thought, she got off the bed with an effort, paused to gather her strength and headed toward her bathroom. She relieved herself while she waited for the temperature of the water to adjust and then climbed into the shower shakily.

Her mind filled with flickering images of the things she remembered as she soaped her sponge and began scrubbing herself, prompted by the twinges she felt with every touch, every movement. As she rinsed, she examined herself for bruising, looking for anything that would substantiate her certainty that what had happened was real. There wasn't a trace of a bruise on any part of her body that she'd been convinced was bound in some way, though. Her nipples and areolas looked chafed and so did her clit, but not raw and lacerated as she was certain they should have.

She'd felt more than tongues and the suction of mouths! She'd felt teeth! She was certain of it, as if whoever it was knew the very moment sensation began to dull and used their teeth to optimize awareness again.

She paused at that thought, considering it. At the time, she'd thought they were growing more excited and less cautious of damage they might cause, but as she considered it, she realized that it hadn't seemed like a loss of self control so much as a determination not to allow her to avoid feeling.

Even the ice used to cool her hadn't been used to numb her from feeling, although it had briefly. It had been used to optimize sensation after she'd been exposed to so much her body was struggling to protect her by dulling her awareness of the stimulation of her nerves.

*They* had. She'd felt three mouths and three cocks—all at the same time. It boggled the mind trying to figure out how they might have been ramming their cocks into her at the same time as they were gnawing a breast or her clit, but the alternative was to consider six rather than three and she found that was hard to swallow. It was hard enough to consider the undeniable fact that there had to have been three to have done what was done to her, but as wild as that was, six simply defied belief.

She couldn't imagine being in the same room with three men and not hearing anything to indicate it. The only thing to support that was what they'd done, which would've been impossible for one.

It flickered through her mind that she should report the assault and just as quickly reluctance filled her. She'd bathed. If there'd been any evidence, she'd washed it away. She realized abruptly that there hadn't been, though. Considering how many times those three cocks had pumped into her, she should've been awash with semen and yet she hadn't noticed any at all.

Condoms?

They had to have been wearing them, she decided, relieved about that at least.

But how had they gotten in? How had they bound her like that without waking her? What had they used to bind her? And on what surface, now that she thought about it?

Stepping from the shower, she turned it off, dried herself carefully, and wrapped up in the damp towel. She left the bathroom then and moved around her apartment. Every door and window was locked and not one room seemed it might have been the room where she was used as a sexual slave and tortured within an inch of her life—with more pleasure than she could stand.

She hated even to admit that to herself. She should be hysterical and catatonic after what had happened to her! She should feel soiled, particularly when she knew she'd felt a lot of pain and she'd reacted as if she'd felt nothing but pleasure.

It was worse than that, actually. The pain had almost seemed to intensify the pleasure and that realization should have made her feel like puking. She should be disgusted—with herself if not whoever had done it.

There was no getting around the fact that she was appalled. No one in their right mind *enjoyed* pain.

Brushing that thought aside, unwilling to examine it, she went in search of something to drive off the weakness that persisted. She didn't see anything that really appealed to her, mostly because she simply felt too weak to have the energy to prepare it. Finally, she settled for a piece of wheat toast and a glass of juice.

When she'd finished, she decided she was just too exhausted to think straight. She still took the time to check all the windows and doors again, to reassure herself that they were all locked, before she returned to her bedroom. As soon as she entered the room, uneasiness wafted through her. Her heart began to hammer a little faster—almost as if some part of her *knew* that this room, her own room, was where she'd been bound and sexually tortured.

It wasn't rational, she told herself. It couldn't have been this room.

But then where? Was it even possible that she could've been transported from one place to another without knowing it and then back again? Because she'd been in her own room when she went to bed and she'd awakened in her own bed.

Drugs? It seemed like the only answer and yet she couldn't think how she might have been drugged.

She couldn't think straight at all! Shaking off her thoughts, she decided to leave her bathroom light on and climbed into her bed again. For a while, she lay staring at nothing in particular while her mind continued to scramble around for answers. Finally, her weariness overcame her again, though, and she fell into a deep chasm.

She woke to the same strange sense of floating that she had before, as if she was drifting between the dream world and the real world and unable to fully capture either. Dread curled in her stomach, but unlike a typical dream, or nightmare, she seemed almost as cocooned from that emotion as she was from true awareness.

She knew it wasn't a dream, however, the moment she tried to open her eyes and discovered they wouldn't respond to the command. Almost as if she was a puppet, with no command over her own body, she felt her arms pulled behind her back and then tugged downward until her back arched, thrusting her chest out. Her palms settled against a flat surface and then something that felt like wide metal cuffs clamped around her wrists, holding her in place. She discovered she couldn't twist her shoulders either, though, or her torso. While she was still trying to understand that strange phenomena, she felt her legs drawn into place. Her knees bent as her legs were pushed close to her body and then her bent legs were spread wide, so wide she could feel air brush along her entire cleft as the flesh parted moistly. Something clamped on the flesh that formed the outer lips of her sex and pulled them up and back until her clit was fully exposed.

She wasn't lying down as she had been before, she realized a handful of moments before she felt pressure against the mouth of her sex. Her heart leapt into her throat and tried to strangle her as the pressure swiftly increased. She hadn't had any stimulation to help her produce moisture—not that she could possibly have produced enough to make engulfing anything that huge easy or painless.

It defied reason that almost the instant she felt the initial penetration, moisture flooded her channel and yet, as she'd thought, it did little to help. The pressure increased to burning pain regardless of the moisture as she was stretched to the very limits of what her flesh could take without fracturing. She panted for breath as the thick shaft was driven home, her mind weaving in and out of darkness. Relief flooded her when the pushing stopped as the head came to rest against her womb. Internally, she struggled to adjust to the invasion.

She was distracted before she'd managed to acclimate when her clit was seized. It couldn't be a mouth, her mind screamed, and yet it felt like one—hot, moist, pulling frenziedly at the sensitive bud until she felt her body scaling toward a peak. She hit it when a mouth abruptly clamped onto each of her breasts and began suckling them as frantically as her clit, gasping and groaning as the convulsions rocked her, her belly cramping as the muscles along her channel clenched around the shaft.

She was still shuddering with it when she felt her buttocks pried apart and a second shaft that felt almost as big as the first, was driven into her so fast and so deep, she blacked out briefly. She wasn't deprived of awareness more than a handful of seconds. She came around when they withdrew in tandem and drove into her again. Unlike before when one was driven in while the other withdrew, they continued to thrust into her in sync and each time they did, she felt like her body would explode from the twin pressures.

And her body still responded with mounting pleasure.

She hit orgasm twice more before she reached a surfeit of what she could endure and fainted.

She roused again with reluctance, realizing even as she did from the uncomfortable tightness in her lower body that she was still mounted on both shafts. As awareness penetrated her mind, they began to move, driving in and out of her with such force and swiftness that she began to come again within moments and continued to spasm until she lost consciousness again.

She groaned when she woke once more to the realization that she was still impaled on those twin shafts. They began to move before she'd achieved full awareness. It wasn't until she'd convulsed so many times that she felt herself falling into the well of darkness again that she realized the mouths had vanished from her breasts and clit and the entire focus had been on driving into her.

That changed when she woke once more. As soon as she roused, the mouths fastened onto both of her breasts and her clit. When her channel began to spasm in imminent release, she realized both cocks had been withdraw. Almost on the thought, the thickest of the two was rammed into her channel and began driving frenziedly until she passed out, completely overwhelmed by the ceaseless rapture that rocked her body.

Light was filtering through her window shades when she surfed toward consciousness again. An internal search told her that she was sprawled limply on top of her bed, completely naked.

She hadn't gone to bed that way. Feeling drunk and thoroughly disoriented, she half climbed half fell from her bed. Her legs gave out, dumping her painfully in the floor, which set off pain in every direction. Waiting until the worst had passed, she got to her feet shakily, looked around her room vaguely and, when she located the door of the bathroom, headed inside.

There were deep bruises beneath her eyes from lack of sleep. Her head swam with weakness and she gagged on her toothpaste and nearly threw up. It took all she could do to stand beneath the shower spray long enough to bathe off quickly.

She lost the towel she'd wrapped around herself as she left the bathroom again, but she didn't feel like bending over to pick it up. Heading straight to her kitchen, she grabbed the gallon jug of water she kept there and drank until her belly felt bloated from the water and nausea washed through her. She still felt dehydrated, but she set the jug down and searched for something to put in her empty stomach.

Settling for a piece of toast because she didn't feel up to doing anything else or waiting, she dropped weakly onto one of her stools and nibbled at it, trying to wrap her mind around the weakness and the sense of disorientation.

Memories flooded her mind, horrendous images. Shuddering, she pushed them from her mind with an effort. Feeling a little better once she'd eaten the toast, she got up and fixed a pan of soft scrambled eggs, another piece of toast, and grabbed a glass and filled it with juice. Despite the fact that she felt like she was about to starve to death, she didn't manage to eat much more than half of what she'd cooked.

Still feeling weak, and miserable beyond that from her full stomach, she considered going back to bed. Reluctance immediately assailed her, though, and instead she headed into her living room and collapsed on her couch, trying to summon enough energy to boot up her computer and work. She struggled with the need to work and the need to rest for a few moments and finally settled her head on the arm of her couch and dozed off.

The room was full of light when she woke the second time, making it clear that it was nearly noon or maybe even past that. Jolted by that realization, she sat up, rubbed her eyes to shake off the dregs of sleep and booted her computer.

She was a little startled when she logged in to her orders file and saw how many orders she'd had—startled and excited until she saw the date. She stared at it in disbelief for several moments and finally moved her cursor to the corner of the screen. Instantly, the day and date popped up.

That couldn't be right! It should be Tuesday, not Wednesday!

She'd gone to bed Monday night and woken on Wednesday?

How could she have lost an entire day?

It abruptly occurred to her how thirsty and hungry she'd been when she'd woke up, ravenous. She'd thought that was because her rest had been disturbed, though!

Disturbed by .... What?

Getting up abruptly, she prowled the house, searching for any sign of intruders. Nothing looked out of place, though—nothing except the burned candles from the ritual she'd performed and the pentagram she'd drawn on the floor with 'magical' sands.

Shaken and confused, she returned to the couch and stared at the screen for a while, her mind on the dark memories.

As dream-like as it had seemed, it couldn't have been, not when she had physical proof that it was reality in the soreness and stiffness!

And yet, there was no sign that anyone but her had been in her house—none! That defied belief. She might be able to swallow the possibility that one man had crept into her house and left no sign—beyond the invisible signs she *felt*!—but she couldn't accept that three men had been in and left no sign that they had.

And she was absolutely certain it was three!

A thought occurred to her abruptly, but it was simply too wild to accept. She struggled with it for a little while, but then it dawned on her that if it was true she'd been completely out of it for two days, that also meant she hadn't gone to see her mother.

That thought was enough to make her dismiss everything else. Bounding from the couch, she dashed into her room to dress. She felt a pang with every movement, but she resolutely ignored it. Grabbing her purse when she was dressed, she hurried back into her living room and scanned her bookshelf for a book, just in case, then headed out and drove to the hospice where her mother was to spend her last days on Earth.

The nurse on duty gave her a disapproving look when she let her in. "She's asked for you. I told her you were tied up, but you'd be here when you could."

Cara felt her chest tighten with a mixture of remorse and fear. Nodding, she headed to her mother's room and went in.

## Chapter Three

Disappointment flickered through Cara when she reached her mother's room and discovered she was sleeping. Shame immediately followed. It was the only time her mother was completely free of pain, she knew, regardless of her mother's attempts to pretend she was fine.

Settling quietly in one of the easy chairs in the room, she took the book out that she'd brought and opened in, studying the table of contents. Ordinarily, she brought a magazine or a novel to read—either to her mother or to herself if her mother was resting. The ritual she'd performed the night before was still very much on her mind, though, and she'd grabbed a book of the occult to see if she could figure out what, if anything, she'd done wrong.

Aside from allowing herself to believe in hocus pocus when she ought to know better!

When she'd read back over the description of the summoning ritual, though, she couldn't see that she'd failed in any part of it—with the exception that she hadn't waited for the full moon.

Very likely that was all it had taken, she thought angrily. The author of the book was insistent about that point—that the gateways of the other worlds could only be opened at specific times and under very specific conditions.

Unless there'd been something impure about the candles she'd used, or the paint for the pentagram or, horror of horrors, the sand she'd used to mark the protection boundary!

Deciding she'd have to check all of them when she returned home, she turned to the section describing various demons that people had dealt with in the past—what they were capable of, what motivated them, or seemed to, and how to avoid their trickery. A strange feeling swept over her when she reached the section describing the incubus. Her skin prickled all over and more importantly, the hair at the base of her skull.

Shivering in reaction, she paused, searching her mind for why she might have such a reaction to what was, after all, nothing more than voodoo whodo. She didn't *really* believe in this tripe!

Ok, so she was willing to keep an open mind to an extent—the extent that she was desperate enough to try anything at this point—but it certainly hadn't worked!

Of course, she acknowledged that she hadn't followed procedure to the letter and there was a tiny bit of doubt that lingered in her mind that it hadn't worked for that reason, but that still didn't explain the reaction. *All* of them should creep her out!

She realized after a moment that it wasn't just reading about the incubus that had caused the reaction. Reading about it had triggered something buried deep in her subconscious. The problem was, she couldn't grasp it and it seemed the harder she tried the further she was from reaching it.

Breaking off the search in the hope that it would come to her when she stopped struggling to reach it, she focused on her reading again. The errant thought flitted through her mind again after a few moments, this time prompted by the statement that the incubus generally appeared in one's dreams.

Frowning, Cara paused once more, wondering if that was the answer to the strange sense of ... almost familiarity. Had she dreamed about it? Was that the nightmare she couldn't remember?

Her mother diverted her from pursuing it. Hearing a change in her breathing, Cara glanced at her sharply, feeling her heart leap uncomfortably.

Her mother smiled wryly, but apparently decided not to address the fact that Cara grew alarmed any time her breathing changed. "How long have you been here?"

"How long have you been asleep?" Cara countered.

"Why? So you can tell me you've been here the whole time?" her mother asked with amusement.

Cara grinned. "It hadn't crossed my mind!"

"Right!" Her mother chuckled a little breathlessly, but her expression grew sharp as she studied her daughter. "You look awful today. Are you coming down with something?"

Cara rolled her eyes. "Gosh, thanks, mom! That bad, huh?"

"Maybe you're working too hard. You look tired."

"I wish! Business is good but unfortunately not good enough to work me to death. I just didn't sleep well last night."

Her mother eyed her skeptically. "You're sure that's all it is?"

Cara smiled with an effort. "I'm sure."

"So ... how were sales yesterday?"

"Good." Cara frowned. "I'm wondering how reliable our source is for those ritual candles, though."

Her mother's brows rose. "I checked him out myself. You've had problems?"

"No, not really. I had a complaint ... but they probably just didn't perform the ritual like they should have. You know how some people are! They think they can take short cuts and still have the same results."

Her mother looked uneasy. "You need to be careful who you sell to. I know we need the money, but this isn't anything to mess around with. It's potentially dangerous. You shouldn't sell to anyone who isn't serious about these things—and by serious I mean really careful."

Cara smiled with an effort. She'd never really understood how her mother, who was so level headed about most things, could believe in the occult like she did.

She was almost sorry she didn't have the same conviction! Maybe that was why the ritual hadn't worked, she thought in disgust? Maybe it had to be performed by a true believer?

What sort of magic was that, though? If it only manifested for 'believers' then how could anyone else believe in it?

"You know I'm always careful to run a background check on anybody that orders the hard stuff. I was just ... concerned. Do you think any of the stock might have gone bad? I mean deteriorated or anything?"

Her mother shook her head. "It isn't like bread, Cara! It doesn't get stale or rot! I'm sure everything's fine."

They discussed business for a while longer, avoiding any discussion about her mother's illness as they generally did. The expression on her mother's face when she launched into a discussion about expanding once she got better unsettled her. She knew what was coming when her mother fell silent. "Cara ... you know I'm not going to come home again, don't you, sweety?"

Cara felt a lump the size of her fist swell in her throat. "Don't talk like that!"

Her mother fell silent again. "Baby, it doesn't help to bury your head in the sand. I don't have long now. You need to prepare yourself."

Cara fought a round with her emotions. "Can we talk about something a little more cheerful?"

Her mother bit her lip, seemed to consider for a few moments and finally nodded. "Met anybody of interest?"

Cara uttered a sound halfway between a laugh and a sob. Where was she supposed to meet anybody? The business they'd once run together took every moment of her time. She couldn't actually afford the hours she spent with her mother everyday and they both knew it. "I saw a hunk when I went out for groceries last week. I think he might be the new store manager."

Her mother looked suitably impressed. "Married?"

"I didn't get close enough to see a ring," Cara admitted. "Well, I did, but I was too preoccupied to notice if there was a ring."

Her mother smiled. "He must be good looking!"

"I said he was a hunk, didn't I?"

Her mother seemed inclined to fantasize about the make believe manager she'd invented and Cara went with it since it seemed to make her mother more lively and cheerful.

"You should consider doing a love spell—I mean, if you see he isn't taken already."

"Maybe I will," Cara said, deciding to end the visit on that note since she could see her mother was tired. "We'll talk about it when I come tomorrow. I need to get back and finished filling all the orders."

Despite the cheerful discussion toward the end of their visit, Cara felt her shoulders slump with dejection as she left. Every effort had been made to make the hospice a cheerful, homey place, but it was an impossible task when no one ever left to go home once they arrived.

As she usually did, she focused on her work as soon as she returned home. She'd developed a powerful ability to concentrate and block out unwelcome thoughts by simply shuttling them to the back of her mind each time they arose. She was so intent, in point of fact, that she didn't even think about her suspicion that she'd had a nightmare about an incubus again until she settled to eat her solitary supper.

Her skin prickled all over as it had before the moment the thought popped into her mind. Her stomach muscles clenched, too, although not in a way she could consider a fear reaction, particularly when her nipples stood erect at the same time. It was purely sexual.

Shaking her head at herself, she struggled to dismiss the thought and the reaction it had prompted. Maybe her mother was right? She really did need to get out!

Actually, she was more inclined to think she just needed to get laid! Now certainly wasn't a time to consider a romantic liaison, even if she'd actually had someone in her sights—which she didn't. She was having a hard enough time dealing with her mother's illness without also having to deal with relationship issues! Especially considering her previous failed attempts!

Not that she'd ever had a really serious relationship. She'd dated quite a bit in high school and throughout college, but although she'd felt an obligation to carry many of them to the next level, that was when it petered out—earlier if she didn't feel any interest in carrying it to the next level. They were too demanding of her time and too selfish to reciprocate. She supposed if she'd actually cared, it would've hurt when she discovered they demanded complete faithfulness from her while they had at least one other girlfriend on the side, and some of them more than one. Instead, it had simply pissed her off. It had seemed to her that the guys she was most inclined to consider on a more permanent basis were the worst about cheating.

Deciding finally that she just had a streak of self-destructiveness where men were concerned a mile wide, inevitably choosing the worse, she'd decided to focus on building up the business for a while. That had been several years earlier and, although she'd occasionally run across a man that piqued her interest, nothing had come of it. She'd reached a point in her life where the most desirable had already been selected and she didn't have any interest in marrying merely for the sake marrying—because it was traditional and expected.

She didn't think it would've crossed her mind again for a long while, if ever, except that her mother had begun urging her to find someone.

She knew why. Her mother was as worried about leaving her alone in the world as she was fearful of being left alone. She was almost tempted to try to find somebody and get married just to give her mother peace of mind, but by the same token, she knew it couldn't be right for her. She didn't feel like she had the time to devote to it and, in any case, she was so deeply in debt now no man in his right mind would want to saddle himself with her.

The idea of getting laid had some merit, though. It was a great stress reliever—when it was good. Unfortunately, when it was bad it only created more stress.

Maybe she should check out some of the hook-up sites online and see if she found any interesting possibilities?

It was dangerous, of course, but what wasn't these days? You could get killed in your own bed in your own home if some psycho decided to break in.

That thought prompted memories she'd been working to suppress—the strange 'dreams'. She'd managed to pretty well put them out of her mind once she'd convinced herself that there was no way that anyone could have been in the house with her. She still didn't think it was possible that it could've been real, no matter how real it had seemed. What would the point be in such a thing? Rapists didn't generally come in threes or even in pairs and except for trying to make sure they couldn't be identified, she didn't think they made much attempt to cover the fact that they'd been there.

It couldn't have been real. She knew it couldn't. But then, how to explain the soreness?

Had it been such a powerful wet dream that she'd acted it out? Done it to herself?

She found that hard to swallow. As far as she knew she wasn't prone to doing anything in her sleep. She felt sure her mother would've spoken about it if she had any tendency to move around in her sleep and she doubted such a thing would've gone undetected all these years.

Maybe the soreness was just the results of having come so hard? She didn't remember much of it very clearly, but she did remember that she'd had an explosive climax. It actually seemed like there'd been more than one, but she thought that was probably just a trick of the subconscious mind. One, she could believe considering how long it had been for her. More than one seemed to be stretching it a little too thin.

Dismissing it finally, she cleaned up after herself and went into the living room. After staring at the remains from her ritual a few moments, she decided to clean up the candles at least. She didn't see the point in removing the pentagram when she would be trying the spell again when the moon was full and even the thought of removing the protective circle made her uneasy in an indescribable way.

It was as she collected the book of spells that was, for some strange reason, across the room from the circle where she'd performed the spell that a memory abruptly surfaced. It was across the room because she'd thrown it—and that was also why so many candles had been overturned. A shiver skated through her. Moving back across the room, she stared down at the circle of protection or, more specifically, the *broken* circle.

The book had skidded through it when she'd flung it away in anger, she remembered abruptly. She'd been too upset to really notice it at the time or care. Her uneasiness intensified as she stared down at it, though, and remembered what her mother had said about it being too dangerous for skeptics or the unskilled novice.

She struggled to dismiss it for a few moments, trying to tell herself it was ridiculous to feel so alarmed about what was really nothing more than scattered sand. She couldn't shake the jitters, though, and finally searched the spell book until she found one regarding the repair of a protective circle.

It had a ritual, but it also emphasized that repairing the circle might be a matter of too little too late—closing the barn door after the cows had already escaped.

The spell hadn't worked, though, she reminded herself, feeling a little less uneasy. Getting up decisively, she went to her workroom to gather what she needed and set about re-establishing the protective circle. She was tired when she finished, but she felt better, however silly she knew it to be.

After checking all the doors and windows, she headed into her room, took a long, hot shower to help her relax and climbed into her bed. Within moments, she felt herself drifting toward oblivion.

A mixture of dread and anticipation coiled inside her when she found herself floating on the edge of awareness again. She struggled to decide whether she was dreaming or if she was actually awake, or nearly awake.

Déjà vu wafted through her when she realized she was lying face down and that the surface beneath her felt far too hard to be her bed. She was struggling to figure out why it seemed familiar when she felt her arms move, seemingly of their own accord, out to her sides until they were parallel to her body. When they stopped moving, she tried to continue the movement and curl them beneath her head only to discover that they felt disconnected from her mind, refused to obey the command. She was still trying to figure that out when she felt a compression of her breasts that seemed to defy any of the laws of physics. They should be flattened tightly against her chest when she knew for a certainty that she was lying on her stomach.

Regardless, the pressure increased until her breasts felt as if they'd been squeezed into an almost tubular shape, until it became uncomfortable enough she tried to shift to ease it. The discovery that she couldn't move made her heart begin to pound a little harder and when it did, she felt the blood begin to pulse hard enough in the ends of her breasts to make it clear that only the base of her breasts were compressed. Her nipples tightened, stood erect and then began to feel more and more swollen and more and more sensitive.

Despite the tendency her mind seemed to have to float in an almost disconnected way, she struggled to focus on moving her torso to relieve the pressure as it grew more and more pronounced. She was distracted by the movement of her legs. Like her arms, they seemed to move of their own will. Her knees bent under the pressure and still her legs slipped upward until her thighs were parallel to her body just as her arms were, pulling against her cleft until the moist flesh there parted. Something clamped on the fleshy outer lips of her sex, sending a jolt of surprise through her. It didn't feel like hands, or fingers—she wasn't certain what it felt like, but it peeled them back until her clit was fully exposed and, once it had, she felt something encircle her clit, compressing the flesh at the base. It made the blood pool in her clit in the same way that the compression of her breasts had made the blood pool in her nipples—except worse. It swelled tightly far more rapidly, becoming so sensitized that when something hot and moist clamped on to it, it catapulted her toward deepest darkness, knocked the breath from her. Her mind screamed at the intensity of the sensation but as with any dream she discovered that she couldn't make a sound. She could only struggle to make sound, gasp for breath, feel the torment of screaming nerve endings and have no way of escape.

It felt like a mouth, she decided when the sensation had dulled enough to allow her mind to function—not enough to give her much in the way of relief. Her body, contrary to logic or her will, responded by opening itself to the stimulation, pumping more blood into those areas most sensitive already. The muscles along her sex quaked, pushing a flood of moisture into her channel.

She'd managed to catch her breath when twin tormentors latched onto her nipples with the same ferocity as her clit had been seized. Like a yoyo, she was pitched toward the brink of complete unconsciousness only to be snatched back. Her skin prickled all over as her body abruptly convulsed in orgasm. Before it had the chance to complete the cycle, she felt pressure against the mouth of her sex, but the warning was brief. Whatever it was impaled her so swiftly she barely had time to register the sense that she was being ripped apart before it slammed into her womb and was withdrawn almost as swiftly only to be driven into her again and again.

Pain and pleasure pelted her from every direction until her mind seemed incapable of determining which she felt most or which to react to. The quaking from her first climax had barely receded when her body began to tremble on the verge of another. The rise was rapid. The pull on her clit and breasts and the pounding thrusts of the shaft drove her upwards and into fresh spasms of rapture before she could even assimilate the rise.

Another thick shaft penetrated her rectum even as she

began to fall toward Earth again. She groaned, tried instinctively to evade the pain and failed. For many moments, the fear filled her that her body couldn't take both and yet it did and it responded by building toward another climax as they thrust into her frenziedly.

She reached a surfeit of what she could endure in the way of pleasure and pain when she hit her third climax. Darkness swallowed her.

She didn't believe she'd had much respite. When she coasted toward consciousness again, everything on her body was still sizzling and pounding. Slowly, her body cooled enough to take the edge off of her discomfort. Almost the moment she achieved that state, the mouths clamped onto her breasts again, sending a shockwave through her. She gasped, struggling to catch her breath. A cock was shoved between her jaws. Before she could decide whether to merely allow it to slide in and out, she felt the muscles of her mouth tighten around it, her tongue curl to cup it and she was sucking at it almost as frantically as the mouths tormenting her were pulling at her breasts.

The cock jerked a warning just as her clit was seized. Mindlessly, she sucked at the cock as if it was a lifeline. Fluid filled her mouth as he ejaculated. Surprisingly, it seemed to boost her own arousal higher, lift her closer to climax. The taste wasn't like come—not like any she'd ever had in her mouth. It sent a dizzying wave of warmth through her when she swallowed, almost as if she'd gulped a shot of strong alcohol.

The cock that was rammed into her sex drove the thought from her mind. She began to climax almost before it fully penetrated and was withdrawn. Her mind seemed to fragment. She was aware of all of the stimuli at once and, at the same time, unable to focus. Pleasure seemed to roll over her in ways almost too intense to bear. She thought it *was* too powerful and yet she couldn't escape. There was no choice but to endure.

And when she finally succumbed to darkness and emerged on the other side, she was taken to the same nearly unbearable heights again and again.

\* \* \* \*

It was a nightmare that jolted Cara awake and yet the moment she awakened, it began to fade and by the time she'd struggled toward full awareness all she was left with was the sense that something horrendous had happened.

And weakness.

And soreness, as if she'd been through a meat grinder.

She was too tired even to groan in her misery. She lay staring at the light against her eyelids for a while, too unnerved to consider trying to seek sleep again and too tired to feel like staying awake. It was thirst that finally drove her from the bed, the sense that she would die of dehydration if she didn't quench it.

Realizing as soon as she sat up and her head swam that she was in no condition to make it to her kitchen, even crawling, she staggered into the bathroom, filled her hands with water and drank until she could feel it sloshing in her stomach. Nauseated from filling her cavernously empty stomach with water, she made her way back to the bed with an effort and sprawled out again. She wove in and out of slumber for a time, wanting to sleep, needing to, and yet afraid to yield to it.

After a time the nausea passed and some of the disorientation. She was still empty, though, and since she felt like she might make it to the kitchen, she got up and left her bedroom in search of food. She didn't feel like preparing anything when she got there but she found a pack of salty crackers and munched on a few while she waited for the frozen dinner she'd thrown into the microwave to heat.

The food improved her considerably. She still felt unaccountably weak and battered, but a hot shower chased a good bit of that away. Unfortunately, it also made her feel weak again.

By the time she'd managed to dress herself and drag herself into her living room, she discovered it was nearly noon. Settling on the couch, she propped her elbows on her knees and used her hands to support her head, trying to figure out what the hell was wrong with her. She felt like she'd been on a ten day drunk and gotten the shit kicked out of her sometime in the rounds.

She hadn't drank anything at all, though.

And she'd lost a day. Again.

That discovery alarmed her but the sense of urgency to rush to her mother that accompanied it pushed the churning thoughts to back of her mind. The nurse condemned her with her eyes when she rushed into the hospice, flooding her with both resentment and guilt, but she ignored that, too.

To her relief, her mother seemed no worse than the last time she'd visited—no better, but it was a relief even to discover that she hadn't gotten worse. Her visit was a trial, more difficult than usual. Her mother was alarmed at her appearance and Cara spent most of the time trying to sooth her mother's anxiety and divert her—when it was her mother who was so terribly sick!

She was so distressed by the time she left, she indulged in a crying jag in her car before she could compose herself enough to drive home. By the time she'd reached her house again, though, she'd arrived at a conclusion about her state and her missing time that replaced her distress with a healthy dose of both fear and anger.

## Chapter Four

Cara found it difficult to accept the idea that flickered through her mind like a ghost but it returned over and over, becoming more solid each time as it brought bits and pieces of memories with it. Parking her car in her drive, she stared at the house for several moments as if she actually had the power to divine what was inside, what might be waiting only for her to enter the dream world to have her within its power again.

The house looked unchanged, however. It was the home she'd grown up in, tiny, beginning to show its age, but basically the same.

Getting out of the car after a few minutes, she headed inside with a purpose. She thought she actually *had* gone off the deep end, but she didn't see that it was any more insane to do what she had in mind than it had been to perform a summoning ritual to start with.

It occurred to her that she might have underestimated the danger from the beginning. Just because, deep down, she didn't really believe such things existed, it didn't necessarily follow that they didn't. Even science now generally accepted that there were alternate worlds, alternate universes where anything might be the norm.

If she considered it from that perspective, then she had to accept that it was at least possible—but could she also accept that the rituals and charms had any validity?

That was much harder to swallow, but the fact remained that something strange had been happening to her and it had begun directly after she'd performed the summoning ritual. Maybe it was a psychotic break, but if it was, then maybe she needed more 'magic' to protect herself anyway?

She shook the thoughts off as she passed through her living room and headed directly to her workroom. It was dusk. She seemed particularly vulnerable when she was sleeping and she wasn't going to sleep again without first doing her utmost to conjure some sort of protection, no matter how crazy it seemed to her.

Settling on the stool in front of her worktable, Cara took the spell book and flipped through it, searching until she found a protection spell. Marking the spot, she began going through the other books her mother had collected over the years, comparing notes until she finally decided she'd found the strongest charm that seemed likely to fit her particular situation.

It was a shame she didn't know the name of the demon she seemed to have summoned—or even what sort of demon he was, although she was pretty sure it had to be an incubus because it seemed to be using her dreams as a conduit. It would've made it easier to banish the bastard, but she would get around to that in time. First, she had to protect herself.

Taking one of the necklaces she'd designed that contained a particularly flawless piece of quartz, she gathered candles and began to recite the protection ritual, focusing it on the piece of jewelry. When she'd repeated it the third time, she saw to her surprise that the quartz seemed to be glowing. Certain she must be mistaken, she reached for it, carefully touching it with her finger and discovered it was not only glowing, it was warm to the touch.

It comforted her, made her feel as if the spell had actually worked. Unfastening the latch on the chain, she carefully placed the charm around her neck. She felt better, safer, the moment she'd fastened it and smoothed the chain so that the quartz settled between her breasts.

Getting off the stool, she gathered candles, the special paint and the protective sands and headed into her bedroom. She considered the bed for several moments and finally decided to crawl under it since the room was too cramped to move it. The cramped quarters, the dust bunnies, and the dim light made it difficult to paint the pentagram, but she finally completed it. After studying it to make certain she'd done it right, she inched out from under the bed again and set the paint and brush aside.

The urge struck her when she'd stared at her bed for several moments to draw the protective circle around the entire room—or better yet, the house. She discarded the idea after a moment. The larger the circle, the weaker it was. She wanted something strong. She had a bad feeling that she needed something really strong. After lighting the candles and setting them on every surface around the bed, she opened the spell book and began the ritual chant, slowly circling the bed and pouring the sand in a thin stream along the floor. When she reached the head of the bed, she discovered a miscalculation. She hadn't thought to move the bed away from the damned wall!

She considered it for a moment and finally decided she couldn't afford to break off the ritual at this point. Instead, she sprinkled the sand behind the head board and kept going until she'd completed her first circuit. Beginning again, she made a second and then a third circuit, chanting and pouring the sand.

She felt strangely drained when she'd finished, almost lightheaded, but she dismissed it. Clearly she hadn't been getting much rest or she wouldn't look as if someone had punched her in both eyes, and beyond that, she'd lost two days over the last four—missing a lot of meals in the process. Adding that to the burden of stress she was already carrying around, it was small wonder she didn't feel worse.

Gathering her paraphernalia, she returned everything to her workroom and headed into the kitchen to fix something to eat. She needed something substantial and strengthening, she decided once she'd studied the contents of her freezer. She took out a steak, examined it for freezer burn and then tore the packaging off and sprinkled it with tenderizer. Turning her broiler on to heat, she tossed a potato into the microwave, fixed herself a salad and headed into her room to take a quick shower.

She was on the point of removing her charm when it suddenly occurred to her that it certainly wouldn't do her any good if she wasn't wearing it! She didn't particularly want to bathe with it on, but she did. Drying off afterwards, she slipped into a robe and headed back to the kitchen to finish up her meal, settling with it on her coffee table instead of at the kitchen table.

Eating alone only emphasized her mother's absence and she rarely ate in the kitchen any longer, preferring the company of the TV occasionally, but usually her computer. Business first, she decided, booting the computer. The steak cooled while she worked, but she ate more than half, most of the potato and the salad, and she felt much better when she'd finished—physically, anyway. The orders she'd gotten weren't anything to get too excited about. After studying her website, she decided she needed to introduce some new products and settled to examining possibilities at her supplier's site. When she'd finally made her selections and ordered, she got up, cleaned up the mess from her meal and checked the doors and windows.

It was obsessive, she knew. No one lived in the house now except her and she rarely opened a window since she had central heating and cooling, but it was a comfort thing to check the doors and windows nightly—just in case she'd unlocked one for some reason and forgotten—and also to make sure no one had tampered with any of the locks from the outside.

Reassured on that count at least, she turned out the lights and headed to bed. Uneasiness began to gather inside her as soon as she entered her room. The temptation to leave a light on as she had when she was a child smote her and after wrestling with it a few moments, she yielded to it, flipping the bathroom light on and leaving the door slightly ajar.

She wasn't used to the light and she discovered that although it comforted her on one level, chasing away the deep shadows in the room, it was distracting, making it even harder to relax than usual. Eventually, perseverance, the hot shower, the heavy meal, and too little rest joined forces against her uneasiness and she found herself drifting toward sleep. It seemed she'd barely reached that peaceful plane when something woke her. Her eyelids felt like lead when she tried to lift them, but after a brief struggle, she managed it.

The apparition at the foot of her bed sent a jolt through her. His gaze locked with hers the moment her eyes opened. Fury emanated from him. "What is this?"

Cara was too frightened to begin to understand the question. In horror, she watched the demon pace around her bed. He paused when he reached the foot of the bed again, glaring at her furiously.

"You think this puny protection spell can keep me out!" he roared at her.

Cara blinked, dizzy with the jolt of fear that went through

her when he bellowed at her, but as it receded a tiny spark of rebellion arose. "Obviously it has or you wouldn't be standing there, you bastard! You'd be in my bed trying to fuck me to death!"

Something flickered in his dark eyes. She had the feeling her counterattack had taken him by surprise, but he showed little sign of it for all that. In fact, the taunt seemed to enrage him more. "You summoned me, mortal she-dog!" he growled.

If he hadn't called her a bitch, her fear might've overcome the spark of anger. The fact that he had only made her angrier. She sat up. "I summoned you to heal my mother, you son-of-a-bitch! *Not* because I felt like I needed a demon to fuck me! I could get a man for that, and it would be a hell of a lot more satisfactory and not nearly as wearing!"

"I made you come as you never have before!" he bellowed at her. "I gave you pleasure such as no mortal could!"

"Funny, but I don't actually remember any of that," Cara said coolly. "I just remember being sick the next day!"

She could tell that didn't go over well. That time, he merely roared at her, as if he couldn't find words to express his fury. "Remove the spell! Give me what you summoned me for!"

"No."

His eyes narrowed. "You will regret denying me."

Cara narrowed her eyes back at him. "I don't think so, you treacherous son-of-a-bitch! We had a deal! You make my mother well and *then* you can have whatever you want! Otherwise, I'm going to banish you back to the world you came from and find someone who *will* honor the deal!"

He looked a little taken aback. "I will do it ... in my own time! First, I want to taste what you're offering and see if it pleases me!"

"You *tasted* all you're going to you son-of-a-bitch! In fact, never mind! I don't trust you. I can see you can't be trusted at all. There's a full moon next week. I'm going to send you back and find a demon that's a little more trustworthy."

The comment enraged him all over again. "You think I'm at your beck and call because of your little chants and charms? You think you can banish *me*? Do you know who I am, woman? I am *Baelin*! The most powerful of all incubi!"

Cara studied him almost dispassionately. "Good to know. If the protection spell works on you, then, it should work on the rest of them. I don't suppose you'd be willing to tell me if the others would be powerful enough to heal my mother?"

"You will not find out, you arrogant little mortal bitch! I will not allow you to open the gateway! I will prevent any others from crossing over! And I will make you rue the day you crossed me!"

"You *are* a nasty bastard, aren't you? *I'm* arrogant? Because I expect you to earn your damned pay? I sure as hell wouldn't have been dabbling with this shit if I hadn't been desperate to find help for my mother! It sure as fuck wasn't because I was anxious for a demon lover to suck the life out of me!"

He narrowed his eyes at her thoughtfully. "If I give you what you want, how can I trust you to give me what I want?"

"How could I trust you not to take it back?" Cara countered. "You're right. This isn't going to work. I thought it was a simple enough bargain. I was willing to do whatever you wanted for your help, but you've broken my trust and I don't want anything else to do with you! Go away! Go back to where you came from!"

Flouncing onto her side, she punched her pillow and settled down again, pulling the cover over her head. She could hear him muttering under his breath and stalking back and forth around her bed. Uneasiness wafted through her that he was chanting some spell that would counter the one she'd woven but after a few minutes, he seemed to vanish. Cautiously, she lowered the cover and peered around the room. When she didn't see any sign of him, she relaxed fractionally, but she discovered she was too shaken from the encounter to truly relax. Eventually, her weariness got the best of her and she slept, but only fitfully.

\* \* \* \*

As tired as she was when she woke up, Cara realized very quickly that there was a world of difference between the way she felt that morning and the times before—since she'd summoned the demon. It made one thing patently clear. Her mother was right. She had no real idea of what she was dealing with or how dangerous it was.

Not that her mother knew *she* was the idiot who'd been playing with the spells when she didn't know what she was doing—thankfully!

As angry as she still was over the fact that the bastard thought he could take 'payment' without performing the service she'd asked for, though, she realized she'd also underestimated exactly what she was giving in payment. She'd been so relieved when she discovered he—Baelin—wasn't anxious to kill her and collect her soul it hadn't dawned on her that fucking a demon wouldn't even *begin* to compare to an affair with another human! She'd figured it wouldn't be pleasant. They were evil creatures after all. It *had* occurred to her that she was very likely to find it more torturous than pleasant or even bearable, all things considered. It *hadn't* occurred to her, though, that he would be sucking the life out of her bit by bit while he was at it!

She'd read that—somewhere. It just hadn't made an impression on her—because she'd thought it was ridiculous! If only a few days of playing with the demon could so exhaust her, however, she had to seriously rethink her bargain!

The entire thing was pretty much an exercise in frustration and futility otherwise. Her mother would be spared—maybe—not the terrible, slow death she was enduring now, because she'd already suffered so much—but she would live and it still seemed worth it to her to promise almost anything to give her mother the years she would be deprived of otherwise. How happy would her mother be, though, if *she* was alone?

In some ways, she thought she preferred leaving her mother than being left, but she realized that was purely selfish, especially when the idea was to prevent her mother's suffering. Leaving her with grief, maybe even guilt if she realized what her daughter had done to save her, wasn't ensuring her mother's health and well-being.

She had to think of a way to pay that would still allow her to have some semblance of a life with her mother. The problem was, nothing actually came to mind. She didn't recall any kind of spell in any of the books that seemed to fit what she needed—semi protection. They all seemed to be all or nothing. She could prevent Baelin from getting to her by wearing the charm and sleeping within the protective circle, but that was just going enrage him and it didn't allow for the 'payment' she'd offered. And regardless of what the bastard thought, *she* was honest! She paid her dues!

She considered the threat she'd thrown at him, but, truthfully, she doubted she would be able to summon anything better. He might be less trustworthy than the rest of them, but everything she'd read seemed to indicate that none of them could really be trusted to do anything except try to trick whoever summoned them. So what to do? Just give up? Send him back and try to accept the unacceptable? That she'd finally found a ray of hope for her mother but she lacked the skills to manipulate that damned demon even if she *could* summon one?

She didn't think she could. She hadn't been able to accept when she'd thought there was no hope at all. How could she simply give up, now, when there *was* some hope?

After going through every book they had on the subject, however, frustration began to get the best of her. She hadn't found anything she thought would work and, unfortunately, the only person she knew who might know of something that could help was her mother.

It took her a while to come to the conclusion that she really had no choice, but when even several hours spent on the internet searching had turned up nothing, she decided she was going to have to risk it.

Before she left for her visit with her mother, though, she went back to her workshop and wove a protection spell around a locket she'd bought for her mother the week before. After wrapping it, she collected her purse and a book and went outside to cut a few flowers in the garden to take with her.

Her mother was awake when she entered her room and sitting up in bed. Hope instantly surged through her that Baelin had actually decided to honor the bargain they'd struck, but it plummeted as soon as mother spoke. "I know you don't walk to talk about these things, Cara," she began as soon as they'd exchanged greetings and she'd settled in the chair she usually used, "but we've avoided it as long as we can, darling."

Cara stared at her mother unhappily, realizing her mother was just as determined to talk about final arrangements as she was to avoid discussing them. "We still have plenty of time to talk about things like that, mom, and it's depressing. I came to cheer you up. Look! I brought some flowers from the garden."

To her relief, her mother smiled happily at the sight of the flowers, taking them and sniffing each one to enjoy the scent, studying them, touching the velvety petals. "They're beautiful," she breathed with pleasure.

"I'll get rid of the last batch and fill the vase with water," she chattered anxiously, hoping to distract her mother. "The roses are doing fabulously. The bushes are full of buds. I'll bet I could bring you a new bouquet almost every day."

Her mother sent her a look that made her heart sink when she returned with the vase. Deciding to ignore it, she focused on arranging the flowers in the vase. "I brought you something else, too."

"Really? What?"

Cara threw a smile over her shoulder. "It's a surprise. I'll get it in just a minute."

"Animal, vegetable, or mineral?" her mother guessed.

Cara chuckled at her mother's playful mood. "Hmmm. I guess mineral would be closest."

"Bigger than a bread box?"

"Smaller."

She frowned thoughtfully. "Mineral and smaller than a bread box," she repeated musingly. "A rock?"

Cara smiled. "It was one on it."

"Something to wear? Or something to look at?"

Cara considered it. "Both."

"Oh! Give me a better hint."

She knew her mother was exaggerating her excitement about the gift, but it still lightened her spirits. "Why don't I just give it to you?"

Moving to her purse, she took the small package out and sat down carefully on the edge of the bed, handing it to her mother. Her mother quickly unwrapped it and then stared at it a little doubtfully. "A broken heart?"

Cara bit her lip. "It's a locket." She shrugged. "It was actually designed for lovers—two halves of a heart, one for each to wear, but it's for love so I figured it was just as appropriate for us. I have the other half." She pulled the chain up to show her mother and then took her mother's necklace and showed her that it opened. "I put a tiny picture of me in yours and you in mine. And this is my birthstone."

Her mother's chin abruptly wobbled with emotion. She covered her mouth with one hand. "It's beautiful, baby! Thank you so much."

Cara thought she was going to break down and cry, too, as she hugged her mother tightly. Sniffing, she released her and leaned away. "Let me help you put it on."

Her mother sat still while she pushed her hair out of the way and put the chain around her neck. When she'd fastened it and leaned back to study the effect, her mother smoothed a hand over the chain and touched the locket, smiling. "I don't need this to keep you close to my heart, darling, but I love it. Thank you."

Cara had been afraid she was about to ask her to make sure she was buried with it. She was so relieved when she didn't she had to struggle with her emotions all over again. As much to head off her mother before she could turn to the subject again as to distract herself, she launched into the tale she'd woven. "I needed to ask you something."

Still studying her locket, her mother flicked her a questioning look.

"It's business. I have this weird customer that has an even weirder problem and I've looked through everything trying to find an answer for her and come up empty. I thought you might know something I could recommend, though."

"Something about a spell?" her mother guessed.

Cara rolled her eyes dramatically. "Yes. She bought a summoning spell a while back for this problem she had and now she says she has this new problem. She summoned a demon to take of her problem, but the demon won't do it unless she agrees to ... uh ... have sex with him. She's willing to do it, but she knows she can't trust a demon and she wanted to know if there was some way to protect herself without warding."

Cara's belly clenched when she met her mother's gaze.

"You haven't been playing with the black arts, have you?"

Cara felt her face redden. "Oh come on, mom! You know I don't believe in any of this mumbo jumbo! Seriously! I need it for a customer. I mean, aside from the possibility of making another sale—which is always good—I feel responsible since I sold the idiot the summoning spell to begin with—especially when you'd told me not to sell anything that powerful. Swear to god I checked her out thoroughly before I did it!"

Her mother frowned, clearly scanning her memory for anything useful, although it was also clear that she didn't entirely believe the story Cara had cooked up and wasn't happy with it even if it was true. "I don't know," she said finally. "The trouble with messing around with demons is that it always leads to *more* trouble!"

"Yes, I know they're evil."

Her mother sent her a sharp look. "In a sense. In a way they're no more 'evil' than a mortal who's completely selfish—they just don't consider how the things they do effect the mortals they play with. Don't get me wrong, they're just as apt to purposefully do harm. They have ungovernable tempers and no one to even come close to controlling them, or punishing them for giving free reign to their tempers—except their masters. But there again, you have to consider just how prone people would be to do whatever they pleased if there weren't any consequences. I'm afraid mortals really don't have the right to pass judgment. If any of them had that sort of power they'd be just as dangerous and just as thoughtless of others.

"I'm more inclined to think of them as being like ... an overgrown toddler in their terrible twos," she added with amusement. "They're used to getting their way and they throw some terrible tantrums when they're thwarted. They *are* dangerous—*all* of them. Some of them *are* pure evil, but I think a lot of them are just ... self-centered and careless."

Cara felt a flutter of uneasiness as her mother's comments resurrected her memories of her encounter with Baelin. She supposed she could see her point—He *had* behaved rather like a sulky child denied his treat—but it was really hard to think of something that damned scary, muscle bound and probably six and half feet tall, as 'toddler like'. She supposed emotionally speaking, that description might actually hit the nail on the head. He was a toddler grown up into a great, big scary savage that had never had any nurturing or discipline.

He might also be pure evil.

Unfortunately, she had no idea whether he fit into the pure evil category or the thoughtless savage category.

She frowned almost as soon as the thought crossed her mind. He'd certainly displayed an ungovernable temper when she'd thwarted him but aside from tossing out unnamed threats—that were scarier, maybe, because she didn't know what he might do—he'd seemed far more focused on getting his 'treat' than punishing her for denying it. If he'd been evil, wouldn't he immediately have focused his wrath on her mother?

It made her feel like throwing up when she realized that, but she'd made it clear how important her mother was to her and her mother had been vulnerable. She hadn't even had enough sense to make a protective talisman for her mother *before* she'd challenged him!

It didn't matter that she hadn't actually believed any of it. She'd summoned a dangerous being from the netherworld without first seeing to her mother's protection!

Maybe he'd just been too pissed off to think about it, though? Or maybe he had thought about it but didn't want to give up the leverage?

She didn't think she should allow herself to begin to think he wasn't pure evil. Self delusion could be a very dangerous thing, especially in her current situation.

"I don't dabble in the black arts, myself. You know how I feel about that!" her mother said after a few moments, redirecting her mind to the conversation. "Of course, if the customer lives halfway around the world, this won't be any help at all, but there is Lazarus."

Cara blinked at her mother. "Lazarus?" she repeated blankly.

Her mother shrugged. "I feel guilty even to recommend him. She'd be dealing with someone almost as bad as the demons—maybe worse. He knows the black arts, though, better than anyone else I know. He'd have a lot better idea of how to deal with demons."

"He lives around here?"

"Oh no! Well, not close. He lives in Augusta. Of course, he might not agree to see her anyway and, if he does, he'll want payment up front and he's really expensive! But he does know his stuff."

Cara's belly tightened with nerves. Dangerous *and* expensive and she was so broke already! Well, it wouldn't hurt to contact him and see if she could afford his services. "How would the customer contact him?"

"Oh, his site is on the favorites list. You could get the link there and send it to her."

Disconcerted at that discovery, Cara studied her mother curiously for a long moment. "Well, I have to go! I hate to rush off, but I have a lot of errands to take care of that I've neglected. I'll be by to see you tomorrow."

Despite her anxiety about the man her mother had told her about, Cara's spirits were higher when she left than they had been in a while. Rushing home, she booted her computer, found the link, and contacted Lazarus, staring at the screen and waiting hopefully for a quick response.

## Chapter Five

The drive to Augusta took longer than Cara had anticipated, mostly because she got pulled over for speeding. Sulking over the damned ticket, she pulled back onto the road when the bastard left and watched her foot and the speedometer the rest of the trip. It was still nearly dark when she reached the edge of the city and since it was unfamiliar to her, she wandered around for a while before she finally found the house she was looking for.

It was a creepy old Victorian and seemed the perfect setting for a man that considered himself a warlock and practiced black magic.

Expecting someone who looked like a lunatic, Cara was startled when a neatly dressed man who looked no more than thirty answered her knock.

"I'm looking for Lazarus."

He scanned her from head to toe. "You're 'in desperate need of help controlling a demon'?"

Cara nodded jerkily. "I'm the one that wrote to you."

He stepped back and gestured for her to enter. When he'd closed the door, he led her to the front parlor—as the Victorian's referred to them. It looked like it had the original furnishings if it came to that. Obeying his silent invitation, she settled on the edge of the sofa, clasping her hands in her lap nervously.

"Before we get down to this ...."

Thus prompted, Cara opened her purse and handed him the roll of money he'd requested. Instead of counting it, he stared at it a moment and then pushed it into his pants pocket.

"Now, as I was saying, before we down to this, I need some background information."

"What sort of background information?" Cara hedged.

"Everything about your dealings."

Cringing inside, but with the reflection that he was a stranger she never had to set eyes on again, Cara explained.

Instead of looking at her like he thought she'd gone off

the deep end as she'd more than half expected, or laughing, he frowned thoughtfully when she'd told him all she could remember. "And he referred to himself as Baelin?"

"He said that was his name."

Lazarus smiled faintly. "Doubtful. Their name is powerful in itself and they don't share their true name."

Dismay flickered through Cara since she knew it *was* important. It was far easier to banish one and keep them from returning if one knew their real name. "Oh. It didn't occur to me that he'd lie about it."

Lazarus' dark brows rose. "You don't have much practical experience, do you?"

"Uh ... actually, no. My mother is the one that's 'in' to this sort of thing."

"Well—it's done now. My question is, are you absolutely certain that you want to try to control this demon? You'd be much better off to simply banish him. I can't emphasize enough just how dangerous attempting to control them is."

Cara dragged in a shaky breath. "I know. If I hadn't been desperate to start with, I wouldn't have even tried summoning him. I need to be able to control him."

He narrowed his eyes speculatively. "In general, people that summon demons are more interested in having their needs fulfilled and getting rid of the demon as quickly as they can."

Cara frowned at that. "Well, maybe that's why they don't trust humans," she said a little tartly. "If they're always getting cheated in a deal. I'm willing to pay. I thought it over before I summoned him. I just ... I can't let him have free reign. I don't think I'd live very long. And besides I think I need it just to get him to do his part of the deal."

Lazarus shrugged. "Well, you have the right idea in that, at least. I wouldn't want to be in your shoes if he manages to slip the leash, but it's possible you can leash him—not easy, but doable."

Cara glanced at her watch.

"In a rush?"

She smiled a little uncomfortably. "Sorry, but yes. I made a protective charm, but I'd feel a lot better being within the protective circle at home before I go to bed, if you know what I mean."

He nodded. "Alright then—there are two possibilities and

both of them are highly risky and nearly impossible to achieve. Probably the most dangerous of the two is also the one most likely to succeed. You'll have to ... uh ... seduce him."

Cara gaped at him. "Uh ... ok."

"What you're after is a lock of his hair. With that, you can weave a control spell and the easiest way to get a lock would be while he's ... uh ... occupied. Now, the reason I suggest seduction is that you aren't at all likely to get what you need if you simply remove your charm and allow him to come to you. Demons tend to be rather brutal beasts and the incubus in particular is a sexual sadist. He receives nourishment, if you will, whether his ... victim is enjoying what he's doing or not and, since mortal women don't typically enjoy sex that's quite that rough, they tend to bind them with their magic so that they aren't bothered by the woman's attempts to fight them or escape. If he binds you, you're screwed, literally and figuratively. You won't get the chance to touch him and you won't get the chance to get the hair you need."

It was really stupid that her heart rate sped up at the description he'd given her of the 'love practices' of demons. She would've felt better if she could've indentified it as pure fear, but it was hard to dismiss the fluttering of her kegel muscles. "So ... you're suggesting I hide a pair of scissors under my pillow and wait until he's busy ... uh ... fucking, and snip off a lock?" she asked doubtfully.

"Pull it out," he said dryly. "I don't think the scissors are a good idea at all."

"Pull his hair out?" Cara echoed.

He nodded. "In the throes of passion, of course. Believe me, once he's focused he isn't likely to notice you plucking a few hairs. The trick will be to be convincing enough he actually thinks it is passion. If he's suspicious, he'll notice the attempt to get his hair and he'll know exactly why you want it."

Cara nodded, but she actually didn't feel a lot more confident now that he'd explained it. There was a strong possibility, as far as she could see, that just trying to get a way to control him might be the end of her, especially since she'd have to give up the protection she had to go after it.

"You said there were two possibilities?"

He shrugged. "I'm not sure there's even any point in telling you. It would require a ... sharing, a blood binding in a sense, although it needn't necessarily be blood as long as it's essential bodily fluids. I don't think it's likely he'd go along with pricking fingers and making a pact but, in essence, that's what you'd be trying to do—except without his knowledge."

Cara blinked at him. "Like a kiss, you mean?"

He made a snorting sound that might have been a laugh. "Demons have no interest in kissing, believe me! They don't make love. They assault. In any case, I don't know that that would qualify. It certainly wouldn't be as effective—unless .... I suppose it might work if you managed to bite yourself hard enough to bleed. Then it would, basically, qualify as a blood bond, particularly if you also bit him."

"Yuck!"

He shrugged. "We are talking about having sexual intercourse with a demon," he pointed out dryly. "They're beasts, highly dangerous beasts. Alternately—and even less likely, his semen would do, but I've actually never heard of an incubus coming, so that's really reaching—actually they *do* reach orgasm, but they don't produce semen. Their orgasms work in reverse to our own. We expel energy and usually bodily fluids in the process. The demon sucks the energy we expel as their nourishment."

Oddly enough, the moment he said it an image popped into her mind—highly carnal. Had she dreamed it, she wondered? Or had Lazarus planted the suggestion and her imagination done the rest?

She frowned. "I don't see how that would work for making a talisman."

"It would actually work better—if it was doable. Then you'd have the essence of the beast inside you, captive, and all you'd need to control him would be a spell and a 'safe' word, a word that would thrust him away when you needed to. You wouldn't even have to utter it aloud. It would be sufficient to invoke the word in your mind. The hair would work, but there's always the possibility, if he's a particularly strong demon, that he could get it away from you—and that would be ... disastrous for you. About the only thing that enrages them more than not getting their way is being controlled by a mortal."

Good to know! She didn't know if he was trying to scare the piss out of her or not, but he'd certainly succeeded. Collecting the control spell and the instructions on invoking it, she left and headed home. It was a long, hard drive and she was so exhausted by the time she finally got back in the wee hours of the morning that she could barely drag herself inside. Almost as soon as she hit the bed, Baelin woke her.

"Where have you been?"

There was suspicion as well as fury in the demand. Cara managed to lift one eyelid high enough to pinpoint him and verify that he was completely enraged. "Well, god! Like it's any of your business!" she said testily. "Go away. I'm tired and I want to sleep."

"Do you think you can dismiss me like a … *servant* with impunity, woman?" he bellowed furiously.

She lifted her eyelid to look at him again. "Please? I'm really exhausted. I know you're a demon and you probably don't understand because you probably don't get tired, but I'm a feeble mortal and I do."

Briefly, he looked disconcerted. "You did not tell me where you were," he growled a little sullenly.

"I went to see a man."

"You gave a mewling mortal man what you will not give me?" he roared, instantly furious again.

"I said I went to see a man," Cara said testily. "I didn't say anything about fucking! Get your mind out of the gutter."

"What did you go to see this man about?"

Cara struggled to gather her wits. "Supplies for my business," she lied.

"What is this business?"

"I sell occult stuff online."

He apparently drew a blank. "Sell stuff? For what purpose?"

"To make a living. We can't conjure what we need, in case you haven't noticed. We have to work, get paid, and use the money to pay for things we need—like medical care."

"You went to see your mother."

Surprised, she opened her eyes and looked at him. "I go

see her every day—except I missed a couple of days last week—because of you!" she ended angrily.

He was silent for several moments. "You took her a protective charm," he said tightly.

"Yes, I did," she admitted, closing her eyes again. "I don't trust you not to hurt her to get even with me because you're mad with me."

"I cannot heal her if I cannot touch her," he said tightly.

That got her attention. She sat up and looked at him hopefully for a moment before it occurred to her that he was probably just dangling a carrot. "I'm not falling for that again."

"I never agreed to the bargain!" he growled.

Cara's lips tightened. "Fucking me was part of it, damn it! I had every reason to expect you to hold up your end of the deal when you crawled into my dreams!"

He narrowed his eyes at her. She narrowed her eyes back at him. For a split second, she thought she saw a gleam of humor in his eyes but it vanished so quickly she decided she'd imagined it. "I've decided that I will heal her a little for what you already paid. But you will have to remove the protective spell if you want this."

Cara gaped at him. "A little?" she asked tightly.

"You only gave a small payment."

She struggled with the urge to call him a conniving bastard and finally suppressed it. "So we're talking about a payment plan, now?" she asked tightly.

"I will make her a little better each time you give to me what I need."

Cara studied him speculatively. "How many payments?"

He looked outraged and then furious. "How much is your mother's life worth to you?"

Cara felt the blood drain from her face. She really didn't have a lot to bargain with and he knew it as well as she did. "You were the one that suggested payments."

"Only as a means to establish trust in this bargain," he retorted.

"So what you're saying is that I'd keep right on paying forever? Until I'm dead or don't appeal to you anymore?"

"I did not say that you appealed to me now," he said coldly.

That was a deliberate slap in the face if she'd ever heard

one. "Don't make me cry!" she said tightly. "You don't honestly think I *want* to appeal to you or that it hurts my feelings that I don't?" Of course it did, but it was a wound to the ego, she assured herself. She'd live—maybe, if she could tie a knot in her tongue and stop provoking the bad old demon that wanted to do horrible things to her every time she pissed him off.

"It is not important to you?"

She shrugged. "Ok, so we're talking about apples and oranges. I get it. You just want to feed and I'll do. It's no more personal than a choice between a hamburger and hot dog. So I don't know why you're so pissed off that I'd like to have some idea when I stop being dinner! I told you before that I was willing to pay the asking price, damn it! I just want to know what the asking price is."

"Everything I want," he growled, clearly still angry. "I do not understand why you would ... haggle over it when you enjoy what I do to you."

"You keep saying that, but I don't remember. All I do remember is feeling like hell the next day—or rather when I finally manage to come around—which, to date, has been the day after. And I was so ... drained and sore I could hardly walk! If that's any indication of what it's like getting fucked by you, then it worries me! You clearly don't plan on taking many payments or you'd be a little more careful when you're feeding!"

He looked disconcerted. "You are not that ... fragile," he said a little doubtfully.

"I beg your pardon? I think I'm a better judge of that than you are!"

He narrowed his eyes at her. "I would be willing to give you two days to rest."

"A week?" Cara demanded, outraged.

"A month."

"I wouldn't last a damned month!"

He glared at her. "What seems reasonable to you?"

"A couple of times a week."

"To rest?"

"To fuck."

"That is not enough!" he snarled. "Five times a week."

"Three. That's every other day—basically."

His lips tightened. "Four."

She studied him speculatively. "Look, I might get used to it if you weren't so damned heavy handed and you'd give me a little time to recover between times! If you're looking at something long term, you're going to have to take that into consideration! Every other night is pushing it, damn it! Two or three nights between, at least at first, would be better."

He turned away from her angrily, pacing back and forth around the perimeter of her bed. "Every other night," he growled finally.

Cara considered trying to argue for better terms and finally discarded the notion. It was something that he'd at least considered her frailty at all! "Alright. Agreed."

His eyes lit. "Remove the protection spell."

Cara gaped at him. "Nothing doing! Damn it! You agreed to make my mother better! It was *your* suggestion! And so far I've made at least two payments and you haven't done anything except ... feed!"

"I am hungry now!" he bellowed.

"I want my mother to be better!" she yelled back at him.

His lips tightened. He began to mutter and pace again. "Then come. We will go and I will take some of her pain and then I will feed."

"I can't go in there at this time of night!"

"I can take you there."

Cara debated. As badly as she wanted to go directly to her mother, though, she realized she simply wasn't up to the challenge of trying to leash Baelin at the moment, and she didn't dare simply remove her protection. "I'll go at my usual time tomorrow," she said implacably. "You can meet me there."

"It will not help her to see me!" he growled. "I must visit her dreams."

"She usually falls asleep before I leave. You can come then."

"Why can we not do it now?"

"Because I'm too tired to face it at the moment. I told you I was exhausted."

After glaring at her furiously for a long moment, he vanished.

\* \* \* \*

Cara was still tired when she woke the following morning

after her long drive and Baelin's visit. Despite that, she felt more hopeful than she had for a long time. She tried to quell it, tried to caution herself against allowing herself to get too hopeful, but it was largely a useless effort. She rushed through both her household chores and the business related tasks that needed attention.

When she'd finished those, she settled to studying the spell she would need to cast and checking to see that she had everything she needed to perform the ritual. Satisfied when she saw that she was as prepared as she could get, she fixed herself a light lunch and retired to her bedroom in hope of getting a nap that would help her be more alert later—when she knew her wits would have to be sharp.

She wasn't in the habit of napping, no matter how much she felt like taking one, and she didn't really expect to fall asleep. She supposed she was a lot more worn out that she'd realized, though, because she not fell asleep, she slept for nearly two hours. Alarmed by that discovery, she rushed around getting ready for her visit with her mother and dashed off.

Her mother was already drowsing when she arrived. Disappointed, she pulled the chair closer to the bed and sat down, holding her mother's hand and talking quietly to her until she drifted off. As hard as she'd worked to bury her head in the sand, she knew her mother was slipping away a little more every day. The morphine they gave her kept her asleep more than awake—which was something to be grateful for even though it didn't allow them much time to visit because it kept her relatively pain free. It was still hard to accept that she'd begun to spend far more time watching her mother sleep than visiting with her.

Wondering if Baelin would keep his word, she bent her head, resting her forehead on her mother's hand, hoping against hope that he wanted her enough to fulfill his end of the bargain.

She shouldn't have allowed her temper to get the best of her, she thought morosely. It was all very well to excuse herself on the grounds that she was stressed by her grief, her money problems and very little rest, but she couldn't expect Baelin to excuse her on any grounds.

She'd begun to think that she might have made him so angry the night before that he wouldn't show when she lifted her head and discovered that he was standing on the other side of her mother's bed, watching her. In spite of everything, she felt hopefulness surge through her again. "You came!" she gasped, smiling at him gratefully.

He tilted his head, looking at her strangely. "I can do nothing with the protection spell," he reminded her after a moment.

Cara jolted to her feet and reached for the clasp of the necklace. She was about to remove it when a terrible fear seized her. She looked at Baelin, realizing she had no reason to trust his intentions and every reason to distrust. "You won't hurt her?" she asked, intending to demand it. Instead, she felt her eyes fill with tears and her chin wobble as it came out as a plea.

He frowned. "I agreed to the bargain between us."

Cara swallowed with an effort, still hesitant to remove the protection and leave her mother vulnerable. "Swear to me that you mean it! That you're here to help. You won't hurt her."

Anger flickered in his eyes. "On what?"

Cara felt a jolt run through her. What would a demon swear on? "Anything that is dear to you—or at least important."

His gaze flickered over her. "I swear on ... you. I want you and if I fail your trust, I know you will not give me what I want."

His comments sent a shockwave through her, but relief along with it. She removed the talisman and stepped back, watching uneasily as Baelin moved closer. Lifting his hand, he lightly touched her mother's face and then her chest and finally her belly. "It's uterine cancer."

He flicked a look at her. "It is everywhere."

Cara swallowed with an effort. "I know. It spread."

Touching her mother's face again, he nudged her jaw down and leaned close. For a moment, Cara thought he meant to kiss her. Instead, hovering a scant few inches away, he inhaled deeply. Confusion flickered through her. She didn't know what she'd expected, but this certainly wasn't it. The second time he sucked in a deep breath, she saw what looked almost like a vapor or smoke drifting from her mother's mouth and drawn into Baelin's. It was a sickly greenish hue. He swallowed, exhaled and sucked in another deep breath. More of the vapor poured from her mother, thicker now, becoming more solid in appearance.

When Baelin straightened abruptly, she glanced at him. Alarm flickered through her when she saw his face had taken on a greenish cast. He looked around a little desperately and strode into her mother's bathroom. She grimaced, feeling her stomach churn when she heard him begin to hack and then gag and vomit.

She glanced at her mother, more because she was afraid his distress would rouse her than because she expected to notice any difference. She was stunned when she did. The grayish pallor had vanished from her face. She was still pale, but Cara could see, very lightly, a more normal pinkish color to her skin—and not just her face. When she'd examined her arms, hands, and upper chest, she saw her skin tones had improved there, as well.

She didn't think it was just a trick of the light or merely imagination. She could see with her own eyes that the shadow of death had lightened its hold on her mother. A thrill went through her that made her dizzy. She glanced at Baelin when he emerged from the bathroom.

He scanned her face. "You are satisfied?"

Sucking in a joyful gasp, she rushed around her mother's bed and flung herself at him, intent upon hugging him in her gratitude. He jolted away from her. Dismayed at the rejection, Cara sent him a look of hurt, which was when she saw he'd clamped a hand against his chest. "What happened?" she gasped.

His lips tightened. He dropped his hand, displaying a burn in roughly the shape of the talisman she was wearing, although it took her several moments to link the two. She clamped a hand over her mouth, flicking a quick look at his face. "I'm so sorry! I didn't mean to do that! I wasn't thinking!"

The anger left his face, replaced with a look of confusion for several moments, and then speculation. "You are satisfied?" he asked again.

Cara smiled at him abruptly. "Yes! She looks so much better I can hardly believe it."

He gave her a look.

She stared at him blankly. "Oh!" She felt her face redden. "I'll meet you back at my place."

## Chapter Six

Cara was reluctant to leave her mother despite the promise she'd made to Baelin. She hovered for a little while, staring at her, struggling with the doubts that began rise almost as soon as the first excitement began to wane. She wanted desperately to stay until her mother woke up so that she could see if there was an improvement as she thought.

Finally, though, realizing that it was likely to anger Baelin if she made him wait too long, she gathered her things and headed back to her house, struggling with the emotional roller coaster she was riding. Throughout the drive, she teetered between doubt and certainty, between exhilaration and fear, between enthusiasm and depression.

She hadn't considered Baelin might actually be waiting for her as she'd suggested. Even when she'd told him she'd meet him at her house, she'd thought he wouldn't come to her until she was asleep. He was standing in her living room when she entered the house, though.

Joy filled her the moment she saw him. Closing the door behind her, she pulled her charm off and dropped it blindly on the table near the door, rushing across the room as she had in the hospice and flinging her arms around him to hug him tightly in thankfulness. He stood stiffly in her embrace for a moment and finally settled his arms around her a little awkwardly.

Remembering she'd burned him with her protective charm earlier, she lifted her head and kissed the spot even though it had already vanished. She discovered when she looked up at him that he was staring down at her with a look of utter confusion. Her heart twisted in her chest and warmth flowed through.

He didn't understand, she knew, because he had no concept of love, but demon or not, bargain or not, he was her hero. He'd helped her mother when no one else could. On impulse, she lifted her hands to cup his face in her palms and then pushed upward on her toes until she could match her mouth to his. He stiffened when she pressed her lips to his, but even as she began to pull away, Baelin opened his mouth over hers. A jolt of surprise went through her and scattered in the wake of the heat that poured into her. She didn't know if it was desire arising from profound gratitude or simply a chemical reaction to him as his essence poured through her, but it didn't matter. His mouth on hers felt good. The bold rake of his tongue along hers felt better than good. His taste and scent were euphoric drugs that made the heat rise swiftly and the hunger of his kiss made it permeate every pore and set fire to her nerve endings.

She'd forgotten Lazarus' warnings and his promptings until one of Baelin's sharp teeth nicked her tongue and the taste of her blood briefly mixed with his taste in her mouth. A mixture of guilt and doubt flickered through her, guilt for even thinking about plotting against him after what he'd done for her and her mother, and doubt as to whether she should still distrust him.

She dismissed both from her mind almost immediately, too focused on the heat he created in her to think straight at that moment, to want to think at all. The heady desire was too much temptation to enjoy to the fullest to ignore. When he broke from her lips to suck in a harsh, ragged breath, she focused on his neck, nibbling, sucking at his skin and then moved lower, stroking her hands over his smooth skin, enjoying the hard bulge of the muscles beneath.

When she'd thoroughly explored his chest and arms with her hands, she stroked one hand down his belly and grasped the thick member nudging her belly. It sent a flicker uneasiness through her, but far more hunger when she discovered she couldn't curl her fingers all the way around it. Her mouth went dry. Her throat closed, prompting her to explore his cock with her mouth.

He began to tremble ever so slightly as she worked her way down his belly with her lips, encouraging her to a boldness she might not otherwise have felt. Settling on her knees at last, she studied the mammoth cock in her hands for a moment and then leaned toward him to take it in her mouth. He made a sound when her lips closed around the head as if he'd been punched in the belly. The sound spawned a rash of Goosebumps, made her belly clench and moisture fill her channel.

After sucking greedily at the knob of flesh for a moment, stroking the ridge around the head with her tongue, she pressed it deeper into her mouth. Using both hands to stroke the length of his shaft that wouldn't fit in her mouth, she pulled on the flesh that would eagerly, becoming more feverish as her own heat surged hotter and hotter. He clamped his hands on either side of her head, tightly, stilling her movements for a moment and then relaxed, allowing her to pull at his cock with her mouth.

Dizzy, consumed with a need to draw his pleasure out, to bring him to culmination, she worked his cock in and out of her mouth more and more feverishly, stroking with her hands, sucking with ravening fervor until he abruptly stiffened. His cock jerked in her mouth. Her heart hammered harder in her chest and she began to suck harder. Abruptly, a warm fluid jetted into her mouth. The taste was indescribable—nothing like she'd experienced before, sweet and salty at the same time. It inflamed her. Swallowing, she tried to draw more, lapping at it until he'd begun to shake so badly she thought he might collapse.

Abruptly, she found herself on her back on the floor, naked, sprawled beneath him, completely disoriented since she couldn't recall how she'd gotten there or when he'd removed her clothes. He moved over her in a sort of maddened frenzy, biting and sucking at the flesh of her neck and upper chest, pulling fiercely at her breasts. A flicker of alarm went through her at the savage passion she'd unleashed, but the voice of caution drowned beneath his onslaught as the muscles along her channel began to clap together in climax.

She gasped, arching upward against him as it shook her. It seemed to jar him from his focus on merely gnawing on her. He caught her knees, pressing her thighs toward her chest and then outward and spearing the head of his cock into the mouth of her sex. The flesh strained to engulf him and failed. She slipped along the floor. It seemed to madden him further. The next time he thrust, she felt as if she'd been glued to the floor. Her flesh yielded screamingly to the force he exerted, knocking the wind from her lungs as he impaled her in one powerful stroke.

The burn of her tortured flesh consumed her mind for

many moments while he pumped into her feverishly. It eased after a few moments, however, and her flesh began to respond with pleasurable ripples to the steady abrasion of his cock along the walls of her sex. She caught his shoulders, struggled to curl her hips to meet his lunging thrusts, and felt the tight hold on her ease until she could counter his powerful thrusts. Almost at once, she felt the muscles along her channel quake threateningly. Lifting her head, she bit down on the flesh of his shoulder as her orgasm exploded through her, uttering keen cries of rapture.

He shook all over, released a deep, rumbling groan. She felt his hips jerk with the force of his own climax. He pressed deeper, almost as if trying to climb inside of her, curling his big body around hers as he shuddered and jerked with the power of his release.

For many moments after they finally stopped shuddering, the lay tightly entwined, gasping hoarsely from their efforts. Cara's heart had barely returned to its normal rhythm and her lungs ceased to labor for breath when he pulled his cock from her and shifted downward to cover her mouth with his.

It was no lover's salute. There was hunger in his touch, almost as much as before. Cara groaned inwardly, weary enough all she wanted to do was to lay like a slug and enjoy the aftermath of the most explosive climax she'd ever experienced. It occurred to her forcefully, though, that the hunger she felt in his kiss wasn't mere passion. It was the need to consume her energy to renew his.

Still, she protested when he finally released her mouth and made it possible. "Could we move this to the couch? This floor is murder on my ass."

He jolted away from her to stare at her blankly for a moment and then lifted his head, scanning the room, she thought. Before the thought had completed the circuit in her brain, however, she felt herself sinking into the cushions of the couch. Twice more, he roused her to heights she'd never before attained, carried her through three more explosive orgasms and then dropped her into a deep pit of complete exhaustion.

Confused by her lack of response, Baelin lifted his head to stare down at the woman, Cara, somewhat resentfully. It didn't abate when he discovered she was asleep. It escalated. The impulse instantly swept over him to enter her dreams and continue but almost as quickly as it struck him a strange sort of reluctance followed. He wanted her to touch him as she had before. He wanted to feel her moving with him, striving to attain release, pushing him toward his own.

Dismissing the urge to enter her dreams after a moment in favor of rousing her to fill his need for a response, he went back to sucking at her soft skin hungrily. She made a whimpering sound, but she remained perfectly limp and he stopped again, debating whether to enter her dreams after all or not.

He discovered it wasn't nearly as desirable to him now that he'd tasted the passion she'd willingly given him. That realization confused and annoyed him, but he realized he couldn't dismiss it once it had occurred to him.

She'd said she was willing to give to him every other night if he would heal her mother. He hadn't realized in what way she meant to give. Truthfully, he'd thought she only meant that she would remove her charm and allow him to feed. He hadn't expected her to rush to him, to kiss and fondle him and drive him into such a frenzy that he'd spilled his essence into her mouth.

That memory caused a flicker of alarm. He narrowed his eyes at her sleeping face speculatively, suspecting treachery for the first time. Truthfully, he hadn't had enough mind about him before to even consider it. Now that he had, he wondered if her sleeping meant that she was innocent of plotting against him or if it indicated nothing beyond the weakness of her mortality.

Closing his eyes, he felt her with his mind and discovered with a touch of dismay that her energy was far weaker than he'd expected.

Resentment followed. He wanted more, gods damn it! He still hungered!

It occurred to him after a moment, though, that he had never known a moment when he didn't hunger and that he felt far closer to complete satisfaction than he ever had before. Was it worth it to risk her fragile life force by feeding more? Or would he discover that he had irreparably damaged his play thing?

Did he want to wait a full day for more?

He didn't. He particularly didn't when he knew that he must expend more energy in healing her mother before she would give to him again. It wasn't much of a bargain considered in that light. She was only giving back what he'd expended to earn her favor.

He considered that sullenly for a few moments before it occurred to him that it wouldn't take more than a few sessions to pull the malignancy from her mother and maybe one or two more to repair enough damage that her body could do the rest. Then he wouldn't have to expend himself at all. He could simply feed on his Cara and enjoy.

Unless she turned on him and sent him back through the gateway.

She would find that very difficult, however, once he'd fed on her for a time. Already, despite what he'd expended on her mother, he was stronger. Beyond the gateway, he'd had to subsist on the little energy that filtered through and that had been pure torment, barely sustaining him, giving him just enough to keep his hunger raw.

He wouldn't give up the comfort of feeling so fulfilled after so long a time of torment!

It flickered through his mind that he was in her world now. Even if he fed on her so recklessly that she withered and died, there were others—many others that he could feed on.

He focused on her again, considering it, wanting to try to appease his hunger completely for once. That odd reluctance gripped him again, though. He struggled with it a few moments and finally flung himself away from her angrily. Mayhap she'd woven some spell on him? He searched, but aside from the fact that he detected a minuscule amount of his essence within her, he could find nothing.

Dismissing it finally, he abandoned her. He needed distance, he decided, to consider whether he wanted anything else to do with this bargain. He was free to decide. She hadn't bound him when she'd brought him through.

* * * *

As weak as Cara was in the aftermath of Baelin's 'feeding', her spirits were high when she readied herself the following day and rushed the hospice to see her mother. The nurse's face was tight when she arrived and her heart sank. "She's worse?"

Confusion flickered in the woman's eyes. "I don't know. She's in more pain than she's been for a while, but her vitals seem to have improved a little."

Anger warred with Cara's anxiety as she left the nurse and headed into her mother's room. She saw immediately that the report was all too true. She had only to look at her mother's face to see that she was struggling with pain. Her anger escalated as she moved to the bed and took her mother's hand, scanning her pale face anxiously. "How are you today, mom?"

"Fine," her mother lied.

"Do you need more morphine?"

Her mother shook her head. "No. I've had enough. I'm alright, just a little more ... uncomfortable than I was yesterday. Don't mind me. How are you doing?"

Cara struggled with her anger and her worry and finally managed to beat both back enough to focus on trying to distract her mother. It was wearing, though, and she was so relieved when her mother finally drifted off to sleep that she had to struggle to keep from bursting into tears and wailing like a frightened child. With the best will in the world, though, she couldn't keep the tears from gathering in her eyes and running down her cheeks.

She was so blinded by them she didn't even notice Baelin at first. He'd already moved to the bed to peer down at her mother before she realized he'd come. Instantly, her anger surged upward. "What did you do to her? You were supposed to make her better! She's in more pain now than she was yesterday!" she hissed at him furiously.

He stared back at her, his own face hard with anger. "She is more *alive* today than she was yesterday," he growled. "If you want her to be free of pain then allow her life force to escape the vessel that feels it."

Cara stared at him with a mixture of hurt, outrage, and doubt for several moments and finally turned to study her mother's face. The lines of pain had softened as she slept and Cara realized that she could still see a far healthier pink to her mother's skin than before. For almost a week before Baelin had helped her, her skin had had a sickly bluish-gray pallor, a sign, she knew that death was near.

Swallowing a little convulsively, Cara met Baelin's gaze again. "I'm sorry," she said sincerely. "I shouldn't take out it on you just because I'm worried about her." She bit her lip. "It hurts me to see her in pain, but you're right. There's no way to avoid it if she's to get better."

Baelin looked disconcerted. "You feel pain when she does?" he asked curiously.

Cara smiled wanly. "I love her. It makes me hurt when I see she's in pain, but I don't feel her pain. I wish I could. I wish I could take it and make it mine so she wouldn't hurt so much."

"If you could take her pain you would also take her place," Baelin said harshly. "Do you want that?"

Cara felt her chest tighten with fear. Did she? Could she endure what her mother had? "I'm afraid," she admitted finally. "A coward, I guess. I should be willing, shouldn't I? If you truly love someone you should be willing to sacrifice your life for theirs."

She saw that Baelin was studying her curiously when she met gaze again, not with condemnation. "You were willing. You offered it to me to save her."

The tightness in her chest eased. She smiled at him, although her eyes filled with tears again. "Thank you."

He frowned. "For what?"

She shrugged, brushing the tears from her eyes with her hand. "I don't feel quite as bad about myself."

He shook his head at her. "You confuse me, mortal."

Cara sniffed, but she couldn't help but chuckle at his expression. "I know. There's really no explaining it, you know. It's just the way I feel and I don't know how to share that so that you'd understand."

Anger flickered across his features briefly, but he seemed to dismiss it. "Remove the talisman and I will take more of her sickness."

Cara hesitated, wondering if it was safe to remove so much so quickly, but she reached for the catch on the chain when she felt Baelin's piercing gaze and removed it. He stepped closer as soon as she did, sucking the sickness from her mother's ravaged body as he had the day before. This time when he stumbled into the bathroom to expel it, she felt more than the revulsion she'd felt the day before, though, wondering for the first time how much it cost him to do it when it made him throw up so violently. Removing her own charm, she dropped it on the bed and met him when he came out, curling her arms around his waist in an embrace meant to comfort. "It must be very hard for you," she murmured.

He'd stiffened when she embraced him, but he settled his arms around her lightly. "What?"

"Taking her sickness. I hadn't considered it, but it must hurt you."

She heard him swallow convulsively. "It does not hurt that much," he said slowly.

She tightened her arms around him and turned her head to place a kiss in the center of his chest. "I don't like that it hurts you at all," she murmured, "but I appreciate it more than I can say that you're willing to do it for my sake."

She heard him swallow again. He lifted one hand and settled it a little heavily against her skull, almost as if he was trying to urge her to kiss him again.

"It is a reasonable exchange for what you give me," he murmured a little hoarsely.

Cara smiled against his chest and then rubbed her cheek against him and placed another kiss there. "Is it?"

"Yes."

He sounded ... almost uneasy and Cara felt a flicker of amusement. Pushing herself up to her tiptoes, she kissed his cheek. "I'll meet you at my place."

He frowned, looked as if he might something and then apparently thought better of it. Heat flickered in his eyes. Abruptly, he vanished.

Cara grinned. He thought she'd forgotten their deal—that he had to let her have a day of rest between his 'feedings'. It pleased her that he'd even considered reminding her, and she was certain he had even though, in the end, he'd dismissed the urge.

She discovered when she turned to look at her mother that her eyes were half open. Wondering if her mother had just awakened or if she'd seen Baelin, she searched her face. It occurred to her, though, that her mother couldn't have seen him. It would certainly have alarmed her if she had!

"I thought you were sleeping."

Her mother's eyes closed again. "I had a strange dream,"

she murmured.

Relieved, Cara moved to her and leaned down to kiss her forehead. "Rest. I'll be back to see you tomorrow."

\* \* \* \*

Cara studied the spell Lazarus had given her, trying to decide whether she really wanted to cast it or not. She had what she needed to do it, but did she really and truly need it?

Despite the fact that Baelin had betrayed her trust when she'd first brought him through the gateway, he had done as he'd promised after they'd wrangled over it. Sighing after a few moments, she set about preparing for the ritual. She didn't feel as if she needed it, but she didn't think she could trust her feelings any longer. From the moment Baelin had first begun to pull her mother's sickness from her, he'd become a hero in her mind, someone to worship and shower with adoration.

It was no hardship at all to be his lover, as wearing as it was, as certain as she was that he was consuming her life force each time and might well drain her completely if the mood struck him. He hadn't merely been boasting. He gave her far more pleasure than any lover she'd ever had of the mortal variety.

He was still a demon, however, and still contemptuous of mortals. Regardless of how she felt about him, she knew she meant nothing to him. And that meant he might tire of her and discard her or he might tire of her and simply take everything before he moved on.

She needed the protection of the spell even if it made her feel guilty to cast it after all Baelin had done for her. Even if it didn't matter to her that his motives were purely selfish and didn't change the way she felt about him, the very fact that she *did* know his motivation was self-serving should have relieved her of any sense of guilt. It didn't, but she had her mother to think about. She was bound to have a long convalescence even if he succeeded in removing all of the cancer. Her mother might never really regain her health after what the cancer had done, and that meant that she was needed and had to consider more than her own wishes.

She didn't feel any better when she'd finished casting the spell, any less guilty of betraying Baelin's trust, but she set it aside. She had no intention of actually using it unless she needed it to protect herself.

If she never had to use it, he never had to know, and if she did then there would be no reason to feel like she'd betrayed him, she reasoned.

The piercing look he gave her when he appeared at her mother's bedside that evening sent a fresh wash of guilt through her, though, until she realized that he'd noticed the absence of her protective charm.

Stupid, she mentally berated herself! Why hadn't she considered that it might make him suspicious?

She looked away, focusing on her mother as he lifted his gaze, wondering if she had aroused his suspicions. If she had, though, she couldn't see it in his expression when she finally looked at him and he curled his arms around her readily when she went to him after the healing session. When she finally stepped back and looked up at him, he caught her face between his palms and leaned down, covering her mouth in a kiss just sort of savage.

Her heart was beating so fast when he lifted his head again it felt like it would beat its way out of her chest. "Meet me at my house?" she said a little hoarsely.

His eyes gleamed with the heat in them. "No."

Surprise jolted through her. She stared at him in confusion. "No?"

He shook his head slowly, his gaze flickering over her face. "Rest. I'll come to you on the morrow."

Cara studied him anxiously, wondering if he was already getting tired of her. "You're sure you don't want to come tonight?" she asked a little plaintively.

A faint smile curled his lips. "I am certain I do, but I am also certain that you need to rest, my fragile little mortal."

Cara smiled back at him, feeling a little better—still worried that he'd figured out what she'd done or that he was growing tired of her—but somewhat appeased. She should've just been relieved, she thought wryly. She'd been with him three nights running and every day she woke feeling weaker and less rested than the one before.

She couldn't quite convince herself, though, that he hadn't instantly figured out that she'd woven a control spell for insurance.

## Chapter Seven

Feeling a presence hanging over her, Claire opened her eyes. It would've been a lie to say that she didn't feel a jolt of alarm ripple through her, but it passed quickly and she studied the demon with wary interest. She'd never actually seen one, although she'd certainly read a great deal about them.

In a way, he looked pretty much as she'd thought one must. He was tall enough and brawny enough to seem like a giant although she doubted he was much more than six feet tall, possibly as much as six four. His flesh was the angry red of a blistering sunburn, his eyes black as were the five inch horns protruding from his scalp, the bat-like wings curled against his back and the long, board straight hair that hung several inches past his broad shoulders. He was not only humanoid, he was appealingly proportioned in the length of arm, leg, and torso, and had the bulging, ropey muscles of a body builder.

Not entirely proportionate, she mentally amended when she'd scanned his length. He was hung with the damnedest dong she'd ever seen on any male animal! It looked downright lethal! Wryly, she decided, considering what he was, it shouldn't have come as such a shock. Dragging her gaze from it with an effort, she scanned his torso to his face.

That certainly was nothing like she would've expected. If she had to describe it, she would've said he was sinfully handsome. It certainly wasn't the sort of face one would expect a monster would hide behind. But then maybe he looked the way he did because of what he was—a predator of mortal women? Maybe it was a glamour and not his true face? Then again, she couldn't dismiss the possibility that the incubi were naturally handsome in the way predators were inclined to adapt to their needs. It must certainly make it far easier to captivate mortal women with a face as flawlessly beautiful as his that was also undeniably male and as enticing in that sense as the body that went with the face, promising delight to the senses.

She seriously doubted he was in the habit of giving delight, regardless. He was an incubus, after all. "You're the demon Cara summoned to help me," she said after a few moments when he said nothing, just continued to study her as if he was trying to understand something about her and couldn't quite grasp it.

Something flickered in his eyes, surprise she thought.

"I am the incubus, Baelin."

She lifted her brows at that, tilting her head curiously. "That isn't your true name, though. Is it?"

His gaze moved over her face. Instead of answering, he posed a question of his own. "Cara told you that she'd summoned me?"

Claire smiled, uttered a snort of amusement and irritation. "Of course not! She thinks she's fooled me. She worked so hard, I let her think so. She ... worries too much already. I didn't want to add to her distress." She frowned. "What did she offer you to help me?"

He frowned, his lips tightening. "The bargain is between me and Cara," he said in a low growl of warning that he wouldn't tolerate interference.

Claire's lips tightened. She released an irritated breath after a moment. "I can guess. You're an incubus, after all," she said dryly. She bit her lip. "Would it ... sway you even a little if a mother asked you not to harm her foolish, impetuous child?"

Confusion flickered over his face. "Cara is no child."

Anger flickered through Claire. "I know you don't understand, and you're right, she's grown now—but she's still my child. She'll always be my child and I'll always worry about her welfare. I'd banish you to protect her if I could, but you and I both know I can't or you wouldn't be here." She studied him frankly for a moment when he didn't offer the assurance she'd hoped for. "Why are you here?"

He frowned. Turning away, he paced restlessly back and forth across the room several times and finally stopped again, scanning her face. "Cara has your face."

Claire smiled in spite of her anxiety. "Except younger—because she's my daughter. It's like that with mortals as often as not, although just as often a child looks like exactly what they are—a cross between their mother and their father."

"She is not like you, though."

"No," Claire agreed. "Just a little, but she's more like her father—especially her impetuousness."

He seemed to be struggling with a question he wanted to ask. She couldn't decide if that was because he couldn't quite decide how to phrase it or if he just wasn't certain of what he was looking for. "She welcomes me into her body because she is impetuous? Or because she is grateful?"

Claire felt her face heat with discomfort. "Oh! I'm not sure I want to have this discussion! In fact, I'm sure I don't even if it was wise, and I don't think it would be. Besides, I'm entirely certain Cara would be furious with both of us if I did, even if I thought it was safe to discuss it with you."

"Why? You know I'm an incubus and what my needs are. She knows this, too."

Claire bit her lip. "It's far too complicated for me to explain. You wouldn't understand it anyway. You aren't human and this concerns feelings and emotions you've never experienced."

Anger twisted his features. "I'm no stupid beast, regardless of what either you or your spawn believe!"

Claire was taken aback both by his anger and the confusion that had caused it. "I don't think you're a stupid beast and I can't believe Cara does either. Truthfully, there are so many things that figure in to such things that it's really hard for us to understand and even harder to explain. Suffice to say, Cara and I have always discussed pretty much everything—even to relationships with men. But there's a line neither of us cross because we respect each other's privacy. Sex isn't the same for humans. It's an expression of love and desire, or simply passion, or a need to find release from stress." She thought it over and shrugged. "I suppose to us it's almost a feeding, as well. It certainly lifts our spirits!" she finished with a touch of amusement.

He frowned. "You are saying you don't know why? Or that you do know and don't want to tell me?"

"She hasn't confided in me," Claire said pointedly. "She's been trying hard to keep me from finding out what she did to save me. I could guess, but it would only be a guess."

"And yet you know her," Baelin said shrewdly.

Claire considered his question. It occurred to her after a moment that it wasn't likely to create problems for Cara even if she did tell him what she thought. Cara was sensible—most of the time. She would've gone to Lazarus for the spell she needed to protect her. "I think it's a little of both and also desire for you," she said finally. "I think she's just impetuous enough to show her gratitude with enthusiasm but, however grateful she is, she feels more than gratitude or she wouldn't continue to welcome you."

"Not even to honor our bargain?" he demanded sharply.

Claire sighed. "It's really hard to summon enthusiasm for something you don't really want, no matter how grateful you might be to a man," she said dryly. "She might try to fake it to spare your feelings, but there would be no real warmth. You'd know that as soon as you … uh …." She shifted uncomfortably. "When a mortal woman desires, they … uh …." She stopped again and cleared her throat. "They're wet to help a man enter them."

He looked thoughtful. It was almost amusing to see the gears turning in his mind. She would've been willing to bet money that he'd been so consumed by his own interests that it was something he hadn't noticed.

Maybe it hadn't been such a good idea to tell so much? She still didn't see what harm could come of it, though, beyond the fact that he would know whether Cara truly wanted him or not, and that might not be a bad thing for him to realize she didn't. He seemed just a little too … possessive of Cara to suit her.

As tender hearted as she knew Cara to be, as vulnerable as she'd been when she'd thought she was facing being alone in the world, she didn't think Cara could possibly have developed any sort of attachment. She sincerely hoped not! She was doomed to misery if she had. Regardless of his curiosity, Baelin was a beast—not a stupid one, certainly—but definitely in the sense that he had no humanity. He was a creature as far beyond human understanding as humans were to him.

Baelin left the woman, retreating to a place that he'd found that suited his desire for solitude, far enough away from the humans that their noises, their chatter, and the noises of their machines didn't disturb him. He'd gotten the answer that he'd gone for, but he wasn't certain what to make of it, mostly because, try though he might, he couldn't recall that Cara had ever been wet for him. He was almost certain she had not for he could not recall a time when entering her had been easy.

That angered him until it suddenly occurred to him that he wasn't a man at all! Her body hadn't been designed for his but for puny man dick! Not that he'd ever seen one, or cared to, but her sweet little cunt was far too tight to have been designed for anything approaching his girth! He thought he could safely assume from that that man dick was puny beside demon dick!

That thought pleased him so much he forgot about being angry for a span of time, until his mind wove its way back to the question he still didn't have an answer for. He would've simply dismissed it as immaterial save for the bigger question in his mind.

Once he had completely healed the mother, would the daughter turn upon him and try to banish him again? Or, nearly as bad, weave a protection spell around herself that he could not overcome?

He dismissed the last. She had a sweet little cunt and it pleased him a great deal, but there were many more, he was sure, that were as sweet and would be just as satisfying. Why should he care if she would have him no more?

The more important question was whether she would continue to feel enough gratitude to refrain from trying to send him back.

He realized that he had been hopeful the mother would say that Cara felt love for him. He'd seen what she was willing to do for love and he knew if she felt it for him then he needn't concern himself that she would banish him once he was done—or try.

It was a delicate situation and damned confusing when he could not tell how Cara felt about him! He couldn't stop healing her mother or Cara would be angry and she wouldn't lavish him with the kisses and touches that he'd begun to hunger for almost as much as driving his cock into her until she came and he was bathed in the energy she released. He wasn't certain *why* he hungered for it except that it seemed to feed him as her energy did.

But if he continued to heal her mother she might stop anyway.

It angered him that he couldn't think of a solution that would make him easy in his mind. Finally, he decided that he would have to focus more on Cara the next time he was with her and see if he could tell if her desire was real or feigned. The love .... He couldn't think of any way that he could determine whether she felt any of that or not.

He realized he had no choice, though, but to continue as he'd begun. Disappointing her seemed the surest, and fastest, way to lose what he wanted.

It infuriated him to know that, to acknowledge that he felt powerless when he would've far preferred to demand what he wanted. Despite the fact that he was absolutely certain that she hadn't woven a magical spell around him like a noose, though, he *felt* like he was bound and he didn't like either that feeling or the gut churning anxiety that swept through him every time he thought about how angry she would be if he disappointed her.

He almost felt as if he would *prefer* to be banished than to see accusation in her eyes instead of the warmth he'd come to consider his due, or if she turned away from him and wouldn't kiss him or touch him anymore. It was disgusting that he did, but he couldn't think of any way to change the way he felt about it.

\* \* \* \*

Cara couldn't help but be relieved that Baelin had insisted that she rest. He'd agreed that he would only expect her to welcome him every other night, allowing her a night's uninterrupted sleep, and then promptly 'forgotten' it, and she hadn't wanted to turn him away. She wasn't exactly sure of why she hadn't wanted to. It certainly wasn't because she was needy. He never failed to satisfy her to the point of being nearly comatose. She was beyond well and truly satisfied. She was exhausted from being satisfied.

She didn't think it was even because she was worried that displeasing him might make him decide to leave and renege on their bargain.

In all honesty, and as crazy as it sounded even to her, she was worried that she wasn't giving him what he needed to sustain him, partly because she didn't like to think of him suffering and partly because she couldn't dismiss the fear that he'd find someone who *could* handle his appetite.

She didn't actually acknowledge that, however, until he failed to show the following night. One day, she could feel relieved about. Two deeply worried her. If she could've just convinced herself that he was being considerate it wouldn't have been so bad, but she wasn't sure he actually believed she was as fragile as she claimed.

Not that she *was* fragile! Not on the human scale, anyway. She was sturdy, strong, and healthy. She just didn't stack up all that well to a demon.

\* \* \* \*

The shock was so sudden, cut so deeply, that Cara felt like she'd hit an invisible brick wall when she stepped into her mother's room and saw that the bed was empty. She stared at it unblinkingly for a split second and glanced toward the bathroom. The door was standing ajar and the room clearly empty. Afraid to allow the thoughts struggling to form in her mind, feeling as if she was crumbling to dust, Cara turned and exited the room in a daze.

The hallway was empty. She headed blindly toward the entrance. Thankfully, the nurse was at her station although she hadn't been when Cara came in. She stopped at the desk, struggling to form words. "My mother?" she croaked finally.

The nurse looked up at her and jolted to her feet when she saw the look on Cara's face. "It's alright! We sent her over to the med center for some tests. I tried to call, but I didn't get an answer."

Cara leaned weakly against the desk, struggling to right the world that seemed to have turned upside down. The nurse helped her to a chair. Flopping weakly into it, she leaned down and covered her face with her hands. "She's alright?" she managed, her voice shaking with the tears of fright already clogging her throat.

"They're running tests. Let me get you some water."

Cara nodded, but she barely heard her. Her mind was still scrambled by the shock of seeing her mother's bed empty and the fear that had instantly lanced through her. She dragged in deep, calming breaths, trying to get her runaway emotions under control. It was the only thing she could grasp and hold on to—the need to protect herself. "Where did you say they took her?" she asked when the nurse returned and cupped her hand around the paper cup filled with water.

"They should be bringing her back shortly."

Cara stared at her. "Shortly?"

The nurse studied her for a few moments. "Let me make a call and see what I can find out for you."

The cup shook as Cara lifted it to her lips and drank, her mind focused on trying to decipher what she could hear the nurse saying in an attempt to learn what she was told. The nurse looked at her uneasily when she'd hung up and Cara felt her heart sink right down to her toes. "What did they say?" she gasped.

"They're still running tests." She paused, seemed to wrestle with herself. "The doctor said to send you over and he'd talk to you as soon as he'd studied the results."

Cara jolted to her feet almost before the woman had finished speaking. The nurse blocked her path. "Why don't you sit down for a few minutes and collect yourself before you go? I don't think you should be driving."

Cara tried to look 'normal'. "I'm fine," she said, glad now that she'd managed to keep from having hysterics.

The woman actually looked concerned. "You don't look fine."

"But I am," Cara said tightly, pushing past the woman abruptly and heading out of the hospice. She wasn't, though. She was crushed. She didn't understand, not all! Her mother had seemed to getting better every day!

A surge of hopefulness flooded her at that thought. Maybe that was it? She'd improved so much they'd decided to run tests?

She was afraid to let herself believe that even though she thought it was a good possibility.

What else could it be, though, she wondered as she unlocked her car and got in, staring blindly through the windshield? A relapse? Was she frightening herself for nothing?

Abruptly, she wished that Baelin was there, that he would hold her and make her feel better. She didn't want to face whatever was waiting at the med center by herself.

It was crazy. He was a demon. He wouldn't understand her need for comfort—at all. He wouldn't know how to give it. And even if he was willing to go with her for moral support, it wasn't as if she walk in to a hospital with a demon!

She wanted him, though, so badly she couldn't breathe. The tears she'd been struggling with broke through the dam and filled her eyes and ran down her cheeks. "Baelin," she sobbed. "I need you."

She'd barely choked the words out when he materialized in the seat beside her. It flickered through her mind how shocked anyone would be who chanced to see him, but she dismissed it, surging toward him and burrowing against his chest. To her relief, he curled his arms around her.

"What is wrong?" he growled sharply, an edge to his voice that she knew instinctively meant that he'd expected to find her in trouble—and not of the emotional kind.

"I don't know!" she wailed.

Clearly he couldn't think of anything to say to that. "Why are you weeping?" he asked after a prolonged pause. "Are you hurt?"

She shook her head. "It scared me ... so ... so bad!"

"What?"

Cara sniffed, trying to bring her emotions under control. "They took my mother to the hospital for tests. I didn't know and when I went in her room and she was gone I thought ... I thought ...."

"You thought?" he prompted.

"I thought she was gone!" she wailed, sobbing all over again.

"You said that she was gone," he muttered, clearly confused.

Cara dragged in a shaky breath and lifted her head to look at him blankly until it dawned on her that he hadn't instantly grasped her fear that her mother was dead because he didn't think in those terms. She sniffed, swallowing convulsively, mopping her face with her hands. When she looked at his chest, she saw she'd wept all over him and mopped the moisture off his chest, as well. "I'm sorry." She settled her head on his shoulder, feeling the shock and fear and grief slowly fade. "I just needed to be held."

He was silent for several moments. "You summoned me because you needed to be held?"

Put that way, it sounded a little lame even to her. She

sniffed again. "I was upset." She lifted a hand to one hard pec, stroking it lightly. "I needed someone strong to make me feel ... stronger. This was a bad idea, wasn't it?" she muttered, realizing as she calmed down that he was tense, maybe even angry that she'd summoned him when he couldn't understand why she'd done so.

He glided one hand lightly along her back, almost as if he was hardly aware of the action. "Your mother is better," he said finally, his voice gruff, as if he more than half expected her to challenge the statement. "I know this."

She'd thought so—until she'd found her mother's bed empty. She supposed she'd lived with that fear at the back of her mind so long that that was why she'd instantly leapt to the conclusion that her mother had died the moment she took her eyes off of her. It was amazing that it took no more than his assurance to convince her she'd had hysterics over nothing. "The nurse didn't know anything except that they'd taken her to run tests. I think I could've gotten a grip if that hadn't instantly made me think bad thoughts." Sighing shakily, she finally pulled away from him, meeting his gaze with a good deal of discomfort. "I didn't really think you'd hear me or that you'd come. I didn't mean to ... alarm you or anything."

"I was not alarmed."

Cara studied his face doubtfully. "Are you pissed off with me?"

He looked at her curiously. "I'm not angry."

She thought he had been, but it was a relief that he wasn't anymore. "I should go. The nurse said the doctor would tell me something when I got over to the hospital."

He frowned. "You do not ... need me any longer?"

She studied him a little wistfully. "I wish you could come with me. I know you can't," she added hurriedly, smiling faintly. "The hospital staff would pass out if I showed up with you."

His gaze flickered over her face. Abruptly, the demon, Baelin, vanished and she found herself staring at a man wearing a suit. She blinked several times, wondering if she really had lost her mind. "Baelin?"

"It is a glamour to make me appear human."

She gaped at him. "You can ... of course you can! You'll go with me?"

He smiled faintly. "That is the reason I donned the glamour."

Cara smiled back at him. "Thank you! I didn't want to go alone just in case ... in case it's bad news."

As distracted and on edge as Cara was, she noticed everyone stared at the two of them as they went into the hospital. She couldn't say that she was surprised. Baelin was a handsome demon and, with a human glamour, he looked movie star gorgeous. The doctor flicked an assessing look at him when they finally found their way to a consultation room. Cara hadn't even noticed she'd been gripping his hand frantically since they'd entered the hospital. "This is ... uh ... my fiancé."

The doctor nodded and extended a hand. Baelin stared at it for a long moment and finally mimicked the gesture to Cara's relief. When Baelin took a seat, she planted herself as close to him as she could get, grabbing his hand again and staring at the doctor anxiously while he studied the folder he'd brought in. The doctor finally shrugged and met her gaze. "We have some good news for you so you can stop looking so anxious. Your mother's cancer seems to have gone into spontaneous remission."

Cara gaped at him in disbelief. "Really?" she managed finally.

The doctor looked more confused than excited. "I've never seen anything like it." He paused. "Quite honestly, I don't know what to make of it. But, we've run the tests several times. There doesn't seem to be a mistake."

Cara sucked in a joyous gasp. Squelching the impulse to fling herself at the doctor and hug him with an effort, she turned to Baelin and hugged him instead.

The doctor looked troubled when she finally looked at him again and her heart sank. "Don't ... don't get too far ahead of yourself. It looks good, but ...."

Cara swallowed. "But?"

"Cara ... Your mother was in the last stages. There's a lot of damage ... a lot. I'm not sure how much of a difference this is going to make. It might give her more time, and I feel like I need to emphasize that—*might*. I'm going to keep her here at the hospital for now so we can run some more tests and keep her under close observation."

Cara nodded a little jerkily. "But she's better?"

The doctor studied her with empathy. "Don't get your hopes up too high, Cara. These things ... well, we've seen spontaneous remission before and sometimes the patient recovers fully. That's not going to be the case here. You need to try to accept that. Even if the cancer disappears completely, we're looking at some serious problems with a lot of her vital organs." He frowned. "At the moment, it might be the least of our worries, but she's also addicted to morphine and she'd have to be treated for that eventually."

When the doctor left, Cara looked at Baelin hopefully. "Can you ...? Do you still think you can ... make her better?"

His gaze flickered over her face. "Yes."

Relief flooded her. She leaned against him, rubbing her face on his shoulder. "I knew you could."

The tension returned, however, when they went up to see her mother. She hadn't thought beyond having Baelin with her for moral support. It occurred to her the moment the doctor encouraged her to go up to visit her mother, though, that she might well have screwed up royally by introducing Baelin as her fiancé. All the doctor had to do was mention him casually, and she would be facing an uncomfortable interrogation from her mother.

Beyond that, she didn't know how to politely dismiss Baelin so that she could visit without coming up with another explanation for her mother—assuming she was awake. She'd practically begged him to go with her. She didn't want to turn around and rudely dismiss him. She worried over the situation during the entire trek, however, hoping she'd discover that her mother was asleep and she wouldn't have to come up with a lie.

That hope went unfulfilled. Her mother was awake and smiled welcomingly when they entered her room. "You've brought a friend!"

Cara sent Baelin a panicked search for help. He stepped forward immediately and extended his hand to her as he had the doctor. "I'm Baelin ... Cara's fiancé."

## Chapter Eight

Cara was still in a state of pandemonium when they reached her house. She'd been thrown completely off kilter the moment she leapt to the horrible conclusion that her mother's bed was empty because she'd lost her and she hadn't really had a chance to gather her wits since. She'd needed comforting, thought instantly of Baelin, and he'd come. He *had* comforted her, and yet that episode had been nearly as unsettling because she hadn't thought beyond the need, hadn't considered that he wouldn't—*couldn't* really understand a purely emotional need when he was a demon. The doctor had taken her on another emotional roller coaster ride and then Baelin had turned everything completely upside down by introducing himself to her mother as her *fiancé* of all things!

The visit had been short—she thought. It had instantly taken on the nightmarish quality of seeming to move in slow motion while she tried to field her mother's interrogation with a pack of lies she hadn't had time to prepare beforehand. She'd begun making excuses for why they had to rush off directly after his announcement, though, and they hadn't even sat down, so she didn't think it could possibly have been as long as it had seemed.

Her mother had still managed a 'where, when, how, and who' session that had her stammering the first thing that popped into her mind. And the worst of it was that the lies had popped out as soon as they left her mouth and she couldn't remember half of what she'd said.

She didn't have time to address the issue with Baelin, either. The moment they were through the door, he drew her up against his length, tangled his fingers in her hair to drag her head back, and covered her mouth. She struggled briefly to hang on to her wits and gave up the effort as his heat scoured her, sent her tumbling almost instantly into a dark, dizzying whirlpool of liquid fire. Dimly, she realized she'd needed this as much as anything else to bring peace to her world. The hunger of his touch banished the doubts that had been plaguing her over the past several days when he'd failed to come to her.

"I removed the protective circle from the bed," she gasped dizzily when he broke from her lips to gnaw on her throat and neck.

The disorientation increased briefly when she felt a falling sensation and then felt herself settling into the softness of her mattress beneath the weight of Baelin's body. Briefly perturbed over the transition from living room to bedroom in the blink of an eye, she dismissed it in the next moment along with the discovery that he'd disappeared her clothing and discarded his glamour. He sought her lips again, exploring the sensitive cavern of her mouth with his tongue and then thrust it in and out rhythmically when she closed her mouth around the muscle and sucked.

He lifted his head after a moment, sucking in a harsh breath, and pushed himself downward. Clasping a breast in each hand, he sent hard rushes of pleasure through her as he divided his attention between them, sucking and pulling at her nipples with his mouth until she was teetering on the brink of orgasm.

Baelin was so thoroughly caught up in the dark miasma of his feeding frenzy when he felt Cara's body gathering to expel her energy that he almost missed the opportunity he'd been waiting for. Her little breathless gasps finally triggered the memory, however, piercing his absorption and he released one of her breasts. Shoving that hand down between them, he teased her clit briefly, and then rammed his thick middle finger into her sex. The muscles along her channel instantly closed around his finger, spasming. It distracted him briefly, diverting him to the sudden desire to explore the tight little cavern that gave him so much pleasure and he sawed his finger in and out along the passage. The discovery that the walls were velvety soft to the touch inflamed him, set his mind to reeling so that it was a moment before he realized the muscles clinging to his finger weren't just warm. They were moist and coating his finger with that moisture.

She arched her back abruptly, crying out, and he felt the walls of her sex convulse around his finger, almost like a throat swallowing. It sent him spiraling out of control. His own body responded, answering the siren call of hers. His balls seized. His belly tightened convulsively, drawing into him the energy pouring from her body in delicious waves.

He curled around her, struggling instinctively to form a tight ball in defense against the intense pain/pleasure that assaulted him, made more excruciating by the fact that her body wasn't cradling his flesh to ease the strain.

A sense of triumph began to filter through his mind even before his body ceased to convulse. He pulled his finger from her channel, examining the moisture that clung to his flesh almost with a sense of awe that it was for him—*him!* She desired him! Feeling the sense of victory mount, he lifted his head to look at her face. His chest tightened for no apparent reason as he studied her, making it hard to breathe. He swallowed convulsively several times in an effort to dislodge the strange sensation. "You are so wet for me, my Cara," he murmured hoarsely.

She lifted her eyelids a fraction to study him lazily. The tightness in his chest grew more pronounced as she lifted her hands, curling them on his shoulders and trying to draw him closer. He didn't yield to the summons. He succumbed to the need it gave rise to, the hunger to claim what she offered. She was his, he thought with a mixture of pleasure and incredulity as he covered her mouth and relished possession of it, drinking in her essence, her taste, with the knowledge that she was giving it to him.

He'd thought he relished conquering above all else, enjoying taking what he wanted, however reluctantly yielded, maybe more because they couldn't deny him. He discovered that receiving what was given with enthusiasm made him feel far more powerful, drove him beyond the heights of ecstasy he'd found before. He couldn't seem to get enough to fill the aching void he hadn't even known was there.

He lost awareness of everything in his maddened pursuit. It wasn't until it finally penetrated the fog of his mind that she felt far too cool to his touch that he came to himself enough to truly focus on Cara once more. Pure horror engulfed him when he did, sending him spiraling into panic. Gods! He'd taken too much from her! Her life force was so weak it frightened him. He stared at her bleakly, too shocked by what he'd done to think straight.

"Cara? Wake up, my precious!"

Rage surged through him when she didn't respond, when he saw no rise in the weak light left in her. "Why did you let me do this? You *know* I'm a mindless beast! Why didn't you protect yourself? *Why,* gods damn it?" he demanded, shaking her.

For several moments, the panic threatened to swallow him whole. He struggled with it, trying to think how to infuse strength into her. She needed food to sustain her, he realized after a moment, and then discarded it when he realized she was too weak to attain consciousness let alone eat.

It dawned on him abruptly that he'd gotten so carried away with enjoying her several times that he'd lost control and yielded his essence to her. If he hadn't, she wouldn't have gotten what she needed to create the protective spell that had so enraged him when he discovered it, that had cost him so much rest while he worried over when she would use it against him.

She hadn't, though. She hadn't used it when she'd needed it, gods damn it!

He thrust that thought aside, realizing that the only way he could preserve the life force that was so precious to him now was to give back some of what he'd taken. Curling one arm around her, he lifted her limp form to him, cupped her face with his other hand and covered her mouth with his own. Yielding his essence, he discovered, when it was not something he was accustomed to doing, was harder than he'd expected made harder by the fact that she was too weak to pull it into herself. Nevertheless, he persevered, forcing his energy into her until he thought he detected a rise within her.

He stopped to rest, studying her worriedly. The paleness of death had lightened its hold on her, enough that he felt a stirring of her subconscious mind. A little warmth had stolen back into her along with the color. He considered for a moment and shifted her and himself, pushing his cock into her mouth. Her mouth remained slack around his member for several moments, but as he stroked her cheek and slowly pumped in and out, he felt her tongue curl around his cock, felt her mouth close around his flesh as she swallowed. It was enough to make him hard for her. Focusing on gathering his essence for her, he began to thrust a little more quickly. The moment he felt her begin to suck weakly instead of merely swallowing, his body erupted. A choked grunt of agony was forced from his chest as he forced his essence to flow from his body and into hers. He groaned as the convulsion eased, grunted again as the suction of her mouth produced a response from his body and another hard convulsion twisted at his guts.

He was shaking all over and bathed in sweat by the time he decided he couldn't endure anymore and tried to extricate himself. She yielded reluctantly, tightening her mouth around his member and sucking harder, hard enough to draw more from him before he succeeded in freeing himself. Spent, he collapsed weakly against the bed, struggling to catch his breath. When he finally decided his lungs weren't going to collapse and his heart wouldn't explode, he rolled onto his side to study her.

Relief flooded him when he saw her chest rising and falling, saw warm color in her cheeks. The feeling that swept over him threatened to crush his chest again. Swallowing convulsively against the tightness, he gathered Cara against his body, so profoundly grateful to feel the strengthening of the life force within her that it sent him into a turmoil nearly as disruptive to him as the fear and panic of before.

Regardless, as badly as he wanted to escape, to leave her in the hope he could leave the troubling feelings behind, enough anxiety remained that he hadn't given her enough, that she would sink again toward the abyss if he didn't stay, that he couldn't bring himself to let go of her. A strange sort of calm stole over him after a time as he lay staring into the darkness with Cara curled against him. It was almost as disturbing as the roiling emotions of before, though, and just as incomprehensible to him.

When he realized it was nearing dawn, he pushed the tumultuous thoughts from his mind and focused on Cara again, discovering in the process that he had been absently stroking his hands over her as he held her. Disconcerted, wondering if he had been subconsciously mimicking the way she so often touched him or if had been prompted by his own need to reassure himself that she was not slipping away from him, he stared at her, feeling a flicker of anger take hold of him along with the certainty that she had *done* something to him.

He didn't know *what* she'd done, beyond turning him inside out and thoroughly rattling him, but it was *her* fault! He'd never experienced such fear, such total panic in his life and he would be happy never to experience it again!

He would not have felt it at all if she had done what she should have, he reminded himself. She had the protection spell! She should have used it, gods damn it! Why leave it in his hands when she had to know that he was a mindless beast when he was feeding!

To *make* him feel those things, he realized abruptly! She'd done it to torment him! She'd *tried* to scare the life out of him and she'd damned near succeeded!

If he had not come to himself when he had, she would be dead now and *then* who would have the last laugh! It would have served her right!

Slipping from the bed when she sighed and rolled over, he glared at her sleeping form for several moments, resolutely ignoring the relief he felt that she was sleeping naturally, and then transported himself beyond the confined, suffocating walls of her dwelling and flew off. He expended just enough anger and angst circling high above the city and glaring down fiercely at the mortals beginning to stir and run about like ants to feel hollow and tired and thoroughly confused all over again when he settled in the crumbling, abandoned factory that he'd claimed as his lair.

\* \* \* \*

Cara yawned and stretched, wincing at the sore muscles the movement caused her and then smiling to herself as the memories of the night before flooded back. The smile vanished after a moment and she frowned at the discovery that darkness shrouded the memories. She couldn't remember falling asleep in the middle of Baelin's lovemaking, but she decided she must have since the very last thing she remembered was coming the third time in their third, wild session.

Cringing inwardly, wondering if Baelin had left angry, she pushed herself up, fighting the familiar weakness and thirst that always followed a night with Baelin. It took an effort of will to drag herself through her morning ritual and into the kitchen to find something to chase the weakness. It disturbed her that it persisted even after she'd packed enough food and liquids into her stomach to feel bloated and nauseated. Usually, she began to feel a little better as soon as she'd eaten something and quenched her thirst.

Dismissing her concern after a moment, she focused on rushing through her tasks so that she could make a trip to the hospital to check her mother's progress. Dismayed when she discovered she'd lost an entire day, she abandoned everything, however, and dashed off.

It was a damned shame she was so panicked to get to the hospital and make certain her mother was alright that she didn't devote any time to the story she needed to cook up to explain her *fiancé!* Her mother was far more alert than she had been then when she arrived. She knew she was in trouble the moment she saw the militant glint in her mother's eyes.

"I was worried about you when you didn't come yesterday."

"Oh, mom! I am sooo sorry! I've just gotten so behind with everything that I was trying really hard to catch up and lost track of the time. I should've called."

Her mother studied her speculatively. "It didn't have anything to do with your new *fiancé?"*

Cara gaped at her in dismay, feeling the blood rush from her face and then surge back in a fiery tide while she scrambled to come up with a story her mother might swallow. "About that ...," she said, uttering an unconvincing chuckle, "he's really hot, isn't he?"

"Oh, yes he is!" her mother agreed. "Was that a glamour or does he always look that yummy?"

Cara blinked at her mother, scrambling to find her footing. "He does look glamorous, doesn't he? Almost like a movie star."

"I didn't say he looked glamorous. I asked you if that was a glamour. Never mind. I know it was—not that he isn't a handsome specimen in his true form—but what were you thinking to summon him?"

Cara looked around for a chair since she didn't see that it would be at all helpful to run. She'd have to face her mother sometime, after all. "Uh ... I'm not sure I know what you're getting at," she persevered when she'd plopped weakly into a chair.

"Cara, really!" her mother said testily. "I'm sick. I'm not feeble minded. You and I both know my cancer didn't just ... go into remission without some help."

"Isn't it wonderful!"

Her mother frowned at her, but she relented after a moment. "Cara ... don't think I'm not grateful. I am. And I completely understand how hard this has been on you, but how do you think it makes me feel to know you risked so much for me? That you put your own life in jeopardy?"

Cara stared at her a moment. "Dearly loved?"

Her mother struggled with her emotions a moment and burst into tears, lifting her arms toward her. Sniffing at incipient tears herself, Cara surged from the chair and into her mother's arms, hugging her tightly. "Yes, it makes me loved, but it also makes me feel terribly guilty and afraid for you," she said when she pulled away to look at Cara. "Did you at least go to your father for that protection spell?"

Cara gaped at her. "My father?" she repeated blankly. "Lazarus? That weird man is my father? Good god, mother! He's barely older than I am!"

Something flickered in her mother's eyes. She pursed her lips sourly. "He's as old as I am! I told you he dabbled in the black arts! That's why I left him."

The discovery threw Cara into turmoil. She'd always assumed her father was dead—or a very bad man. Her mother had never actually explained the absence of a father. She'd simply tried to reason through what might have happened by herself when her mother evaded her attempts to find out about him.

"You did go to him for the spell?" her mother prompted.

"Yes," Cara said absently, turning everything over in her mind and trying to picture the man she'd met with her mother.

"And you performed the ceremony?"

Cara blinked at the prompting, realizing abruptly that her mother must have seen right through the tale she'd woven about a customer in need. "You knew it was me?"

Her mother shook her head at her. "Cara, darling, you are the most transparent person I know! You couldn't make a poker face if your life depended on it! Everything you feel shows on your face. Of course I knew it was you! And you didn't answer me!"

Cara nodded uncomfortably. "I actually felt guilty about it. Baelin's ... well, we got off to a rocky start but he's really very trustworthy. I don't actually think I need it."

Her mother sighed with irritation. "Baby ... he's a demon," she said gently. "There's no such thing as a trustworthy demon. I'm just glad you had enough sense to weave the spell."

Anger welled in Cara. "He isn't like that! He's ... you'd

have to get to know him to understand. I agree he's a little rough around the edges and he's pretty thoughtless at times, but when I was so upset the other day because I found you gone and didn't know what to think about it, I called him and he came right to me. And he just held me. He didn't expect anything for it. He has the capacity for gentleness whatever you think."

Claire looked at her daughter in dismay. "Of course he came, sweety! You summoned him. That's part of the binding spell you use to control them when you open the gateway."

Cara stared at her mother uneasily. "The binding spell?"

Claire turned white. "You didn't open the gateway and summon a demon without the binding spell, Cara! Tell me you didn't!"

Cara looked away uncomfortably. "Of course I didn't!" she lied. "I wasn't thinking about that when I summoned him—that he *had* to come. He was still just as sweet as he could be!" she added stubbornly. "He wasn't even very mad when he realized I wasn't in trouble, like he'd thought, just upset. And I think the only reason he was angry at all was because it scared him when he thought I was in trouble."

"Cara ...," her mother began hesitantly, "you haven't ... grown attached to him, have you?"

Cara felt her face redden. "Of course not! That would be stupid, wouldn't it?" she responded, swallowing a little convulsively. It occurred to her forcefully that it wasn't a lie, precisely. She hadn't grown attached. She'd fallen in love with him in spite of his wealth of imperfections— maybe because of them. She didn't know. Until her mother had suggested the possibility, she hadn't actually acknowledged how much he'd come to mean to her, not even when he was the first person she'd thought of when she was so upset.

He needed her, though. Maybe he didn't think so, but she knew he was the way he was because he needed someone like her to love him—needed *her* to love him. How could he understand something he'd never experienced if he had no one to teach him?

She discovered her mother was studying her in patent dismay when she emerged from her thoughts. "You can't tame this beast, Cara. You can't gentle him. He will never care about you. You're nothing more than a meal to him. He might be fond in that sense, but that wouldn't stop him from discarding you without a thought if he grew tired of you. It wouldn't make him hesitate even a moment if he perceived you as any kind of threat. Even if it was possible, and it isn't, he is not of this world. He doesn't belong here and you certainly don't belong in his! He could never truly understand what it is to be mortal because he isn't. Your entire life will be no more than a moment to him, and just that insignificant."

Dismay flooded Cara as she acknowledged that everything her mother had said was true. She nodded. "I know. It's just ... I'm so grateful to him for giving you back to me when I thought I would lose you. I am fond of him ... because of that, you know, not the way you're worried about."

Her mother looked cautiously relieved. "I thought as much! You're too sensible to act like an idiot like I did with your father. He was so very charming, though!" she said wistfully. "And great in the sack."

Cara gaped at her mother, horrified. "That's way too much information!"

Her mother blushed, but shrugged. "We're grown women—both of us now. You aren't harboring illusions that I'm not a woman just like you are?"

She rather thought she preferred harboring her damned illusions! "Of course not! It's just ... well you haven't really had any relationships in my memory. It's a lot to absorb."

"Well, I didn't want to be dragging men in when you were little and confusing you. Besides, the few I dated seemed to resent you and I couldn't have that. Anyway, I never really got over your father. It wasn't as hard to live without a man in my life as it might have been if I could've found anyone who compared. I was a little lonely at times, but I had you."

Cara smiled with an effort, abruptly seeing history repeat itself. She knew her mother was right about Baelin. She'd always known he would leave eventually, but she was certainly never going to find a man that stacked up to him. And the worst of it was that she wouldn't even have a child for solace!

It made her feel like crying to realize that, but she

resolutely pushed it from her mind. "It's not too late," she said, as much to distract herself as her mother. "You'll be well soon. Baelin promised and I know he'll keep that promise. You could always renew your acquaintance."

Her mother blinked at her. "Oh! I couldn't do that! He plays with really scary stuff! That's why I left him to start with. It was just too ... nerve wracking, and I lived in dread that something awful would happen to him because of his practices.

"Besides, the son-of-a-bitch looks younger than me now! Even if I still appealed to him, which I doubt—you can imagine how tongues would wag if we were seen together—with him not looking much older than my daughter!"

Cara shrugged. "They do that these days, actually. I can't say that very much has changed over the years, but there are plenty of women who date younger men today. And why shouldn't they? Men have never been constrained by the age thing! Nobody makes their life miserable over it."

Claire shook her head. "I've let you guide me completely off topic! I'm relieved that you have the sense not to be taken in by Baelin. They are tricksters! But you need to be very careful in your dealings with him. Regardless of how much you've grown to trust him—which you certainly shouldn't!—despite your gratitude, don't hesitate to use the spell your father gave you if you feel threatened. It won't hurt him. It *will* repel him and protect you.

"Assuming he does actually keep his word and I get well enough to go home, I'll handle the banishment. I know how tenderhearted you are and how much it would crush you to do it, especially if he managed to convince you it was harmful to him—which it isn't! If I don't, if he betrays your trust and I begin to sicken again, you'll have to do it, but I don't think it'll be as hard for you under those circumstances.

"Don't wait, though! Don't give him a chance to use his wiles against you. They're very clever and very good at manipulation and although I know you're clever, you're very susceptible to users like him."

## Chapter Nine

No amount of pondering, Baelin discovered, brought him any closer to understanding any of the things plaguing him and, since it didn't, it also didn't bring him any closer to a solution for ridding himself of the emotions that churned in his belly until he could find no rest. If it wasn't bad enough that he'd turned to pure jelly with the terror that had seized him when he'd thought that he had destroyed his frail little mortal, he relived it over and over in his mind as he paced, trying to think. And it wasn't one whit easier to deal with in retrospect than it had been when it had happened!

As many times as he thrust the thoughts away, they came back and each time, he felt the same stomach churning nausea, the same frightening sense of helplessness. If he'd felt *any* of that while he was draining the life out of her, he wouldn't have to endure torturing himself with what he'd done.

It wasn't even logical, by the gods! He'd certainly *almost* drained her of her life force, but he hadn't. She'd still been alive—barely—but still alive! Not so far gone that he hadn't been able to rekindle it and feed it with some of his own energy to bring her to safety! Why torture himself with something that had *almost* happened? It hadn't! It wasn't reasonable! He'd stopped in time.

He'd noticed his little flower was wilting because he was such a greedy bastard he'd tried to take more than she had to give!

That was why he felt so sick with ... guilt and remorse every time the memory presented itself again, forced him to look at what he'd done, he finally, reluctantly acknowledged.

He was still inclined to blame her for the whole damned mess! He was a demon! He couldn't help what he was, by the gods! If she hadn't known, it would've been different, but she did know. And what was more, she had the means to protect herself! She could have stopped him. She *should* have!

She'd done it to spite him! He wasn't sure what for, but

he knew that must be it. Mortals were spiteful creatures! Punishing others for their flaws! Or maybe she'd done it to teach him a lesson?

It would certainly have done so, but it would not have done *her* any good! Aside from that, how would he have put the lesson to use once he'd destroyed her? He couldn't show her gentleness when she was dead! He couldn't show her that he'd learned to control himself. He couldn't prove to her that he finally, completely understood the consequences of his selfishness and his unwillingness to control himself only because he felt like he had the gods given right to behave just as he pleased at all times! He couldn't tell her that he understood that he had been given a mind to make decisions even while he had been created as a beast that fed upon mortals!

Tired of pacing, he finally crouched beside the wall, cradling his aching head in his hands. His stomach rumbled. He'd been so distraught that he'd burned up his energy and now he was hungry again! If that wasn't the outside of enough, he didn't know what was!

Was he not miserable enough already, by the gods! Now he must be hungry, too?

It was all the thinking about Cara, he thought morosely. He had only to think of her and he wanted her, even when he wasn't particularly hungry.

And that was her damned fault, too! As *if* he could retain any willpower whatsoever when she ... *flung* herself at him each time he saw her as if he was one of the gods instead of a demi-god, one of the spurned ones!

And he did not trust himself to go back. Even now, as miserable as he was about what he'd done, he was afraid he still wouldn't be able to control himself.

Beyond that, he was uneasy about his welcome. He did not think that she would be able to remember, but she would not need to! She would know when she woke that he had used her cruelly. She was soft and delicate, his little Cara! She would be sore and weak and she would know what he'd done. He didn't think he could face seeing wariness in her eyes instead of the light of welcome. He knew he would not be able to bear it if she looked at him with fear or hate! She had never done that! Even in the beginning when he had behaved so badly, she hadn't cringed away from him. She'd bellowed back at him!

She'd been angry, but she hadn't looked at him with fear and loathing!

Would she now? Or would she forgive him as she always had?

He massaged his aching head with his hands, trying to think what to do. He wasn't compelled to return to her, not by any spell. He didn't have to go back. Why risk it—the possibility of being banished to the netherworld again or facing Cara's condemnation—when there was no reason to?

His chest tightened instantly with angst. He wasn't certain if the thought of banishment had caused it or the thought of leaving Cara, but it was a short, unpleasant road to discovery. He thought he was more angry at the thought of being banished than anything else, though he couldn't dismiss apprehension entirely. It was a miserable place for all condemned there, a special torment designed by the gods they'd offended when they'd rebelled long ago, but it was especially hellish for those like himself who depended upon mortals for survival. The occasional soul migrated there to be fought over until one them emerged victorious, but otherwise the only sustenance to feed upon was the weak energy mortals released that filtered through the gateway, and the constant hunger could be maddening.

It was small wonder they couldn't contain themselves when they escaped into a world filled with mortals!

The thought of leaving Cara made him more miserable by far, however.

Anger followed the pain that stabbed through him and he surged to his feet and began to pace again. There were no gods damned choices that appealed to him at all! He would be miserable if he stayed. He would be *more* miserable if he left, and if he stayed and was banished, he would be miserable *and* hungry and he was *sick* of being hungry!

He would be better off if he left, he thought abruptly. He was not used to so many emotions churning in him that he could hardly think! His life had been simple before! He'd had nothing to think about but the pursuit of sustenance—which was all the gods damned pleasure he needed! He did not want this *need* that had been growing inside him to go to Cara! He did not want the constant battle between his instincts and his fear of hurting her!

He *would* go, he decided furiously. He would find

another mortal to give him what he needed who would not *also* twist his guts into a knot! He would find a dozen! Why limit himself to one when there so many? He was hungry now, gods damn it! Why should he be hungry when he was surrounded by mortals? There must be as many different flavors to chose from as there were women!

He was on the point of dashing off to find his first when it dawned on him that he hadn't healed Cara's mother. He'd told her he would.

He did not owe her anything!

Mayhap he would, though, just to show her that he was magnanimous? *Then* he wouldn't have to worry about his conscience bothering him that he'd broken a vow!

\* \* \* \*

For the first time since her mother had gotten sick Cara was tempted to simply call and chat with her on the phone for a little while instead of making a personal appearance. Not that she hadn't dreaded every single visit while her mother was sick! She had. There had been days when it was all she could do to make herself go and watch her mother slowly fade away. In a way, she thought part of the reason she hadn't missed a day—until Baelin came into her life—was because she'd felt a need to punish herself because she was alive and healthy and mother wasn't. That certainly hadn't been the main reason, though. She'd gone despite the dread she'd faced each time that she'd get more bad news and, toward the last, because she'd feared each visit would be the last.

In spite of the doctor's doubts, though, her mother had steadily improved since she'd been transferred to the hospital and Cara's doubts about Baelin's ability and his willingness to help had long since been laid to rest. She didn't feel that she needed to be there for moral support and she'd stopped expecting hourly to discover her mother had died.

She was reluctant to make the trip because she expected her mother to be coming home any time and she had a zillion things that she'd neglected that she wanted to take care of before that.

She was also reluctant because of the lecture her mother had given her the last time about Baelin. She hadn't seen him since and she was too upset about it, she was sure, to keep it from her mother's eagle eyes.

She'd tried to convince herself that he hadn't come because he wanted her to rest up and recover from the last time. That worked the first day. It mostly worked through the second. She had no reason to think he wouldn't come to her that night and yet she just *felt* that something was wrong.

Possibly because, although Baelin seemed to have the best of intentions, he wasn't a very patient man. The last time he'd told her to rest, he'd appeared the very next night. She'd fully expected him to this time—but he hadn't. Reminding herself that it was the first time since the beginning that he'd gotten so carried away that she'd lost an entire day, she decided that explained why he was a no show the following night. He just thought she needed more rest, and really she had. The weakness had persisted. She still didn't feel one hundred percent and that worried her, too, but not enough that she wasn't anxious to see him again.

Except she had a terrible feeling that she wasn't going to, that something had happened. That thought prompted her to go visit her mother after all. If it was purely imagination that something had happened to prevent him from returning, then he would also have missed visiting her mother—she thought.

At least if she did go and speak to her mother, she had some possibility of finding out something. If she didn't and he still didn't show up she would be worried sick.

Her mother was sitting up in bed eating when she arrived. She jolted to a halt at the sight. Her mother had been fed through tubes so long it was stunning to see her eating actual food!

She wrinkled her nose when she spotted Cara. "Clear liquids—blah! I'm hungry enough to eat real food!"

Cara smiled. "The tubes are all gone!"

Her mother nodded toward the door. Thus prompted, Cara closed it and moved to the chair closest to the bed, looking at her mother questioningly.

"Baelin fixed everything," she said in a low voice that was almost more mouth movement than sound. "The staff is having apoplexy right now. I think they're convinced somebody screwed up and misdiagnosed me and they're trying to find somebody to blame."

Cara felt a dizzying thrill go through her. "You're

serious?"

Claire shrugged. "Just guessing. They've been all abuzz since they ran tests on me this morning. They keep coming in and staring at me, like somebody switched patients on them." She giggled.

Cara bit her lip, but her mother's amusement was infectious and she was near delirious with joy and relief besides. "He fixed everything?"

"Seems like. I don't think they would've gotten nearly so up in the air to discover the cancer had gone away— although that did give them a jolt. Anyway, they wouldn't have taken all the tubes out if I'd needed them. And I feel fine—better than fine, actually. I don't know if it's been so long since I felt good that it feels wonderful just not feeling bad anymore, or if I just feel wonderful. I mean energetic, like I could turn cartwheels or something!"

The excitement inside Cara took an abrupt nosedive as that sank in and she realized what a tremendous leap her mother had made. It hadn't even been a week ago that they'd discovered the cancer was in remission and the doctor had lectured her about getting too hopeful. Now she was free of cancer and everything that had been damaged was healed?

Not that she wasn't still thrilled speechless at her mother's recovery! She was. It was just that it also occurred to her that Baelin had fulfilled his end of the deal ... and he hadn't come back.

"You don't look very excited."

Cara shot her mother a guilty look. "I'm thrilled beyond words! It's just ... so much to take in at once. I'd thought the best we could hope for was a few weeks of convalescence. Of course, Baelin is amazing, but I hadn't really thought he could completely heal you so quickly!"

Claire eyed her assessingly. "You're worried that he tried to do too much at once and something happened to him."

It was a statement not a question. The worst of it was, she hadn't actually formulated that fear until her mother put it into words. She swallowed a little convulsively. "Oh, I know he wouldn't do that! He *is* a demon, after all," she said with only slightly forced confidence.

"Exactly!" her mother said bracingly. "You aren't fooling me, Cara. You're worried and it's silly. Beyond the fact that they're far too self-centered to do anything that might harm them for the good of anyone else, he's an immortal. Besides, he looked fine when he left—maybe a little tired, but he didn't have any trouble disappearing."

"You saw him? Last night?"

"Like clockwork—every other night since you two made the bargain."

Cara frowned.

"What?"

She shrugged. "It's just that ... well, he usually comes to see me afterwards, but he didn't last night." Or the night before. "You're sure he looked alright? I mean, the times when I was here he looked terribly ill after he'd pulled the malignancy out. He always threw up and he looked pale and weak afterwards."

"Well, he was expelling it—and who doesn't look weak and pale after throwing up? I don't imagine it's any more pleasant for them than it is us."

"I guess," Cara responded doubtfully and then determinedly dismissed it with the reflection that he probably just hadn't felt up to a visit after doing so much at once. "When do you think they'll let you come home?"

"Lord knows. They're in such a blind panic I don't think that's crossed their minds. I wouldn't be surprised if it turned in to a three ring circus. If anybody starts talking about miracles, though, I'm sneaking out! I am *not* going to get stuck trying to explain this!"

Cara got up. "Well, they're bound to let you out as soon as they've run every test they can think of and see that you're well. I should get home. I've got a lot to do before they turn you lose."

She hugged her mother and kissed her cheek. Instead of releasing her when she'd returned the embrace, Claire held Cara at arm's length. "I wouldn't lie to you, Cara, especially when I can see you're concerned. He was fine when he left and I'm absolutely certain that he's still fine."

Cara smiled with an effort and nodded, but she wasn't comforted or convinced. Beyond being worried about the effects it might have had on him to do so much at once, though, she was worried about what it might mean regarding their bargain. He'd seemed to imply that he expected payment for a very long time and when she'd confronted him about taking pay for work not done, he'd indicated that they would take it a step at a time. He would heal her mother little by little until he trusted her and take small payments until she trusted him.

Why had he abruptly changed the rules? She hadn't really thought he could do it all at once. That was one of the reasons she'd agreed to his terms. Clearly, he could've at any time, though, and he'd still made her only a little better each time because he hadn't trusted *her* to honor her word.

She supposed she should be happy that he'd finally come to trust her enough to make her mother all well, but somehow it didn't *feel* like trust. It felt like washing his hands of her, especially when he hadn't bothered to collect payment in two days!

Anger followed the hurt when he didn't come that night or any night after that. Cara tried her best not to think about it, focusing on work, focusing on all the tasks she'd neglected when she'd been dividing her time between watching over her mother and trying to make a living. She had indifferent success. When a week had passed with no sign of him and her mother called to tell her she would be released the following day, she finally gave in to her emotions and spent most of the night crying. It wasn't as if she dared let down her guard once her mother was home!

* * * *

It was a very good thing he had discovered that he didn't particularly care for the first female he countered, Baelin decided. He'd abandoned her before he could do any harm and it had given him the time to consider his situation with a slightly clearer head.

Despite the fact that he had set out to lay waste, in a manner of speaking, he realized that that would be the surest way to attract the notice of the gods and they would descend upon him in a righteous fury and drag him back to the netherworld. He couldn't afford to behave as recklessly as he wanted to—and he had *wanted* to behave recklessly in the worst way! More cautious after that, he decided he also couldn't afford to confine his hunting grounds to an area for his convenience.

It was almost more work that it was worth, he reflected when a week's hunting had not turned up a single gods damned female that he found particularly appealing. *Not* that he bothered to examine them too closely! He wasn't taking any chances that he might become maudlin over another mortal female! But there was always something that just failed to please. This one was too plump and that one too thin. This one's skin was too rough, the next felt like raw dough. This was screamed enough to give him a blinding headache before he'd so much as touched her, and that one screamed and gave him directions of what she wanted until he couldn't even *focus* on feeding! He had been right in one sense. There were mortal females everywhere he looked, but it was far harder to find one that was just to his taste than he'd expected.

Finally deciding that he was just hunting in all the wrong places, he returned to the new lair he'd claimed—further from Cara—and considered his situation. Acknowledging finally that he really knew nothing about mortals beyond the tales told in the netherworld, which were clearly unreliable, and what he'd learned from Cara, he decided that what he needed to do was to study them. All he needed was a glamour to fit in and since he could change at will he could make certain that he fit in where ever the mood struck him to go.

It was no great surprise to discover that they were always in a rush to go somewhere. He'd noticed that particular behavior already and found it extremely tiresome. He supposed, though, that it had to do with the fact that they were mortal and didn't have much time. They *had* to rush to actually accomplish anything in the time they had.

That deduction disturbed him in an indefinable way. He found it more unsettling, though, when he'd tracked down the uneasiness to the source and realized it bothered him because Cara was mortal. He hadn't considered when he'd rushed off that he might discover if he decided at some point to go back—say to see how Cara was taking his rejection—that she might not be there at all. He tried to dismiss it. He told himself that he wasn't so oblivious of passing time that he would 'forget' and her time would've passed before he considered going back. He couldn't shake the fact that mortals were so fragile, though, and Cara had seemed particularly delicate to him. Truthfully, he'd found that that appealed to him a very great deal. He wasn't certain why unless it was because she was so completely opposite all that he'd known before, but it did.

Unfortunately, it also meant that he couldn't even count on her living the typical lifespan of a mortal—not that he had a clue of what that was beyond short, like a butterfly.

He discovered he couldn't get it out of his mind once it had entrenched itself firmly. Everywhere he went, he saw everything from tiny mortals just hatched to ancient ones creeping along with canes. They marked the time on the watches they wore on their wrists, counting minutes and seconds as if they couldn't spare a moment to merely stop. They had to rush, rush, rush or they would miss something.

He attended births, marriages, and funerals, trying to grasp their concept of time and what it meant to them. The only thing he discovered of any real interest to him, however, was that that strange word Cara had used—*fiancé*—was what the mortal women used to identify the male they'd chosen to marry.

He wasn't certain what to make of that or if it had any significance at all. It seemed—strange, though, that she'd chosen to refer to him as her *fiancé* when she might simply have said a friend, a co-worker, or a boyfriend. They seemed to have any number of ways to describe what they referred to as their relationships and each one was different. Why had she decided to use that one when any of the others seemed to be perfectly acceptable and that one was the only one that meant they'd chosen a mate that they intended to stay with, to have children with?

Not that they did stay with them that he could see. Divorce was a common enough topic that it didn't take long to figure out what that meant and some seemed to get married and then divorced almost as often as others took and discarded boyfriends.

He was a little annoyed when he discovered that scarcely two weeks had passed since he'd left, which was almost no time at all even to mortals! He couldn't help but wonder if their concept of time, or all the rushing, had somehow warped his own sense of time. It had felt like *much* longer or he wouldn't even have checked!

He couldn't help but wonder, though, if Cara might have had time to get over being angry with him. He was tempted to find out, but then it occurred to him that she might be more than angry. He'd been worried that she might hate him now or be afraid of him and he was fairly certain two weeks wasn't long enough for her to get over either of those.

In any case, he reminded himself, he hadn't actually

intended to go back at all. It might be true, and was, that he had enjoyed being with Cara more than he had ever enjoyed anything else since his spawning. He had been miserable almost as much, though. Well, in all honesty, not nearly as much, but it was true that he'd discovered that Cara could make him more miserable than anyone or anything else just as she could make him happier. He missed the first, but he was damned if he missed the latter! If he wanted misery, he had only to return to the netherworld!

By the time a full month had passed, Baelin had lost his appetite and ceased to go out and hunt at all until he reached a point where he knew he had to or perish. He'd sampled everything he came across with relish at first. He'd sampled with a growing sense of desperation after that, glutted himself enough times to discover what overfeeding actually felt like—as much misery as not having enough—and he still hadn't managed to appease the need that clawed at him night and day.

She hadn't even tried to summon him, he thought morosely. Despite the many miles he'd put between them he would've heard. He knew that could only mean that she was glad that he was gone, but *he* was not glad he was gone. He was more miserable than he could ever recall, and that saying something considering the misery he'd known!

He managed to rouse a spark of anger after mulling over it a while, to begin to feel abused. She had discarded him like refuse after he had done what she wanted! So much for gratitude! That sure as fuck hadn't lasted long!

The more he thought about it, the more outraged he was that a mere mortal had treated him with so little respect! He had power she couldn't even *begin* to fathom!

He could steal into her dreams and take what he wanted, by the gods! As often as he wanted it! She could do nothing to stop him. She wouldn't even *know* that he'd taken what she wouldn't give him anymore!

## Chapter Ten

Cara knew she should be deliriously happy without a dark cloud on her horizon. Her mother was well and home again. She'd lost a lot of weight and she was weak from spending so much time in bed, but completely free of pain and growing stronger every day. In that regard, she *was* happy. It felt wonderful having her mother home again, sharing work with her as they had in the days before she'd gotten so sick, sharing meals, entertaining one another—sharing ideas. They'd always had a wonderful rapport and Cara thought of her mother as much as her very best friend in the world as she thought of her as a mother.

The problem with your very best friend in the world *also* being your mother, Cara reflected, was that there were times when she desperately needed someone to talk to when she couldn't talk to her mother. She wanted to. She would've been willing to, but her mother had already been very clear about how she felt about Baelin. She wouldn't listen and commiserate with her about her unhappiness and she wouldn't offer helpful advice. She would lecture her about falling for such a creature and tell her she had to send him back.

She'd asked Cara point blank as soon as she was home if Cara had banished him back to his own world.

Cara had lied through her teeth and assured her mother she had when the truth was she didn't have a clue of where he was and she wouldn't have banished him even if she could. She wasn't *going* to banish him either! For once, she hadn't lied to her mother to spare her feelings or because she'd worried about a scold or disappointing her mother. She'd lied to protect Baelin. She sincerely hoped that if he did come back she would be able to make her mother understand, but if she couldn't .... She didn't actually want to consider that, especially when it was beginning to seem as if it was a moot point.

He'd been gone a month! She'd run the gamut of emotions over it, afraid at first that something awful had happened to him, angry when she thought he'd simply tired of her and left, and then purely miserable because she missed him. She knew, though, that it was time she tried to put him out of her mind and go on with her life. For whatever reason, he'd decided he didn't want to be a part of life and he wasn't coming back.

She supposed it was because he was immortal and she wasn't. She supposed she could see his point in not wanting to hang around. She thought it was completely unreasonable when it would've meant so much to her and wouldn't have cost him a damned thing, wouldn't even have amounted to much of his time, but as her mother had suggested, she could see why he wouldn't spend a lot time considering her wants or needs! But *she* had them the same as he did! As hard as it had been to try to get used to his sexual appetite, it was a hell of a thing that he'd decided to pull up stakes and take off just about the time she was *starting* to get used to it! Now, she was horny all the time, which was *his* fault, when she'd scarcely given sex a thought before.

But did he care? Was he worried sick about her? Obviously not! If he had been, if he'd had any damned consideration at all, he would've at least told her he was done and he was leaving! *Maybe* she would've wept all over him and begged him not to go, and he hadn't wanted to have to deal with it, but he could've left a damned message or something! He could've told her mother. She was sure her mother would've been glad to pass that along!

She'd been tempted, oh so many times, to call out to him and see if he would come as he had when she called him before. She hadn't quite been able to get up the nerve. As much as she'd wanted just to know that he was alright, she supposed, deep down, she knew he was because any time she thought about summoning him she thought about him reacting badly to it and changed her mind. He hadn't been especially happy when she'd summoned him before. He might be *really* angry if she tried it again. And wouldn't *she* feel like a complete fool?

Sighing, she switched her shower off and climbed out. It was the only place she could cry without worrying her mother would hear. She'd been taking a *lot* of showers over the past weeks. Naturally, her mother had noticed and commented on it, telling her she should get something for her allergies since pills would be a lot less expensive than so much hot water.

When she'd dried off and blown her nose, she trudged into her room and sprawled on her bed naked. Thankfully, she was exhausted enough from her latest crying jag and from the hot water that she began to grow drowsy almost immediately instead of lying awake thinking. It almost seemed as if she'd barely sunk beneath the blanket of darkness when she felt the weight of it lifting from her. She drifted for a moment, wondering vaguely what had stirred her and then began to sink again. Feeling a light tug on her arms just before she was completely submerged, she floated upward again. She lost track of the movement almost as soon as her mind registered it, though, and began a slightly drunken internal search. Her arms were above her head, she discovered, crossed at the wrists.

Weird, she thought, almost as odd as finding that she was on her back. She didn't sleep on her back. She was still trying to figure that out and grasp why she couldn't seem to move back into a more comfortable position when she felt her legs slide upward until her limp knees bent. That was strange enough to make her attempt to rouse more fully. Discovery that she couldn't throw off the drugging, disjointed sensation of deep sleep made her heart surge, producing a single, hard beat that failed to pump any adrenaline into her system. It took an effort of will to perform an internal systems check and at that her mind was still wandering aimlessly. She'd just realized her legs were bent at a sharp angle to her body and spread so wide that she could feel cool air wafting over the tender inner flesh of her genitals when she felt a pair of hands coast along the exposed underside of her arms.

That was a circumstance that should have instantly pitched her toward full consciousness and yet she only noted the touch and the movement in an oddly detached way. A fine tremor seemed to move through the hands and into her as they traveled down her arms, along her sides from breast to hip and then up her thighs to her knees, stirring warmth in her belly, making the muscles along her passage palpitate. The hands disappeared for a moment, reappearing when they settled around her breasts, massaging for a moment and then tightening around the base hard enough to squeeze the soft flesh into conical mounds. Blood rushed into them, flowing into the tips until they rose, tightened, and then began to pulse, growing more swollen and sensitive with each heartbeat.

They'd reached a point of true discomfort when she felt a mouth settle over both, clamping onto them and sucking with a ravenous vigor that shot her entire body and mind into instant turmoil. Sparks of fire jolted through her breasts like flaming trails of electric current, charging her so that the fine hairs all over her body stood at attention, awakening every nerve ending. When the heat had snaked its way into her lower belly, a volcano erupted. And yet, she felt almost encapsulated, frozen within the confines of her body, unable to escape either physically or mentally.

She struggled to grasp what was happening when her mind seemed so sluggish and yet capable of registering the intense sensations pouring through her. Something flickered through her mind, and yet before she could grasp it a third mouth latched onto her clit and sent her spiraling toward the blackness that lay just beyond her reach. Instead of the blanket enveloping her, however, she seemed to bounce off of it and float upward again.

Something thick and hard pressed against the mouth of her sex, plowing through her flesh and burrowing deeply so fast her brain had barely registered the burn of flesh stretched almost beyond its limits when it was withdrawn again. That time her brain managed to connect one thought—Baelin. As if the name carried magic of its own, her body erupted in a flash fire. She struggled to suck in a breath as hard, orgasmic convulsions wracked her. The hard flesh pounding into her stopped abruptly as her body reached a crescendo. She could feel it vibrating within her as the quakes of her climax lost strength. Almost before the spasms stopped entirely, the thick flesh withdrew from her completely.

When it did, she felt the bed dip beside her. Warmth wafted through her from the body that settled next to hers. Her own body relaxed limply against the bed and yet her mind still seemed almost disconnected from her body.

"It isn't the same."

Anger threaded the harshly growled words, but Cara

sensed confusion, as well. She struggled toward consciousness, felt almost as if she was swimming upstream against a hard current. Reluctance flickered through her even as she fought to throw off the bindings of her strange sleep, the fear that her mind had conjured a dream to appease her needs. As she emerged, though, she realized the weight next to her was becoming more solid.

Opening her eyes with an effort, she saw that it was Baelin lying next to her just as she'd hoped. He was lying on his back, one arm across his eyes. Remembering the anger she'd heard in his voice, she hesitated, not from fear but because it dawned on her that he was disappointed and angry because he was. After a moment, she curled her hand around his fist and lifted his arm a little so that she could peer at his face beneath.

He moved his arm, staring back at her, his expression hard. There was wariness in his eyes, though.

"Is ... something wrong?" Cara asked finally, unable to think of anything else to say, to uncertain of her welcome to yield to the urge to throw herself at him.

His face twisted. "Everything is wrong!"

Cara digested that with a sinking heart.

He lifted his hands and rubbed his eyes and then speared his fingers into his hair and squeezed his skull. "Send me back," he said hoarsely. "Banish me to my own world."

Cara felt her throat close. "You want to go back?"

He sat up abruptly and cradled his head in his hands. "I cannot bear it any longer!"

The anguish in his voice clamped around her chest like a vice even while his anger made her heart flutter uncomfortably. She discovered it hurt her to see his distress too much to ignore it, though. She lifted a hand and settled it tentatively on his shoulder. He stiffened, but he didn't pull away. "Tell me what's wrong, baby. I'll help if I can."

He dropped his hands so abruptly and whipped his head to look at her that it startled her. She jerked her hand away from his shoulder. His face twisted at the instinctive retreat. "You're afraid of me now. I didn't mean to hurt you."

Confusion flickered through her, but since he didn't seem to be angry with her, she lifted a hand to his cheek. "You didn't hurt me. What makes you think you did?"

He swallowed audibly, his gaze flickering over her face. "Why didn't you use the protection spell to push me away?"

More confusion poured through her, but uneasiness, as well. The urge to deny having a protection spell rose instantly to the tip of her tongue, but she realized it was pointless to lie when he obviously knew about it. "I only did it in case I needed it for protection."

He caught her arms, shaking her slightly. "You *did* need it! Why didn't you stop me?"

Cara blinked at him, feeling the sudden urge to cry. She couldn't for the life of her figure out what he was accusing her of. "I didn't want to stop you. I never felt threatened. Why are you angry with me? Is that why you left?"

He studied her face a long moment and pulled her roughly into his embrace, curling his arms so tightly around her it bordered painful and burrowing his face against her neck. "I nearly killed you!" he growled angrily. "I thought you were so far gone I couldn't bring you back."

Cara digested that with an effort, trying to remember. She couldn't remember much about their last night together, though. She hadn't been able to the following morning. She finally remembered that she'd been weaker than usual, though, that the weakness had lingered long enough she'd begun to worry that something was wrong with her. "You fed too long," she said finally.

He stiffened. "I lost control."

"And you're sorry?"

He dragged in a harsh breath. "I have regretted it every day since. It torments my mind."

Warmth filled Cara's chest and hopefulness. She lifted a hand and stroked his dark hair. "I didn't know. I wasn't hurt or afraid. I would never have known if you hadn't brought me back."

"*I* know. *I* would've known and it would have been more torment even than knowing what I had almost done. I don't think I could have borne it."

"It didn't happen, baby."

He lifted his head and gave her a strange look. "Why do you call me that, woman? I am an ancient!"

Amusement flickered through her. She lifted a hand and

stroked his cheek. "It's a love word."

He searched her eyes and swallowed audibly. "It is?" he asked doubtfully.

She tilted her head back and nibbled at his lips. "What do you want me to call you?"

"It means you love me?"

She smiled against his lips. "It means I adore you."

He drew back slightly to study her face suspiciously. "That is the same as love?"

"Better," she murmured, pursuing his mouth relentlessly.

He took the bait abruptly, covering her mouth with fierce hunger and igniting the fire he'd only just extinguished. She moved restlessly against him, exploring him with her hands, beseeching, demanding. He shifted the two of them to the bed, wedging his narrow hips between her thighs. She lifted against him hopefully. Instead, he broke the kiss, burrowed lower, and suckled her breasts with tender savagery until she was gasping his name feverishly. He broke from her breasts as abruptly as he'd abandoned her mouth moments before, curling around her as he caught her mouth beneath his again and pressing his cock into the mouth of her sex at the same time. The double penetration as he plowed his cock inside of her ruthlessly and thrust his tongue into her mouth sent her scurrying up the mountain toward its peak in a heady rush. He'd barely set a rhythm when ecstasy exploded through her in white hot cascades of fire. She groaned into his mouth, shaking with the force of it.

He shook, as well, tearing his mouth from hers to suck in harsh gulps of air. To her surprise, instead of continuing after a moment as he usually did, he pulled free of her and rolled the two of them onto their sides. She snuggled against him gratefully, basking in the waves of bliss rolling through her. He wrapped his arms around her to hold her tightly against his length as if it was the most natural thing in the world for him.

She was slipping toward sleep again when he caught her hand. She felt something cool glide over her finger. Curious, she drew away from him and lifted her hand. A jolt went through her when she saw the hideously outrageous ring he'd slipped on her finger. The stone was nearly the size of her first joint! Speechless, she turned to look at him questioningly.

"It means you are mine," he said gruffly.

Cara's lips curled. She was about to point out that he was supposed to ask when there was a tap on her bedroom door that jarred her. She whipped her head toward the door, trying to see if she'd locked it. "Yes?" she asked cautiously.

To her horror, her mother took it as an invitation. Pushing the door open, she flipped the light switch on. Contrary to Cara's expectations she didn't gasp in horror. She folded her arms over her chest and leaned back against the frame. "I see the beast's back," she observed coolly.

Baelin and Cara both glared at her. Cara lifted her hand and waved the ring at her mother triumphantly.

"Good gods! You'll need a sling to carry that around."

"*Mother!*" She turned to look at Baelin apologetically. "I think it's beautiful."

"She thinks it's hideous. She's just saying that because she'd madly in love with you and she thinks everything you do and say is wonderful and clever! You can't go out of the house like that, you know."

Cara snatched her cover up to cover her breasts.

Her mother rolled her eyes. "I was talking to him. He'll have to don a glamour if he plans to hang around awhile. The neighbors will be up in arms."

She shook her head at her daughter. "Now what was that you told me about sending him back?"

Cara bit her lip. "I didn't *want* to send him back. He wasn't happy there."

"Oh I expect he's much happier here—like a fox in a hen house. Been off hunting, have you?"

Cara turned to look at him. Baelin swallowed convulsively. "I was hungry."

She looked hurt and he felt like throwing up.

"You left me for somebody else?"

He frowned, confused. "I did not."

Cara was confused then. "You just said ...?"

He wrestled with the realization that sex meant something entirely different to them than it did him—at least it always had before. "I did not feed much," he offered uneasily. "I was hungry."

Cara frowned at him and he held his breath. "Well! You

can't do that anymore! If I belong to you now, then you also belong to me. Got that?"

He blinked at her. "I don't want to feed on anyone else. I never wanted to. I was so ... empty without you I could not think beyond trying to fill it."

Cara's heart melted. "That's so sweet!"

Claire made a gagging noise. "Excuse me while I go throw up."

"Go away, mom!" Cara said, nuzzling her face against Baelin's neck. The door closed with a resounding click. "Now, tell me how much you love me."

He pulled away and looked at her frowningly. "I did not say I did. I said that I needed you. I cannot fill the emptiness without you."

Cara smiled. Curling her arms around his neck, she kissed each corner of his mouth and then the center. "Close enough."

He closed his eyes. "This is what I hungered for until I thought that I lose my mind."

"What? My kisses?"

"The sweet energy that flows into me whenever you touch me."

"It's called love, baby," she murmured.

He held her, basking in the nectar flowing through him. "Will you let me give you some of my essence?"

She pulled away and studied him curiously. "I don't know what you're asking," she said finally.

"I can give you some of myself and you can stay with me, just as you are, for many lifetimes."

"Become immortal?" she asked doubtfully.

He frowned. "I don't know. I only know that if I give to you then I can keep you with me, that it will renew you each time."

"How would you do that?" she asked, sitting away from him to study him with a mixture of doubt and curiosity—pleasure, too, because as uncertain as she was that it was something she wanted, she *was* certain that it pleased her no end that he wanted it.

He grasped his cock. "I can give you my seed. If you will drink it, it is powerful magic."

Cara bit her lip, torn between the suspicion that she was being teased and doubt. He seemed perfectly serious, though. "I've heard that one before," she murmured. "As it happens, though, I've discovered it's something I really enjoy."

His eyes lit with triumph, making her more suspicious. "You will not mind being part demon?"

Surprise flickered through her. "Not if it's what you want. Will you give me some of your magic seed to grow a baby demon?"

He looked startled and then torn. "I don't want to share you," he said gruffly, and then relented when he saw her face fall with disappointment. "In time if that's what you want."

The End

Also available from NCP by author Desiree Acuna:

## DEMON SEED

## BELLY OF THE BEAST

## LABYRINTH OF THE BEAST

## DEMONIC DESIRES

## VALLEY OF SHADOWS

## BEAST MASTER'S SLAVE

Full length erotica available from NCP by author Kimberly Zant:

# SNOW WHITE AND THE SEVEN HUNKS

# SUBMISSION

# SURRENDER

Novellas and short stories:

Fulfillment

A.D.A.M: Wired for Sex

Blood Feud

No Holes Barred: Missing

Blood Sin

Awakened

Reunion

Heart of Midnight

Punished